# BURY Me

## SELENA

# Bury Me

*Willow Heights Preparatory Academy: The Elite*

*Book Three*

selena

*Bury Me*

Copyright © 2020 Selena

Unabridged First Edition

Published in the United States by Selena and Speak Now.

ISBN-13: 978-1-945780-89-9

Cover © Marisa Rose of Cover Me Darlings

*Battle not with monsters, lest ye become a monster.*
*And if you gaze into the abyss, the abyss gazes also*
*into you.*

—Friedrich Nietzsche

# one

*Crystal*

*It's time to go back to school. Time to stop hiding. Time to make the power grab that all this was leading to. But I no longer care. When I look at the perfectly made up face of the girl in my mirror, I see a stranger. No, not a stranger. A doll. She's beautiful, but she isn't real. She's hollow, while the real Crystal is full, bursting with emotions, with chaos, with pain. The real Crystal is a broken mess, bruised flesh and broken bones jutting from torn skin, all hot blood and solid meatiness. This girl in the mirror? She's so unsubstantial she floats. An illusion that could be whisked away by one stiff breeze.*

A tap on my door brings me back to reality. I slip my phone into my bag and stand from the stool in front of my vanity. One last look in the mirror shows me what I've already seen, the girl who is all put together, who looks like a life-sized cutout of me.

"Crys, you ready?"

It's King's voice. My brother, my protector, my keeper. He sounds like this is any other day. Like it's not the day when they get everything they've wanted. The day when the Darlings' throne begins to crumble.

"Coming." My voice is normal, too. Everything is normal outside of me.

But I look at my window before I go. I left it unlocked. Some sick, terrible part of me thought he'd come. Maybe even wanted him to come. But he didn't.

"We're going to be late," Duke yells, thudding a fist against my door.

"Calm your tits," I say, pulling open the door.

All four of my brothers stand in the hall. I wait as they look me over, making sure I meet their approval. Apparently, I do. We all head down and pile into Royal's Range Rover, though King takes the wheel. It's so normal, and yet, nothing feels right anymore.

"I can't wait to see the look on their faces when we walk in today," Duke says, laying an arm over my shoulders. "You did him so good, sis. Like a savage."

I nod numbly. I pray for Royal to turn around, like he used to, to let me lose myself in his coffee eyes, to tell me it's okay. But his face stays turned to the window as we drive.

"We're on the team," King says. "As soon as your ribs heal, Royal, you'll be good to go. Don't worry. We'll make sure Devlin's off the team. You're my QB1. Always."

He holds out a hand, and Royal turns to give him knuckles.

We're almost there. Ready to take our spot at the top. Preston is injured and will be out for the rest of the season. It's already November, so there's no way he'll have healed by the time football is over. Devlin confessed to kidnap and imprisonment of a minor. He'll probably get out of the charges, but it's enough to get him suspended from the team, I'm sure. This town is all about image. They won't want a guy like him representing them.

Which leaves Colt. I may not know him as well as I know Devlin, but he's not a leader. He just wants to have

3

fun and live his life. He craves the spotlight and enjoys the benefits of being at the top. But if it's him against my four brothers, he won't fight. He's not stupid. He'll know when he's defeated.

"What about you, Crystal?" King asks, looking at me in the rearview mirror. "When's that cheer tryout?"

"I missed it," I admit. It was last Friday, when I didn't go to school.

"That's okay," Baron says, giving my knee a quick squeeze. "Coach Snow will understand."

"Make it for this Friday," King says. "You can cheer for us at the game."

I nod, not bothering to argue. Sometimes, you have to choose your battles, and this one isn't worth fighting.

We pull up to the school. The first parking spot, the one the boys fought over for the past month, is empty. King parks the Rover, and we all climb out. I can't help but feel jumpy and edgy being back at Willow Heights. The last time I was here, I was searching for Royal, terrified that I'd find him dead in the office of the Midnight Swans, some fucked up secret society Devlin's family belongs to.

I reach for my twin's hand, but he draws away. It's not a blatant rejection, just a slight turn, a move so subtle I might miss it if I didn't know my brother so well.

"Are you okay?" I murmur to him. But of course he's not okay. The parking lot has fallen silent, and everyone is staring at us. Everyone is watching.

I can't help but wonder if the Darlings are about to show up and throw down. It seems so quiet without Devlin's car here, without the Darling cousins sitting on it, lording their status over the school before anyone even steps through the doors.

"Let's go," Royal says, his shoulders square and broad, his head held high. I'm not the only one who puts on a fake face every day.

We fall into formation next to King, but it's all wrong. I cling to my twin, which leaves the younger twins to fall onto his other side.

"What's wrong?" I hiss at Royal. "Are you just upset about being back here, or are you mad at me?"

I know it's selfish to even ask that question, but he's been freezing me out all week. He talked to everyone but me.

For a minute, I don't think he's going to answer. But just as we reach the wide doors with the school motto engraved above, he pauses. "You fucked him," he says under his breath. "While I was in there, dead for all you knew, you were fucking the guy who did that to me. Am I just supposed to forget that?"

I feel like he just slapped me. He's right—that's exactly what I did. But I thought I'd atoned for that. I gave up Devlin for him. To prove to him that I was a Dolce, that I wasn't a traitor.

But he still thinks I am one.

"I was trying to save you," I say, tears springing to my eyes. "I had to."

He stares at me hard, his dark gaze shadowing mine. "You didn't have to like it."

Without waiting for an answer, he shoves open the doors and strides in, letting the doors swing closed in my face.

I take a deep breath, trying to steady myself. But how do I steady myself when my rock is gone? The earthquake that's shaken all our lives has broken a fault line between us, and I don't know if I will ever cross it, if we'll ever be on the same side again. It's all I can do not to collapse onto the stairs and sob.

Dolce daughters don't make public spectacles of themselves, though. Instead, I hold my head just as high as my brother's, and I let Baron link his arm through mine and escort me into the school like a patrol officer. And I keep on pretending, just like I have for the past year, that everything is fine. That the world isn't crumbling to ruins around me. That everything is sugarcoated perfection in my little candy-colored world.

I'm relieved when Devlin doesn't show up first period. Of course, he's apparently been in jail for a week, so he probably needs time at home. But Colt strolls into sophomore English like he owns the place, as usual. Our eyes meet, and he smirks. I tense, my heart stammering in my chest. This is it. He's going to cut me down, or issue some new decree, or declare open season on me. I'm the

7

Darling Dog, after all. I know I got lucky in that locker room, that Devlin saved me. Yes, we had an audience I'd rather not have had, but he protected me from them. Without him here… Without his protection from the things his cousins could do to me…

Even though class hasn't started, and the teacher isn't even in the room yet, the voices in the room die in an instant when Colt strolls in. Not a whisper breaks the dead silence of the classroom, as if they're taking the ACT that will determine their future instead of watching some high school drama unfold.

Colt's gait is slow and lazy as he moves toward me. I know better than to think there's anything else slow about this boy. I sit up straight, schooling my face into a blank slate even though adrenaline has turned my limbs to mush. He stops in front of my desk. My gaze meets his laughing blue eyes, the ones that crinkle at the corners, hiding the alertness that never leaves them beneath heavy lids. He's not smiling now, though. Not much. Just a little twist at the corner of his lip, a hint of a crooked smile. Then, he reaches out a fist to me.

I stare at it.

He raises his brows, waiting.

I know Colt's game. I know I have to do what he wants, or he'll make it a spectacle. I reach forward and gently bump my fist against his, expecting him to pop me in the face when I let my guard down.

But he just grins and drops into the seat next to mine. Other kids start whispering, still watching. I turn to Colt.

"So, what's next?" I ask.

He shrugs. "Nothing."

"But I—." I break off. I won't say what I did to Devlin. Not in front of the class.

I may not be able to be with him, but I can't pretend I don't care. Not to myself. I owe myself the truth.

"And no more Darling Dog for this one," Colt says to the class, laying an arm around my shoulder. "That honor went back to your friend Winn-Dixie this morning. Some girls are just born to be dogs. And some…" He trails off, his eyes moving over my face, down my white buttoned blouse and my navy skirt and pumps.

"Go on," I say, raising my chin and meeting his eyes. At this point, it seems silly that some unsubstantial words have ever been able to cut through my armor.

Colt sits back in his seat and grins, moving his arm to the back of my seat. "You can put dog ears and a collar and a leash on a tigress, but she still ain't a dog."

And then I remember how much power words can have. I remember because I used them for evil, and they almost took someone's life. I remember, because with one little sentence, Colt has set me free. I'm not the Darling Dog anymore. Now, it's my turn to use my voice to stand up for Dixie.

"What are you saying, man?" asks Shaun, a guy in several of my classes. But I remember him all too well from situations outside the classroom. Shaun ate dogfood in the hall. At the party where Devlin led me around on a leash, Shaun groped me, and I slapped the shit out of him. And later, Shaun tried to grab me again when Devlin wasn't there to protect me, to keep the others at bay. He doesn't play football, and he's not in their crowd, but he's a hanger-on. He's not good enough for the Darlings, but he's good enough for some of their frustrated fangirls, just annoying enough to get their attention on occasion.

"I'm saying," Colt drawls. "That Crystal's not the Darling Dog. She never was."

"Is she a Doll?" Lacey asks, twisting around in her seat and shooting me a resentful glare. She was stripped of her Doll title because of me, and she obviously hasn't forgotten it.

"Nope," Colt says.

"Neither are you," I say to Lacey, tense with anger. I'm so sick of this catty little bitch and her underhanded comments. She huffs and turns away.

"Alright," Shaun says with a grin. "If she never was the Dog, then she's fair game."

"I'm also right fucking here," I grit out.

"Yes, you are," he says, giving me an appreciate once-over.

"She took the whole football team at once, dude," mutters another guy, snickering. "Better nail a two-by-four to your ass so you don't fall in."

"Yeah," I say, giving him a demure smile. "I'm sure a little boy like you isn't big enough to satisfy me."

Colt grins and slides his arm around my shoulder again. "Oh, Sweetie, guys like Shaun don't care about satisfying you."

Shaun's friend starts slugging his shoulder and ragging on him, and Lacey giggles and turns to her friend, both of them whispering and glancing at me so obviously that I have to roll my eyes. I'm grateful for Colt deflecting the attention, but I can't stop dwelling on what Shaun said.

So, there it is. The rumor I knew was coming. It's just what I expected, but it still makes my stomach sour. If there's one thing I know, it's how rumors catch fire and spread, starting with a seed of truth or a lie and then raging out of control, getting bigger until they swallow a person's whole reputation.

I shouldn't care. I know the truth. But as the snickers and the looks, half of them disgusted and the other half thirsty, follow me for the rest of the day, I can't help but feel it, even when I walk with my head held high like I don't feel a thing. I'm strong, but I'm not impenetrable. I may have armor, but it cracks with every blow, with every snicker and dirty look, with every whistle a football player lets out as I walk by.

By the end of the day, I'm planning how to convince my mother to take me back to New York with her. Yes, I had my problems there. Every day I fought the demons that whispered in my ears that I'd been found out, that everyone knew I was a fraud. My brothers may have been royalty, but I no longer felt like their Dolce Princess. When people found out, they began to fight for my throne. They wanted to take me down. Half of being queen is believing you are, after all. Believing you deserve it. I spent my last semester there falling. Falling from grace. Tumbling from my throne.

Here, I had a chance to start from nothing. I was excited to try again. I thought I'd do it right, that I could be just another pretty face in the halls, no one special. And that's what Colt did for me this morning, stripping my titles like Devlin stripped Lacey's. But I'm not a no one. I'm the girl who let the team run a train on her. I'm a girl they've seen led around on a leash like a dog, a girl they've groped and watched a live show of in the locker room. They've seen

selena

me naked. I can't be a nobody any more than I could the first day I walked through those doors.

I'd rather go back to New York. I'd rather run away, just like my parents do, than face this. I'd rather go back to Manhattan without my brothers' protection, fight my way through the next two and a half years as the girl who bullied someone to near death than be what I am here. I hate this school. I hate walking these halls where the ghosts of my trauma wait around every corner. I hate the terror that grips me when I have to walk into lunch in the same cafeteria where my attacker sits, a girl on his lap and his friends around him like he's a monarch, not a monster.

When we get home that afternoon, the house stands big and silent. After having all the uncles and cousins and grandparents around, it's eerily quiet and still.

"Mom?" I ask, moving from the back hallway where we entered into the dining room. I wander into the kitchen, then upstairs to the guest room where Mom's been staying. The bed is made up tight, the room looking as barren as the rest of the house. I step inside, my heart hammering. Mom does not make her own bed. She leaves it a tangle of sheets, with

14

shoes toppled under the bed and dresses flung over chairs. But this room—this room is empty. I can feel the absence in it, and I know better than to hope the new maid fixed it for Mom while she was downstairs.

I sink onto the edge of the bed. I shouldn't be surprised. But my throat aches, anyway. My house is full of brothers, and Daddy will be home soon. Somehow, though, I feel utterly alone as I sit there.

I go to my bed, and I sink down on it and close my eyes. I thought when we found Royal, everything would be good again, that it would make everything okay. But nothing is right. The big house is haunted by the ghost of the boy my brother used to be. And maybe it's haunted by the ghost of me, too.

No amount of ice cream, online shopping, or other wallowing techniques can fix this. When I close my eyes, I just see Devlin's face. I'm supposed to hate him for all he's done. I'm supposed to be happy that I made him fall for me, that I gave back what I got.

But how can I be happy knowing I hurt the boy I love?

# two

*Crystal*

*Yes, I used my body to get what I wanted. Yes, I let a boy use my body—again, I let him. I let him to get what I wanted. Anyone who has a problem with that can go fuck themselves. It's my body to use as I see fit. My choice to do so. Who are you to disagree?*

When I open my locker the next day, a cup of coffee sits right inside, still steaming. I pull it out and look up and down the hall, my heart doing a funny little twist in my chest. Is something still alive in there, some seed of hope that's taken root and is winding up, a tender green shoot that could be crushed under a single careless boot?

People are watching me, but I can't tell if it's more than the day before. I can't tell if it's because I am rumored to like a good gang bang on a Friday night, or if there's some other reason. Am I an idiot to hope? Maybe Lacey put a coffee in my locker, spiced with cinnamon and laced with arsenic.

I get my books and close my locker. My heart nearly stops. Devlin Darling is walking toward me, a cousin on either side of him. A hundred thoughts go tumbling through my mind. Will he talk to me? Look at me? Does he hate me? Does he love me?

I stand there, rooted to the spot, my heart beating so hard I see black spots behind my eyes. I ache for him, for anything. A touch, a smile, a word, a look.

Each step he takes brings him closer and closer. So close I can see the way his shirt stretches over muscles on his broad shoulders, the strength in his jawline, the ice of his blue eyes. And then he's here. He's right beside me, so close I could reach out past Preston and press my fingertips to his skin again, feel the heat of his body, the beating of his heart. I curl my fingers so I won't do it, not even to make sure he's real, to convince myself that it was all real. That I really had Devlin Darling, and I lost him.

No, I didn't lose him.

I threw him away.

As he walks past without so much as a flicker of a glance, my body deflates. The tension sweeps away, and I'm left shaking. I turn and slam my locker, relishing the bang of metal on metal. What is wrong with me? I'm so fucking pathetic I could puke. What am I doing, waiting for a look from Devlin Darling like I'm one of his lovesick puppies, like I really am a dog?

I remember something Dolly said to me, that they ruin the Darling Dog, and when they're done with her, she wishes she could go back, that she had their attention again.

Fuck. That.

I'm not some pathetic dog. Even if no one will ever believe me, and I'll never be more than the whore who took the whole football team at once, I know the truth. Devlin wanted me. He liked me. And I broke his fucking heart.

What did I expect—that he'd come begging for me to take him back? That's not his style, and I know it. I know that he's proud, and he'll probably never look at me again. If I told anyone that I hurt him, he'd deny it to his dying day. And why would anyone believe a whore like me?

But that doesn't matter. I didn't do what I did for the glory, for the reputation points. I did it to hurt him, and I succeeded. Now I live with that. I don't get to cry about it. I'm not the victim here.

I tighten up my pony, toss the coffee in the trash, and go to class. I don't look at Devlin, even though we sit together in science. The next day there's another coffee, and I hold onto a sliver of hope as I walk to class, picturing what we'll say to each other about it. When I walk into the class, though, Devlin's sitting in the seat next to Dolly.

I swallow hard. I know she means something to him, but the first day of school, he refused to sit with her. Apparently, that's better than sitting with me.

I slow when I reach their spot.

"So, that's how it's going to be?" I ask.

Devlin looks at me, his gaze cool and a smirk on his beautiful lips. "No, Sugar," he says. "That's how it already is."

"I'm real sorry," Dolly says, glancing nervously between us with her big blue eyes. "Want me to sit with you?"

She looks like she means it, too. I don't know their complete history, but I was told that she still had a thing for him. I thought people were wrong, that she was into Preston, but maybe not. And who am I to stand in the way of their future together?

I'm no one, that's who.

"No," I say, forcing a smile before letting my eyes meet Devlin's. "I work better alone, anyway."

I drop the coffee in the trash as I walk back to my seat, picturing myself how my classmates must see me. Because of course they're watching. Anything to do with the Darlings, and they want the drama. Well, they'll just have to keep on wanting, because I'm not giving them anything. All they get is an image, a mirage. Something perfect and unreal, like a doll. Every strand of hair smoothed and tamed into place. Flawlessly made up face. Prim and proper dress masking curves that might cause uncomfortable thoughts, whether that be lust or jealousy.

Like a mannequin, a Dolce daughter exists for the sole purpose of giving everyone else a palatable, bland experience that makes them agreeable enough to what they're being sold. Something they want, but not too much. Something they admire but can't quite replicate for themselves. Something that's not beautiful but fashionable, something they crave but in a detached way. I will be that girl. It's all I have left. I sold my heart to keep my name.

At lunch, no one barks at me. But by the time I've walked to the table where I usually sit, I've been eye-fucked by half the school. I'm not sure which is worse, that or the dog noises I used to get. Just as I slide into my seat, thinking I'm free, the barking starts. I look up, dread gripping my heart.

But they're not barking at me. Dixie has arrived. She stops in the doorway, planting her hands on her hips like a badass superhero girl. And a damn good one at that. She seems to have gotten the makeover my brothers suggested. She's wearing black eyeliner and red lipstick, and her red hair is piled on top of her head with a few strands framing her round face. Her outfit consists of black, thick-soled boots, fishnets, a black-and-red schoolgirl skirt short enough to show her thighs rubbing together when she walks, a black leather jacket, and a corset top that shows a whole lot of boob.

She marches through the cafeteria, through the sea of barking dogs, her face flaming red. I tense, praying she won't look at the Darlings table when she passes. She glances their way, but at least she holds back her smile until she collapses into a chair at my table, her back to the cafeteria. Then, a huge grin breaks out over her face.

"Damn, girl," I say. "Way to make an entrance."

"Do I look okay?" she asks breathlessly.

"You look like sex in boots."

"I second that," Duke says. "I'd fuck you in just your boots."

I roll my eyes. "I don't think they'd fit you."

"Better cut it out before Dolly hears you flirting," Baron says to his twin. "Just because we're the sharing type doesn't mean she is."

"What are we talking about?" Dolly asks after mincing over to the table. Hurt twists inside me at her appearance.

22

"My outfit," Dixie says with a giggle.

"And whether I could rock fuck-me boots," Duke says with a grin, pulling out Dolly's chair without standing.

"No," she says definitively.

My brothers all burst into laughter, and I try to join, but I feel like there's a knife twisting in my back.

"What do you think?" Dixie asks, leaning forward eagerly.

"Good god, did you go goth?" asks Dolly, the antithesis of goth, as she looks over Dixie's outfit. She sets down her purse—a tiny, bejeweled unicorn head that can't fit more than her phone and a tampon—and opens her Dr. Pepper while she studies our freshman friend.

That earns her another round of laughter—even Royal smiles. An ugly dart of jealousy pierces through me. He'll barely look at me.

"I thought you'd sit with the Darlings today," I mutter. Because yeah, I'm a petty bitch.

Dolly turns to me. "Devlin is my friend, Crystal," she says. "I know he did some bad shit to you, but you did him wrong, too. And y'all got him and his dad arrested."

"We didn't get him arrested," I say, narrowing my eyes at her.

She holds up a manicured hand. "I'm not taking sides because you're both my friends. Unless you don't want to be my friend anymore."

I swallow hard and nod. "I'm sorry. I'm being a bitch. Of course we're still friends."

"I've known those boys since we were in diapers," she says. "But the Darlings don't own me. No one tells me where to sit."

"You're friends with them?" Royal asks, nodding across the room to the Darlings table. I have to remind myself how much changed in the week he was gone. We told him how the twins ended up with Dolly, and that she took our side and stood up to the most powerful family in town, but he hasn't seen any of it play out in real life.

"Yes," Dolly says, raising her chin and meeting his eyes with a challenge.

"Then I'm telling you where to sit," Royal says. "And it's not at our table."

"Royal…" I start.

"No, it's fine," Dolly says, picking up her tiny purse and her soda. "I know you've been through a lot, Royal, and I'm sorry for coming over here if it's triggering for you."

"It's not triggering me," Royal snaps. "It's pissing me off."

"Okay, you both need to stop," I say, pressing my palms down on the table and staring at my twin. "Dolly's one of my best friends now, and you can't tell either of us who to be friends with."

"You're right," he says. Without another word, he gets up and stalks off, leaving his lunch on the table. My throat aches as I watch him go. What have I done?

I stand, but King's hand closes around my arm, and he pulls me back down into my seat. "Give him time," he says. "He's been through a lot."

"And he doesn't have to go through it alone anymore," I say. "Why is he pushing me away?"

"I'll go talk to him," King says. He gathers his and Royal's food, leans over to plant a quick kiss on top of my head, and walks off.

"Trouble at home?" Dixie whispers to me.

I shrug, pretending I'm fine, that we're fine, that everything is fucking fine.

"Trouble's walking this way," Dolly says.

Colt Darling strolls toward us, taking his sweet time, soaking up the attention he's gathering. When the Darlings are on the move, everyone watches. They've created this environment at Willow Heights, an intoxicating combination of anticipation, fear, and sometimes, payoff. It's strangely addictive, this adrenaline followed by a reward or a punishment, like the rush an addict gets from gambling. Maybe, just maybe, they'll pluck you from obscurity, put a necklace around your neck, and proclaim you untouchable… For a time. Or maybe they'll snap a dog collar on and publicly humiliate you.

Anticipation ripples through the cafeteria as students fall silent, waiting for what comes next, craning to see what he's holding balled up in his fist. Some of them are probably shaking, hoping he won't stop at their table. Some are praying he will. But most just want to hear what he'll say. They want the gossip, crave it, need it like oxygen. Excitement buzzes in Colt's wake because this time, they won the roll of the dice, and it isn't them. But for one person, it is.

Colt stops at our table, and my eyes move down to what he's carrying. "The Darling Dog claims her rightful title," he drawls, opening his hand to reveal a studded dog collar. "Welcome back, Winn-Dixie. I like what you've done with yourself. It's almost like you were waiting for me to put this collar on you all along. Weren't you, girl?"

Dixie nods mutely, her eyes wide as she stares up at him with a dumbstruck expression that makes me hurt for her even as I want to shake some sense into her. Colt gives her an affectionate chuck under the chin before snapping the dog collar around her neck. She ducks her head, her face flaming, as he reaches into his jacket pocket, pulls out a dog ear headband, and settles it onto her head in front of the pile of hair she's fixed into a messy bun.

Suddenly, anger flares bright and hot inside me. "You better take that off her, or you're going to end up wearing it," I snap at him. "Dixie's not a dog. And don't even start threatening how you'll treat me the same. I'm not wearing that, and neither is anyone else at this table, or at this school."

"See, that's where you're wrong," Colt says, giving me an easy smile. "We still run this school, Sweet Thing. You keep thinking you've disrupted things, but you're just providing us with entertainment. Isn't that right?"

He turns to the next table, where everyone nods vigorously, eager to please their rulers.

"And you put on quite a show," Colt says, gesturing a finger back toward his table. "See, we're as solid as ever. You can't beat us. You can either join us, or you can leave this school. There's no third option."

"I don't mind," Dixie says. "I'll be the Darling Dog again."

"See, that's a good dog," Colt croons, his voice almost tender as he hooks his finger into the ring on the front of the collar and pulls it up so she's forced to face him again. "This girl's smart. She knows her place around here. She knows being the Dog isn't a punishment. It's an honor. Right, Winn-Dixie?"

Dixie nods like a bobblehead, and I can practically see her swooning over this guy as he humiliates her. But who am I to talk? I fell for a Darling, too, just like her and every other girl at this school. I'm no better than any of them.

Colt smiles down at Dixie, but there's a vicious glint in his eyes. His voice drops until it's barely more than a purr. "Now, meet me in the bathroom at the start of your next class, and I'll fuck the red right off that pretty pout."

He turns and walks away, leaving her gaping after him.

"Want me to break his arm, too?" Duke asks. "Because I'll do it for you."

"No," Dixie says, shaking her head and staring down at her lunch, her face scarlet. "I—I really don't mind being the Dog."

"Dixie," I begin. "You don't have to do that to get his attention."

She raises her eyes to mine. "No, *you* don't have to," she says. "I am a dog, Crystal. At least this way, people look at me like I'm something... Intriguing. When I'm not the Darling Dog, they call me a dog, anyway—and worse."

"Who?" I demand. "That's bullshit, Dixie."

She shrugs. "Everyone. It doesn't matter. But I'm tired of being called a fat cow. When I'm theirs, no one else dares mess with me."

"She's right," Dolly says. "The Darlings are very possessive about their Dogs and Dolls."

I want to protest, but I have to admit she's right. When I was the Dog, no one except the Darlings messed with me. When the girls put dogfood in my locker, they were publicly shamed.

"I'm not sure it's worth it," I say at last. "What they do to the Dog, it's really fucked up."

"They did those things to you because you fought back," Dixie says. "Not because you were their dog. If they take me to a party, and all I have to do is wear a leash, at least I'm at a Darling party. I mean, when else would a girl who looks like me get to go to a party like that?"

"Since when are the Darlings back on good terms?" Baron asks, changing the subject before I can argue more. "I thought they let Devlin's dad rot in jail for a week instead of posting bail. What gives?"

"The Darlings aren't on good terms," Dolly confirms. "Their families are still on the outs. The police are still investigating Devlin's dad, but y'all—and don't hate me for saying this—he didn't do it. I've known that man since I was born, and he wouldn't hurt a fly."

"Not to mention he'd never do anything that would risk taking him away from his family," Dixie says. "Mr. Darling's a real family man."

"Really?" I ask, quirking a brow. "Because I seem to remember his real mom saying he cheated on her."

"No, no, no," Dolly says, holding up a hand. "That's not even fair."

"Then what happened?"

She opens her mouth and then closes it. "You know, you better ask Devlin about all that," she says at last. "It's not my place to air all his family's dirty laundry. I just want you to know that I'm not saying all the Darlings are innocent, or that they're good people, but Devlin's dad? He's good people."

Carmen and Kaylee the horse-faced head cheerleader walk by, slowing to sneer at us. "Look, it's the whore of

Faulkner. I wonder if she's fucking her own dog. No one else would want her now."

"They've all had a turn, anyway," Carmen says.

"You seem awfully interested in what I do with my vagina," I say. "Maybe you're the one who wants me now."

"Oh my god," she squeals in disgust, like I just used some unspeakably vulgar term. "Could you be any more tacky?"

"I'll ask Coach Snow when I'm done taking your place on the squad," I say with a smile.

"In your dreams, skank," Kaylee says.

"Whoa," Duke says. "I was going to let this go on in case you and Dolly got in a hot girl fight, but no one talks to my sister like that."

I set a hand on his arm to steady him before turning back to Kaylee. "Not in my dreams," I say. "This Friday. Enjoy your time on the squad while you have it."

"This school would never allow someone with a reputation like yours to cheer in front of the whole town," Carmen says. "You're an embarrassment to Willow Heights."

I shrug. "You had a member who ate dogfood off the floor."

"Not even," Kaylee says, her eyes flashing with hatred. "She was off the team the second that happened."

"And you'll never make it on," Carmen says. "You're nothing but white trash in an expensive wardrobe."

"That's not a very nice way to talk to a girl on your squad."

"You will *never* cheer on my squad," Kaylee hisses, her face twisting into something ugly.

"Okay," I say with a shrug.

"And don't you dare even *think* about calling it your squad," she continues, obviously about to lose her shit.

Carmen hooks her arm through Kaylee's. "Willow Heights has class, and our squad reflects that."

"Oh, is that what you call your pathetic pep squad routine?" I ask.

"You'll never make the squad," Kaylee fumes. "I'll make sure of it."

"Okay," I say again, giving them a little finger wave and a smile. "See you Friday, girls."

When they flounce off, Dixie gapes at me like I'm some kind of hero. "Oh my god," she gushes. "You are such a badass."

"She's right," I say with a shrug. "We'll never make the squad. Coach Snow is too smart to add people who the other girls won't work with."

"But… I know the whole routine."

"Oh, we're still doing it," I assure her. "I'm not going to slink away like I'm beaten. But I don't want you to get your hopes up. We can make a point, but we won't be cheerleaders here."

"It's true," Dolly says. "But I'm still in, too. I wouldn't mind showing them what they've been missing out on by not having me on the squad."

Dixie looks back and forth between us and then nods, a grin spreading across her face. "Okay," she says. "I'm in, too. I love your dance, Crystal."

She and Dolly go off to fix themselves up before class, leaving me with the twins as they discuss the latest obstacle in their quest for domination. The Darling cousins seem to be on good terms again, but maybe they're putting on a show, presenting a united front so they can keep their place at the top. After all, if they show cracks in the perfect image they've so painstakingly created here, it would be easy for my brothers to take them down. How can they find out if the Darlings are really solid, or if now is the time for a decisive power move by the Dolces?

As they talk, I go back to Dolly's parting words about Devlin's dad. I can't help but wonder, are we good people?

# three

*Crystal*

*All the haters who call me weak? I don't hate you. I pity you. You think strength is measured by the choice to fight with fists and the loudness of a girl's mouth. Good thing human intelligence isn't measured by what your tiny minds can comprehend.*

"Hey, baby," Shaun says to me in class on Friday. "You got plans this weekend?"

I shut off my phone and glance at the table to the right and one row forward where Devlin and Dolly sit side by side. Whatever their squabbles, they seem to have worked them out. I guess that's what friends do when one person's having a hard time. I'm glad he has someone to confide in, someone who's there for him when I can't be, but it still hurts to know that I'm not that person for him. Still, if the only good I can do is bring them together, I have to be happy with that.

I shake my hair back and turn to Shaun, who sits at the table to my right, behind Devlin. "I don't date," I say. "But thanks."

"Who said anything about dating?" he asks. The other guy at his table slugs him in the shoulder and snickers into his fist.

I give Shaun a tight smile. "I'll pass."

I've been dealing with this shit all week. Maybe Dixie's right about being the Darling Dog.

"I can bring friends," Shaun says. "I hear that's your thing, and I've got plenty."

"No, thanks."

"Aw, come on," Shaun wheedles. "I've seen those tits. I know what you're working with."

Devlin shoots out of his chair and spins around, grabbing Shaun by the hair and slamming his face down on the lab table. "What the—"

Before Shaun can finish his protest, Devlin lifts his head and drives a fist straight into his nose. I hear bones crunch. Blood is gushing from his face, and he howls once before Devlin throws him out of his chair onto the floor. Shaun scurries backwards, screaming curses and trying to hold his broken face together.

"She said no," Devlin growls before he spits on the floor between Shaun's feet.

Shaun hiccups out a sob.

"Devlin Darling," the teacher barks. "There's no fighting in my class."

"There shouldn't be any fucking assholes, either," Devlin says, dropping back into his seat.

"Go to the nurse," the teacher says to Shaun.

Holy shit. She's just going to let Devlin sit there like nothing happened.

I'm shaking so hard I think I'll puke, and I'm glad I didn't drink the coffee I found in my locker this morning.

Did Devlin really beat the shit out of some guy in class just for talking to me? Colt said I was now free of the Darling shadow, that I was nothing to them, neither Dog nor Doll. But obviously I'm not fair game for the average douchebag. Like every time they've made rules for me, they've left out a key factor, making sure I can never win their fucking games no matter how hard I try to figure them out, play by the rules, or break the rules.

As Shaun stumbles out, Devlin sits facing forward, flexing his hand in his lap—his right hand. His throwing hand.

"Is your hand okay?" I ask quietly.

Devlin doesn't turn, but I see his shoulders stiffen. "Now you care?" he mutters, his voice edged with bitterness and so quiet I can't be sure those are his words.

Suddenly, my throat tightens. When my eyes fall to the trail of crimson droplets Shaun left, my stomach lurches. At last, my gaze stops at the splatter of blood on his desk where his nose exploded, and I just can't. I shoot up from my seat and hurry out, trying not to see the blood, unable to see anything else. I make it to the bathroom before I get sick.

Afterwards, I rinse my mouth until there's nothing of the sour taste left. I stand in front of the mirror trying to catch my breath. My lipstick is gone, and my mascara runs down my cheeks in black rivulets. I left my bag in class, which means I have no makeup, no way to fix this. A tendril of panic wraps itself around my spine. I can't go back to class without makeup, without my face on. It's been four years since I went to school without makeup. It's my armor. It would be like showing up to school in my pajamas—without a bra.

But as I stare at my bloodshot eyes, tears leaking from them, I'm so fucking done with that. I'm tired of faking it, pretending, and praying with every fiber of my being that someone will approve of me. I'm tired of having to pass an army of inspectors every morning before I leave the house, like I'm a piece of meat about to be shipped to the grocery store, USDA approved for consumption.

I lean over, turn the warm water on, and splash my face, scrubbing until there's no makeup left to ruin. When I finally stand up and shut off the water, I almost scream. I stumble backward, adrenaline spiking through me. Someone is standing by the door, watching me.

No, not someone.

Devlin.

"What, you're scared of me now?" he asks.

I grab a handful of paper towels and pat my face dry while my mind reels with possibilities. "Considering you spent the last two months telling me every day that I should be terrified, I don't think that would be unjustified."

"You didn't answer my question."

I swallow hard, balling the paper into my fist. "No," I say at last. "I'm not scared of you. You just startled me."

We stand there staring at each other for a long minute. "Are you okay?" he asks at last.

"Fine. Just the sight of all that blood…" I break off with a shudder.

"I wasn't talking about that."

I gaze into his turbulent blue eyes, the distance between us seeming impossibly far. I can't take the first step, though. It's as if we're both frozen in place, rooted on opposite shores of this impossible divide with no boat to reach the other side.

I don't know how to answer his question. Am I okay? No, I'm not fucking okay. My life is spinning out of control. My brother is completely changed. My mother escaped us like we were a trap, without so much as a goodbye note, though she did text when she made it home. The rest of my relatives left, including the grandmother I love and the grandfather who I'm pretty sure killed someone while he was here. My best friend outside my family, for some inexplicable reason, wants to be the Darling Dog. And somewhere along the way, I started counting on this insane boy for support, and then I broke his fucking heart—on purpose.

Because that's what Dolces do.

"I'm okay," I say, nodding. Because that's what Dolces say. "You?"

Devlin leans against one of the sinks, and my eyes drink him in, because damn if he isn't so beautiful it tears me up inside. He rubs his forehead with his thumb before lifting his head to face me. "No," he says, bracing his hand on the edge of the sink. "Crystal, I fucking... What I did to you in that locker room..." He shakes his head, the torment in his eyes unfathomable. "How can you be okay?"

"Devlin, no," I say, moving toward him, my feet suddenly unglued from the floor. I stop in front of him. "Listen, I get it. Your cousin made you prove your loyalty, and you did. It wasn't ideal, and yeah, I wish the rumor hadn't gone the way it did, but it's not like we hadn't hooked up before. It's not like... Like I didn't want you to."

"You said no," he says quietly, his eyes searching mine. They're still as deep as the lake I saw that first day, but the ice is gone, and all I see now is the pain in the depths of that endless blue.

"Devlin," I say, pain twisting in my own heart. I step closer to him, until our bodies almost collide, and raise my hand to cup his cheek. I wait until his gaze meets mine to go on. "You were protecting me from them. I was saying I didn't want them. I never said no to you."

His lips tighten, and then he reaches up and takes my hand, pulling it away from his face. "You did, Crystal. You said no. Twice."

"Not to you," I say, shaking my head. "I can't believe you've been thinking all this time… I'm sorry."

"Don't you dare apologize to me," he growls. "Not after what I did to you."

"Devlin, I know what you're talking about," I say. "I did say no. I said it once to Preston, and once to Colt. I never said no to you. I… I wanted you to do what you did."

My heart is hammering in my throat at the admission.

Devlin stares at me a long minute. "How could you want that?"

"Because I did," I say. "I was never saying no to you. I couldn't if I tried. You know that, Devlin. You know I liked it, even there, even like that. You must have felt that."

Color rises to my cheeks as I remember all those people watching. I didn't care. My body wanted Devlin's, always, no matter what. I was wet for him. I would have come if he had kept going. I'm glad he didn't. It's humiliating enough that they saw me the way they did. I don't need them to have seen me even more vulnerable.

"Fuck, Crystal," he says, his voice low and hoarse. "Are you trying to kill me?"

"No," I whisper. "I know it's wrong, and I've tried, but I can't help myself with you."

"Jesus Christ," he says, pulling away and raking a hand through his blond hair, leaving it tousled in a way that reminds me too much of when we're in bed together. "Crystal, you can't just say those things to a man."

"What?" I ask. "The truth?"

He stares at me a second and then nods. "Yeah."

"I'm tired of hiding," I say. "I'm tired of the lies, and the costume, and carrying the weight of this name. I just want to be myself, like I was with you."

I know I should stop, that I'm laying everything out for him to trample, that I'm laying myself bare for him. But even though I hurt him last, even though it's his turn for revenge, I can't stop myself. I want to lay every part of myself bare. I want to be vulnerable. Only for him.

Devlin swallows and takes my hand, placing it on his chest. He covers my small hand with his rough one, and I can feel the rapid, steady beat of his heart. "I want that, too," he says quietly. "You're so damn beautiful it kills me, Crystal. You should never have to hide who you are, or what you look like, or that heart that's too good for me or your family. Every inch of you is fucking magnificent."

I can't stand to be away from him after touching him. It's like an addict's craving. I broke and took one hit, and now I need more. Now I can't stop. I take his hand, turning it over between mine. "Did you hurt your hand?"

"I'll ice it."

"I can't believe you did that for me," I say, skimming my fingers gently over his red knuckles. They're already swelling. "What if it's really hurt?"

"You're worth it."

We stay there another moment, neither of us moving. My heart is hammering, and I don't dare look at him. I can barely believe I'm touching him at all. I can't risk making him pull away, reminding me that this thing between us is over, that it has no future. That people like us get to keep only memories.

At last, I can't hold back any longer. "Devlin," I begin. "I…"

"Don't," he says, his hand covering my mouth. His blue eyes are soft as a baby's blanket as his gaze caresses my face. "Let's just leave it at that."

"But—" I try to speak behind his hand, but he shakes his head.

"You know we can't be together," he says. "Not after what our families did. And that's for the best, Crystal."

Tears pool in my eyes, and I turn my face away, pushing his hand away. "How is this for the best?"

"Trust me when I say you're better off without me."

"That's why you left me alone all week? Because you think I'm better off without you?"

"I left you alone because you told me to," he says slowly. "And because you were right to. Everything you said that day was true. I'm no good for you, Sugar. Hell, I'm no good for anyone."

"That's not true," I say, my voice breaking. I reach for him, but this time he pulls away, stepping back toward the door.

"Come on, Crystal," he says. "I never deserved a girl like you. I never deserved anything from you. But I'm a guy like me, so I took it, anyway. Now I'm paying for it, and I'm sorry that you have to pay for it, too."

I swallow hard, swiping away the tears on my lashes. "Now what?"

"Now, you go make your family happy because that's what you do."

"What about you?"

The ghost of a smile plays over Devlin's lips. "I'll try not to fuck up anyone else who asks you out. It might take a couple tries, but I'll get used to it eventually. And pretty soon, I'll be just that asshole who punched out a couple guys who wanted to date you. And pretty soon after that, I'll be nothing to you."

"You could never be nothing to me, Devlin," I say. "I…"

"Don't say anything you can't take back," Devlin warns. His eyes search mine, and I watch his cool exterior slide back over his face, the one he shows the world just like I show them the made-up version of me. When it's firmly in place, and his eyes are that impenetrable frozen surface, and his face is hard and haughty, he smiles and pushes open the bathroom door. "See you around, Dolce."

And then he's gone. I melt back against the sink, closing my eyes and breathing deeply, trying to get myself together.

"I love you," I whisper to the silent bathroom, my whisper like the breath of a ghost against the tiled walls. The ghost of what could have been, and what can never be. He's right. If we tried to be together, our families would keep tearing each other apart. We've already torn his apart. I don't want it to do the same to mine.

But god, it hurts. Knowing what might have been, what we could have if we were anyone other than who we are, if we weren't a Dolce girl and a Darling boy.

I take a last breath, shaking my head to clear it. There's no use dwelling on what beauty could be if it existed. We both bear the yoke of our names, and we can't escape that. We're still players on the same board, still opponents. For one moment, we came together, and made magic. But that moment is over.

# four

*Crystal*

I push out of the bathroom and go to my locker, since it's almost time for the next class, and I don't even have my phone to waste the rest of the period on. As I walk down the hall, I feel naked without my makeup, but somehow stronger, too. As if I'm strong enough to fight without armor now.

I'm getting stuff for my next class from my locker when I hear quiet footsteps in the hall. I look up, my heart catching with some pathetic, terrible bud of hope.

But it's not Devlin coming back to tell me he made a mistake. It's the person I've been avoiding all week, the one whose face makes adrenaline shoot through me, my heart race, and sweat break out on my palms.

Preston is right there, so close I can see the dots of blond stubble on his angular jaw. My heart roars into overdrive, my knees nearly give out, and my hands start shaking so hard I fumble my books and they thud back into my locker. I haven't spoken to him since he beat the shit out of me and tied me up in the locker room. I was hoping I'd never run into him without my brothers there to protect me. But here he is.

He stops and looks me over, his eyes so inscrutable it makes me want to scream. "You're still here."

"So are you," I reply, forcing my fingers to close around my book. I wish I had something to defend myself, a weapon. But I know he'd just rip it out of my hand. There's no stopping this boy—or any of the Darling boys. They take what they want, and no one can stop them. Even the coach didn't stop him. I know there's no help for me, that I'm at his mercy if he wants to shove me in a closet and slit my throat with his knife. But I won't whimper and beg. I'll go down with the steel spine and the grace that makes me a Dolce. That's what matters. Not my face.

"You look different," he says.

"You know, it's a miracle what makeup can hide these days," I say. "Scrapes, bruises, ugliness."

He just stands there staring at me, his expression infuriatingly unreadable.

"Go on," I say. "I made it easy for you. Take your shot."

"Now, come on, Manhattan," he says, a tiny smile at the corner of his lips. "Where's the fun in that?"

"Just helping you out," I say smoothly. "You already made me into the school slut. Might as well take the last thing a girl has to hold onto—the illusion of beauty."

"You think you're ugly?" he asks, his head cocked to one side.

Damn him. Why can't he just cut me down? Why does he have to play with me? He looks like he wants to figure me out so he can get inside my head and destroy me from within like a parasite.

"It doesn't matter what I think," I say. "You already ruined me the easy way—by making the world admit that a girl could possibly be a sexual being, too. I know what happened in that locker room. We both know. And yet, the whole school thinks the entire football team ran a train on me. But that's just a reputation, Preston. You know as well as I do that it's not true. You know what I'm made of now. And I know what you're made of."

He leans against the locker like he's settling in for a long conversation. I should walk away. I know I should. And yet... In truth, this psychotic monster fascinates me. I can't stop myself from wanting to study him the same way he studies me. But now he's behind my locker door, where I can only see his legs.

"I could say you're ugly," he drawls. "But I'm not the liar in the family."

I'm relieved he can't see my face. Because he'd see that some stupid, stupid, stupid part of me thrills at that littlest of compliments, really just the crumb of one. Because yes, I may be standing here like it doesn't make my heart race and my head dizzy to be this close to my attacker, like I can spar with him like an equal, but I'm still a girl.

And not just a girl who wants to be told she's pretty, but the insecure little girl who wore the same lipstick for two years because someone said she liked it. The girl who sits at home wondering why Daddy's not showing up for their father-daughter date. The girl who hides under the bubbles in the bath when her mother asks how much ice cream she's been eating, the one who gets up two hours early to make sure she looks worthy of carrying the burden of her own name. I'm not bulletproof. My heart is still a fragile thing, like a butterfly just learning to spread its crinkled wings.

"Well, thanks," I say lightly. And then, because I know the faces we show the world can't hide the ugliness we feel about ourselves, I add, "You're not so bad yourself, Preston Darling."

I'm glad I'm behind my locker door, that he can't see my face. But I wish I could see his. I want to know if that little compliment might mean as much to him as it means to me.

At the same time, I expect him tell me he knows exactly how hot he is, to grab his dick and ask if I want to ride it like all the other girls.

"Why didn't you tell the police?" he asks after a beat of silence. His voice is only mildly curious, as if an assault charge is just another day in the life of a Darling boy. Maybe it is. I have no idea how many girls they've done that to— some of whom Devlin didn't rescue. "I did a number on you in that locker room," he goes on when I don't respond. "And you were with my brother all evening after that. Y'all saw the cops. You went to the hospital. You could have told them I did that to your face."

I take a steadying breath and then swing my locker door almost closed, so I can see him.

"I'm not the rat in my family." We stare at each other for a minute. "There are no rats in my family," I add. "See, that's the difference between a Darling and a Dolce, Preston. My family is good. We don't pick one person to be the liar, one to be the psycho, and one to be the bully, so we can all feel good about ourselves. Isn't that how it works? Because hey, maybe you beat the shit out of some girl and tied her up to be gang-raped, but at least you didn't lie about it."

He stares at me a long minute, those blue eyes making me rage inside, because I can't see a damn thing in them. Finally, he says, "You're not blameless, Crystal. Don't be a hypocrite."

"Oh, what, because I fought back? Because I hit you when you attacked me? That makes me just as bad?"

"Because you're human," he says.

I grab the notebook I need from my locker and close the door quietly before turning to him. "Yeah, I'm human," I say. "I make mistakes. What you did? That wasn't a mistake."

"You hurt people, too."

We stare at each other a long minute. A soft chime sounds over the intercom, and students start to pour into the hall. "You'd better go, Preston," I say. "Unless you want that other arm broken."

He lets out a little scoff, the corner of his mouth twisting up. "See? You think you're so fucking perfect, but why am I standing here with a broken arm and no football career ahead of me? This isn't some stupid prank. That is my *life*, Crystal. Football was my ticket out of here."

By the time he's finished speaking, his eyes are finally showing more than indifference. He looks savage with fury, like a trapped, desperate animal. And I want to feel something for him—maybe I even do feel something—but I can't forgive him.

"That's not my fault," I say, my own anger rising to meet his. "And listen, you can stand here and talk to me if you want, but you know the consequences. Think of it this way. You warned me to leave this school after they broke your arm, and if you want to pretend that I was asking for it because I didn't listen, fine. But now I'm warning you. If you don't listen, you know what my brothers will do. That's on you."

I turn and walk away. Maybe he deserves what my brothers will do to him or maybe he doesn't. But I'm done. I'm done with all of it. I don't want to be around for it. I'm just not a vengeful kind of person. I tried it with Devlin, and it doesn't feel good. Revenge isn't a dish best served cold. It's a dish best not served at all.

# five

*Crystal*

I make it through an entire class period before I run into my brothers. But on my way to my next class, as I'm ignoring a handful of guys taunting me and humping each other as I walk by, I run smack into Royal and King. They come to a full stop when they see me.

"What the hell, Crystal," King says, sounding halfway pissed and halfway shocked.

"So, I guess it's pretty noticeable when I don't wear makeup after all," I say. "No one seemed to care in my last class."

"What the fuck is wrong with you?" Royal asks, grabbing my arm and marching me toward the nearest restroom.

"That's what this is about?" King asks, falling into step on my other side as they bodily escort me to fix my face. "Attention?"

"No," I say, trying to twist away from Royal. "It's about the fact that it's bullshit that I have to wear a whole face full of makeup every day to hide what I look like. You don't do that. Why should I?"

"Because you look like shit like that," Royal says, shoving me into the bathroom. A handful of girls squeal and giggle when they see my brothers.

"Since when do you think I'm ugly?" I demand of my twin.

"Since you stopped looking like a Dolce girl."

"Yeah, well, who made you the judge of what I get to wear? Not everyone thinks I have to hide behind a pound of makeup to look good."

"Who doesn't?" Royal asks, his eyes narrowing and his nostrils flaring with fury. His fingers crush my wrist in their grip, but I refuse to flinch.

"You know who," I say quietly, staring right back at him.

"Say his name to me right now," he growls. "I fucking dare you."

"Where's your bag?" King asks, looking around.

"I left it in science."

He turns to the girls huddled in front of the mirror watching the drama. "Can one of you ladies go get my sister her handbag?" he asks, flashing them a quick smile.

"Sure," Carmen says with a giggle that's nothing like the bitchy attitude she shows me. She's all too happy to scamper away with her friends and help me out if it'll get her points with my brothers.

"Would the rest of you mind watching the door?" he says. "This is a family matter, and we need a little privacy."

They fall all over themselves to obey, batting their eyes and sending inviting smiles our way as they sashay out. I roll my eyes at them, but they're too busy eye-fucking my brothers to notice.

The minute the door closes behind them, Royal jerks at my wrist again. "What do you have to say for yourself, Crystal?"

"Nothing," I snap, twisting to free myself from his bruising grasp. "Now let go. You're hurting me."

"Did you say that to Devlin Darling when he was trying to fuck you?" Royal asks.

"What the fuck is wrong with you?" I demand. "Who even are you?"

"Royal," King warns. "Let her go."

"Me?" Royal asks, ignoring our brother. "Who are you? I left my twin sister and came back a week later to some football team-servicing slut."

"Don't call me that," I say through clenched teeth. "You don't know anything about it."

"Yeah, you're right," he says, shoving me away. "Because you didn't tell me."

"You're one to talk," I burst out, rubbing my wrist. "You've barely said two words to me since you got home."

"Fine," he says, crossing his arms over his chest. "I didn't really want to hear about it, but if it makes you happy, tell me. Tell me all about how you stuck your ass in the air like a slot machine and let every single guy on the football team stick his dick in you while the rest of them cheered each other on. Tell me how you sent them off to the game in high spirits, because what else could get them so pumped up but running a tag-team on my sister?"

"You're disgusting," I whisper.

"The feeling is mutual, little sister."

"Crystal," King says slowly. "Why don't you tell us what happened? Because the rest of us have been hearing about it for the past two weeks, and we all know how rumors twist the truth, but it's not something a man wants to hear about his little sister."

I look up at my oldest brother. He is a man now, eighteen, all tall and broad and destined to bring some girl to her knees before she even knows what hit her. And even though it's none of his business, and it's my body and not his, I suddenly want to tell him. I want to tell him because his dark eyes are filled with such an ache that it twists my heart around and makes me want to cry. I know that no matter what my brothers do, King's number one priority will always be the rest of us. He's a born protector, even if he was born into a world where protecting everyone you love is impossible.

But how do I tell him what happened without getting people killed? Because he will want revenge for this one. No matter what I say, it will come out worse than it was. He'll kill Devlin, and the Darlings will kill him, and it won't stop until every member of both families is dead.

"I can't," I say, dropping my gaze and turning away. "It's too hard to explain, and you won't understand it."

"Try me," King says, his voice gentle but commanding.

"Okay," I say, bracing my hands on the sink and taking a trembling breath. I remember leaning on this sink in a very different situation, with Devlin between my thighs.

And I remember some girls saying I let the Darlings fuck me in the bathroom. If they heard that somewhere, I guarantee they didn't keep it a secret. Which means my brothers probably heard those rumblings as well. I've been struggling so hard here, just trying to keep my head above water, that I haven't thought about how the swirling rumors were getting back to my brothers.

"I've only ever been with Devlin," I say. "I've never done anything else with anyone else. I've never even touched another guy. I swear."

"Bullshit," Royal growls.

I look up. "What?"

"You kissed Colt at Homecoming," he says. "I saw you. Or did you forget I was there while you were busy fucking his cousin? Why should we believe anything that comes out of your mouth? You were lying about all of it, weren't you?"

Damn it. Why did I lie about liking Colt? Royal could always read me like a book. He probably knew I was lying the whole time. And he paid for that lie, more than I ever will, more than I can even imagine.

"I'm sorry," I say. "You're right. Colt kissed me, and I guess I kissed him back. But we went to that dance as friends, like I told you. We were friends."

"And you were fucking Devlin."

"No," I say firmly. "That happened after. You can ask the twins."

"We already know that part," King says. "What happened in the locker room the day the coach asked us to stay late and the rest of the team went in?"

Shit. The coach. The coach who walked away when he saw me with Preston, the one who refused to help. That asshole intentionally kept my brothers from coming in, knowing they'd help me.

I shake the thought away. I don't know that it was him. Maybe they'd already planned to hold my brothers. Maybe Preston told another one of the coaches when he left me there alone and went out to watch the practice from the sidelines, fuming about his broken arm. Did I really end his football dreams? And why is he so desperate to get out of this town where he's royalty, a town that will all but belong to him one day?

"Why should we believe her, anyway?" Royal asks.

"Fine," I say with a shrug. "I don't have to tell you guys anything. What I do with my body is none of your fucking business. I don't interrogate you every time you pump and dump some poor girl. And I bet it's a lot more than a football team's worth. So if I want to let every guy on the team line up to drop his coin in my slot-machine ass, as you so succinctly put it, that's my choice."

"I'll believe you, Crys," King says. "Tell me the truth, and I won't question whatever you say. I just want to hear it from you once."

"Why?" I ask, crossing my arms and glaring at him. "Why does it matter?"

"Because I want to know you're safe here. That you're okay. You looked pretty bad when you came to the hospital that night. And yeah, I know we were all busy worrying about Royal, but that doesn't mean I didn't notice."

"I'm fine," I say, squeezing myself tighter, my throat aching at his kindness. I can handle Royal's anger better than the sympathy and concern I see in King's eyes. If I tell him, he'll hurt Preston more. And Preston will hurt me more—or worse, he'll hurt them. And it will go on and on and on, until someone dies. And even then, it might not stop. Like Preston said, this has gone beyond pranks and petty parking lot quarrels. Lives are being altered irreparably. One look at Royal is proof of that.

"Did Devlin hit you?" King asks.

"No," I say. "He never hurt me."

"Did he rape you?" Royal asks.

"No," I say, shaking my head vehemently. I'm not sure how to tell them without it coming off as worse than it was. Even Devlin thought it was something other than what it was. It was never like that for me. I never said no to him. I said no to Preston, to Colt, to the idea of the team even touching me. Devlin asked if that was what I wanted, if I wanted him to fuck me there, and I told him I did. Didn't I? I remember wanting to tell him yes. Sure, part of it was fear that if it wasn't him, it would be them, but when he wrapped his arms around me, blocking me from their view, I felt him protecting me. He hadn't hurt me. He'd claimed me, told the whole world that I was his. And I had wanted that.

I had wanted it because that was the moment when I knew that he actually cared about me. That I had won, as fucked up as that sounds. I'd been trying to get him to fall in love so that I could hurt him. And that was the moment when I knew I could. When he'd protected me, marked me as off-limits to everyone in the school, even his cousins.

I think it was the moment he realized he cared, too. He took me home, cleaned me up, took care of me. He even made sure I got off, since I didn't in the locker room. He drove me around, risked himself, went against his family to help me find Royal. And I still broke his heart.

A knock on the door startles me out of my thoughts. King doesn't move. He's watching me, waiting. After a moment, Royal goes to the door. Carmen hands in my purse. "Everything okay?" she asks, batting her eyes at him.

"Fine," he says, pushing the door closed in her face.

He hands me the bag. "Get yourself together."

"Why do I have to look the way you guys want me to?" I ask.

"Because you're a Dolce," Royal says. "Get used to it. Mom doesn't sit around the house in a bathrobe with unwashed hair. You know why? Because she was raised with more class than that. We may not have much else, but we have that. Now, put on your makeup, or I'll put it on for you."

"Fine, since I don't want to look like Picasso painted me, I'll put on the damn makeup," I snap. "I still don't get why you guys care so much."

"Because I need a job when I graduate," King says quietly. "And they've already got a lawyer and somebody to do the books. And they look at everybody and everybody's family. We can't look like slobs. This is a big opportunity for me. Don't fuck it, okay? Please?"

"What are you talking about?" I ask, meeting his eyes in the mirror as I do my makeup.

"Come on, Crys," King says. "Have you ever heard me talking about college? I'm a senior. You know I'm not going to school next year."

"What do you mean?" I ask, my heart suddenly hammering.

"I mean, I'm going back to New York when I graduate," he says, his face grave. "I'm going to work for the Valentis."

"What?" I ask, my heart thudding so loud I can hear it in my ears. "Why?"

King shrugs. "Al Valenti is Mom's uncle."

"Holy shit," I whisper. Al Valenti might as well be Al Capone—just a century later. It's one thing to know my family might take loans from the mob, or do a few dirty deeds for them, but this… Fuck. We're not working for the mafia. We *are* the fucking mafia.

Have I met this famous mob boss and not even known about it? I've heard people talk about Uncle Al. I'm pretty sure that as a kid, when we'd go visit my grandparents on Mom's side for the Fourth of July or a Memorial Day cookout, Uncle Al was among the relatives. I might have even been to his house. But it's too hard to remember. I think of all the uncles and "uncles" who've come through our house over the years. It's impossible to know who's actually related or even whose uncle they are. Mom's? Dad's? Ours? Our nonni's?

And then there's the fact that half the ones related to us are only related through marriage. Keeping track of which side of the family they come from is hard enough. I'm definitely lost by the time I'm trying to figure out which side of each of my grandparent's family they're from. But shit. I try to think of anything I know about Al Valenti—not the

Uncle Al slowly forming into a picture in my mind, a rather quiet, watchful man in his fifties who never drew attention to himself at parties—but the legendary mafia boss on the news.

But I don't watch the news unless it's assigned for a class. I'm a normal sixteen-year-old. I watch YouTube videos, social media stories, and occasionally *Your Celebrity Eyes,* the gossip channel. If I'm feeling really gossipy, I'll read Page Six. Which is why I know the name Valenti in the first place. There are a couple notorious socialites around my age who carry the name, no doubt part of his family tree.

"So, it's true," I say at last, dropping my mascara into my bag and snapping it closed, having done my face while I mulled over his words. "Everything the Darlings say about us, that it's dirty money—they have a point."

"Who's side are you on?" Royal asks, narrowing his eyes.

"I think I've proven I'm on your side," I say through gritted teeth. "Though I'm beginning to question whether that's the right side."

"Crystal," King says. "You know how hard Dad works. You know he earned what we have."

"I'm going to class. I'm late." I shove out of the bathroom, and they don't stop me. Now that I apparently look suitable for the great-niece of a mafia king, they're satisfied with me.

# six

*Crystal*

*Is my protective, caring brother really so excited about working for ruthless killers? Is this an opportunity for him, or is he trying to soften the blow and hide the truth by calling it that? King heals and protects. He'd be a good doctor. Not a killer. So, why is he going to work for Mom's family? Was he promised in some grisly exchange straight out of a fairytale, a beautiful daughter's hand in exchange for a firstborn son? Is that what King is? A debt Daddy owes to the mob?*

I don't go to class. I walk past my class, all the way down the hall to the door where Devlin came in that night when we were looking for Royal. Today, the parking lot is full. I find Devlin's car, and I sit on the hood, and I text him.

And then I think about what King said about Dad making his own money. Nonna told me that they owed money to the wrong people, and that's why they came here when Dad was a kid. And that he was determined to make it after that. I can put it all together from there. He came up with a plan to expand my grandparents' little mom-and-pop candy store into an empire. He came up with some ideas for new candies, something of his own to make him stand out. And Devlin's dad helped him.

That's what Mom said. That there was some dispute over a patent, ownership of something. Did she say Devlin's dad tried to steal Daddy's idea? But I can guess what really happened. I know Daddy's cut-throat, that he'd step on anyone to get to the top. So, which one was thought up by Mr. Darling in some brainstorming session? Our famous Dolce Drops? Dolce Sweets or Dolce Pops? And then Dad claimed them all for his own. But if the Darlings hated him and this all ended in a big brawl, why was he working with Mr. Darling in the first place?

That's an easy question to answer. Dad wanted funding, and my grandparents weren't rich. He must have convinced them to work with him, but when they realized he wanted all the credit, and they were going to just back the operation, they must have pulled out.

Which left Daddy with no money. But he knew someone who would loan him money. They'd already lent it to his parents. Someone with bottomless pockets, and an effortlessly beautiful, glamourous, single niece.

I swallow hard, feeling sick.

Maybe I'm being too hard on him. But all my life, I've idolized my father. To find out that he stole someone's idea and funded his empire with blood money—it shatters all my illusions.

Would he marry someone to get in with her powerful family? Mom herself gave me that answer. Daddy's ambition always, always comes first, before everything, including her, and us, and anything else in the world.

When my grandparents moved back to New York, he must have contacted Al Valenti for a loan. Maybe he was scheming on Mom then, or maybe he met her through his connection with them. King is right about one thing, though—Daddy works harder than anyone in this world. But if he took a loan from the mafia, even after he paid it back, it's still dirty money. It's all blood money because the seed was blood money, and you can't grow an apple tree from a pomegranate seed.

"Hey."

I turn to see Devlin standing at the rear of his car, his eyes wary.

"Can you take me home?" I blurt, not bothering with pretenses.

"Shouldn't your brothers be doing that for you now?" he asks. "You made it clear you don't need me around."

"Devlin, that's not fair," I say. "And you know it."

His lips tighten, and he rakes a hand through his hair and sighs. He jerks his chin toward the car, looking down at me in that damn hot way of his. He unlocks the car, and I climb in before he can move because I don't want to know if he was going to open the door for me or not.

"Why don't you have your own car?" he asks, glancing sideways at me as he starts the little Ferrari. The engine purrs, and I lay my head back on the headrest and close my eyes. I need to drive, to get out of here, but he just sits there waiting for my answer, not going anywhere.

"My family won't let me learn to drive."

"Why not?" he asks. "All your brothers have cars. Even the freshmen."

"But how could they control me if I could just leave on my own?" I ask, an edge of bitterness creeping into my voice. I've wanted a license for two years, since Royal got his at fourteen, thanks to some of Daddy's connections who could pretend Royal needed a hardship license, as if he had to go to work and provide for his family.

"And you said my family's backwards," Devlin mutters.

"Yeah," I say. "We're fucked up like that."

His hand falls on my knee, and I try not to gasp aloud at his touch. Just the warmth of his hand on my bare skin makes me want to eat him alive. I have to force myself not to move. If I do, he might stop touching me, and I might crumble to dust and blow away.

"Crystal," he says. "What's going on?"

"What do you mean?"

"You never talk bad about your family," he says. "What happened?"

"I think you were right," I admit, opening my eyes and forcing myself to focus on something besides the heat of his hand shimmering up my thigh, awakening things that are better left dead. "My family is tied to the mafia. My dad stole some candy recipe from your dad and ran off to get funded by the Valentis themselves."

Devlin stares ahead for a second, his other hand resting on the steering wheel. We're still in the parking lot. I'm still itching to move, to do something, like it's all wound up tight inside me and I need to let it out. I need to scream, or drive so fast I can't remember anything but how to breathe, or numb myself with a credit card and a website full of shoes I'll wear once and forget I own.

"That's not exactly what happened," Devlin says. "But yeah, I know your family's tied up in that shit. I told you that before."

"I know," I say. "I guess I just didn't want to know the truth. They've always kept me sheltered from it, and I was happy to stay that way. It's the same with the car. They won't buy me a car because then they'd have to teach me to drive. And they won't teach me to drive because then they wouldn't know where I am at all times. I know they mean well, that they want to protect me. But they also want to see me in a certain way."

"They want to control you," he says.

I start to protest, to defend them because it's my default setting, but then I stop myself. "Yeah," I say. "So, tell me what happened between our dads."

"They were in a class together senior year," Devlin says with a shrug. "It was one of those senior project classes. They were paired up, and they had to come up with some idea for a business and try to start it. No one expects a business to actually succeed when you're in high school, but this school likes to prepare people for the real world, and it looks good on college applications and all that. Dad thought they could make your family's candy business into something big, Dolce Sweets. He just came up with the name and the idea and the first candy together. The recipes, all the rest of it, that's all your family's. That all came later."

"But the whole idea for Dolce Sweets was your dad's?"

He shrugs. "Yeah. They were going to be business partners and keep it going after high school, turn it into something real. Your dad knew some people back in New York who could lend him some startup money, but once my dad found out who it was, he didn't want anything to do with it. So your dad took the idea and ran with it. Literally."

"Fuck," I say, letting my head fall back again. Once, I would have doubted him, called him a liar. But I know it's true. There's too much evidence to back up what he's saying, and nothing but naïve loyalty to back up a denial.

Devlin slides his seat all the way back and pats his thigh. "Come here and drive us home."

"What?" My head snaps up and I stare at him.

"You said you don't know how to drive," he says, a smile tugging at his lips. "This is the south, Sugar. Everybody drives."

"But… What if I wreck?"

"You won't," he says. "I'll be right here to catch you if something goes wrong."

"You just got this car," I say, my protests getting weaker. I really fucking want to do this. But the thought of sitting in his lap while I do it… I don't know if I can handle that.

"And I can get another," he says. "It doesn't mean shit to me."

I wince at the reminder of what my brothers did to the car that did mean something to him. "I'm sorry," I say. "About your other car."

He shrugs. "It gives me an excuse to spend time with my dad building a new one."

*If he doesn't go to jail,* I think. God, this is so fucked up.

I swallow hard before climbing across the seat. Devlin puts the top down so I don't have to duck my head while sitting on his lap in the small car. Then he pulls the seatbelt around us both and snaps it into place.

"I don't think you're supposed to double up in a seatbelt," I say, ignoring the thudding of my heart. "Then we'll both be crushed to death if I wreck."

"If you die, I'm going down with you," Devlin says, squeezing me against him. "Besides, I can't really think of a better way to die than crushed up against you."

"I'd choose a heart attack during sex," I say. "Sorry to the guy who's fucking me, but I'm selfish like that."

"You're twisted as fuck, you know that, Dolce?" Devlin says.

"I think we both know that."

"Stop talking about sex while you're in my lap, or I'll pull up your skirt and fuck you while you're driving, and we'll both get our death wish."

"Fine, what do I do?" I ask, but I can't stop thinking about what he said. I can't stop feeling dizzy and intoxicated from inhaling the scent of him so close to me. I can't stop feeling his body against mine, his strong thighs under mine; his taut abs and muscular chest pressing to my back with each breath; the relentless, demanding ridge of his erection growing under me.

"First, take off your shoes," he says. "I don't know how you even walk in those, but you're not driving my car in them."

"Isn't that illegal or something?"

"Nah," he says. "That's how I learned. You can really feel the pedals, how much pressure to use, with bare feet."

"That's so redneck of you," I tease.

"Shut up and drive."

I laugh, and he guides me out of the parking lot and then through town. He takes the steering wheel when he needs to, coaches me through restarting when I stall out at a stop sign, and taps the brake when I'm not quick enough. And all the time, he acts like he's not hard as a rock under me, like his cock isn't burning into me and lighting me on fire. If it weren't for the fact that I can feel his desire throbbing against me, I'd believe he didn't feel anything for me anymore.

By the time we pull up in his driveway, I'm squirming on his lap, the heat between my thighs an unbearable, wet ache.

"That was quite a ride," he murmurs against my shoulder as his hand finds the seatbelt and unbuckles. The pressure holding our bodies together releases, and an anguished cry ripples through every cell in my body. I bite my lip to keep it from bursting from my lips.

I twist around to face him, my breath already labored, desperation eating me up from within. "Devlin," I whisper. "Can we go inside?"

"I… Don't think that's a good idea," he says, glancing up at his big house.

"Are your parents home?"

"It's not that."

"I'm sorry," I say, twisting around further so I can slide my hand behind his neck. "I'm so fucking sorry I said all those things to you. And I know I'm not supposed to want this, but I don't care. I want it, anyway. I want you, anyway."

"How can you?" he asks, his hand cupping the back of my head and pulling me forward, his hand rumpling my hair as he presses his forehead to mine. "After everything I did to you—how can you do anything but hate me? I fucking hate myself."

"I told you," I say, stroking the back of his neck with my thumb. "I wasn't saying no to you."

"I'm not talking about that," he says. "I'm talking about everything. I don't even know where to start, or how to apologize to you, Crystal. You should despise me."

"But I don't," I say, squeezing my eyes closed. My heart is beating so hard I feel dizzy, and the smell of him is making my head spin. "I care about you too much."

He closes his eyes and takes a deep breath. "Don't say that."

"I do," I insist. "I can't help myself. I'm sorry. I know we can't be together, but I fucking need you, Devlin. I just…"

"Don't cry," he says, his thumb smoothing across my cheek, skimming my wet lashes. I'm not crying yet, but I'm about to. "Tell me what you need, baby. Tell me what to do."

"I need you to fuck me," I whisper. "It doesn't have to mean anything."

He tenses, and I don't blame him. I made him fuck me until he cared about me, and then I ripped his heart out like some heartless bitch who needed it to fill the void where her own should be. Maybe that's exactly what I am, but I can't stop myself. I hold onto him, not letting him go this time. There's something wrong with me, something missing, and only he can make me feel whole.

"I don't know if I'm capable of that," Devlin says quietly, his hands falling to my waist. "And even if I was, I don't think I could be capable of it with you."

I remember what Lacey told me on my first day at Willow Heights, that Devlin didn't sleep around. I hate myself for asking him for this, but not enough to change my mind. I need closure, need to know that I can move on, and I don't know if I'll ever be able to do that with the way we left things.

"Just this once," I say, a tear sliding down my cheek. "Please. For me. I can't have our last time be that time in the locker room. Just let me have this, just one time. Let me feel every moment like it's the first time, for the last time. And we'll pretend the rest of it never happened."

Devlin's jaw tightens, and he just stares at me like I'm some kind of stranger to him, and it breaks my fucking heart.

"I can feel how much you want me," I whisper. "Feel how much I want you." I take his hand and slide it down from my hip, around my waist, and down, burying it between my thighs.

Devlin draws a sharp breath.

I tug up my skirt, pulling it around my hips, and press his fingers to my soaked cotton underpants.

"Fuck," he breathes, his head dropping back against the seat. He closes his eyes, his breathing labored, but he doesn't move a muscle.

I pull aside the fabric and press his fingers to my bare, wet flesh. "Just one more time," I beg. "Let me remember you like this. Just us."

Without a word, Devlin slides his hand down and buries a finger deep inside me. He groans and pushes deeper, lifting his hips to push his cock against my ass. I tilt my hips and grind into his palm, spreading my thighs for him, desperate for him to obliterate me.

His head snaps up, and he grabs my chin and turns my head toward him, his mouth smashing into mine and his finger pumping into me. I moan into his mouth helplessly, rocking against his hand as I bury both hands in his hair and my tongue in his mouth, tasting him and drinking him in like it's the only thing keeping me alive. He slides his hand over my hair, yanking out my hair tie and running his hands through it, mussing it until all the work I did to polish and smooth my long dark mane is erased, and it tumbles around my shoulders in wild disarray.

I don't care. I don't care what I look like. I lift my face and close my eyes, letting the sun bathe me in warmth while I ride his hand. Devlin stretches me open, working another finger past my tight entrance and forcing it deep, pulsing them against my walls while his palm massages my clit until I'm gasping for breath. All at once, I break apart for him, throwing my head back and crying his name as I slip over the edge.

When I open my eyes, Devlin's watching me. My first instinct is to be self-conscious, but he's looking at me like I'm some exotic treasure he's never seen before, and suddenly, I forget why I wanted to hide. He's breathing as hard as I am, his eyes blazing with lust. For me. No one else. No audience, no pretense. It's all for me.

"You're so fucking sexy," he growls. "If you're not on your back in thirty seconds I'm going to cum right here against your ass."

I'm still coming down from my orgasm, but I don't want it to be over. I know this is how it ends, and I'm not ready.

I grab his collar and tug him back as I climb into the back seat. He stays with me, grabbing me before I can get situated and throwing me down on the leather seat. "God, I'm going to fuck you so hard," he says, kneeling up and yanking his belt undone. I barely wriggle out of my underwear before he's on me, plowing into me. I cry out and arch up, my knees tightening on his hips because it's too much, too fast.

"Wait," I gasp. "We need a condom."

"You said you wanted it like the first time," he says, driving into me quick and hard. "Shut up and take it raw."

And god, I do want it like this. I don't want anything between us, ever. I want him driving his thick, bare cock deeper with each thrust, breaching the tightening of my muscles and forcing me to take every agonizing inch of him.

"Fuck, you're so wet," he rasps, gripping the top of the door with one hand as he draws back and slams his cock to the hilt inside me. I cry out when he hits my depth and a throb of pain goes through me, but I don't pull back. I cling to him, gripping his thick shoulders and lifting my hips to receive each punishing thrust, shaking like a junkie finally getting a desperately needed fix. He goes faster, fucking me like a frenzied animal, like an attack.

I open myself for him, letting him take everything, strip away all the fakeness and drama until it's just us, just our bodies that knew what we wanted and where we belonged long before our minds caught up. I welcome his punishment, relish the pain, take everything he gives me. I don't want him to stop. I only want more.

Suddenly, his hand grips my throat. "I'm gonna cum," he growls. "Don't scream."

"Not yet," I say. "Slow down. I don't want it to be over."

"I tell you when it's over," he snaps.

He slams into me again, grinding his pelvic bone against my clit, his fingers tightening around my throat until my panting breaths are only gasps. "Okay," I manage through my restricted throat.

"Should I pull out?" he asks, his breath coming quick.

"No," I snap, wrapping my legs around his hips and my fingers around his taut forearm, letting my nails bite in. "Like the first time."

"Every time is like the first time for me," he says. "You're so fucking tight I want to scream."

"No," I gasp, covering his mouth with my other hand. All I can think about is someone coming out and seeing us like this, fucking in broad daylight like a couple of animals who can't keep their hands off each other, who can't even make it to the house before they rip each other's clothes off.

"You're a bossy little bitch, aren't you?" he asks, smirking down at me as he crushes into me until I can feel his tight balls against my bare ass, ready to explode into me. The sensation sends ripples of forbidden pleasure through me, suddenly, I'm so close I don't know if I can hold it.

"Yes," I gasp, too close to the edge for shame. "Cum inside me, Devlin. Please."

"I could cum all over your belly and those perfect little tits."

"No," I breathe, arching up against him. "Please. I want to feel you fill me up. Nothing else does it. I want it all inside me."

Devlin grinds me down into the seat "You really know how to fuck with a guy's head," he says. "But if that's what you want, I'll fill your tight little cunt with my cum until it overflows."

Biting his lip, he grips my knees, pulling them open and pinning them wide. He arches up so he can watch his cock bury itself inside me with each thrust. I rake my nails down his chest, biting my lip to keep from crying out in pleasure and pain. His hand clamps around my neck again, and he barks at me to cum as he drives in the final time, stretching me impossibly far, his shaft thickening as cum pumps through it and spills into me. His fingers spasm around my throat, and it's too much, I can't take it. My nails bite through his skin and cries tear from my throat as blackness blots out my vision, my toes curl, and my whole body jerks and bows like a butterfly spread wide open and pinned through the center.

He holds me down, letting me writhe against him as orgasm holds me gripped in its teeth, the exquisite balance of unbearable pleasure and wrenching pain wrapping around every inch of my body. Devlin's whole body jerks each time he pulses into me, pouring liquid heat into my parched core as it squeezes him over and over, sucking every drop from him as if he could save us. I can't seem to stop even when he stills. My body is still going, waves crashing over me for minutes on end.

Only when I stop crying out do I realize how long it's been, how rough and sore my throat feels. Devlin releases his grip and lowers down onto his elbows and kisses me, a smirk playing over his lips. "Guess you really do like it when I choke the shit out of you."

"Was I that loud?" I ask, suddenly embarrassed for telling him to stop and then getting loud myself. But god, I needed that. I feel wrung out, and yet, he filled me and satisfied me in a way I haven't been since the last time. Even knowing I got out of control can't cut through the haze of bliss around me.

"I've never made a girl scream like that before," Devlin says. "I wasn't sure if you were coming or dying."

"I wasn't sure, either," I say with a shaky laugh. "You think anyone heard us?"

"I think the whole neighborhood heard you."

"Shit," I say, unable to hold back a giddy, embarrassed grin. "I'm sorry. I couldn't help it. I tried to hold back."

"Don't apologize," he says, tucking my hair behind my ear. "That was fucking hot."

"If you ever gloat about it, I will punch you in the nuts," I say.

Devlin chuckles. "When you're good enough to make a girl scream bloody murder, you don't need to gloat."

"You're gloating," I say, laughing and pushing at his shoulder.

"Okay, I better get my dick out of you before some gangster comes over and starts shooting," he says, kneeling up on the seat and putting himself away. I start to sit, but he pushes me back, his gaze landing between my thighs. He swallows hard, his eyes widening.

"What?" I ask, starting to sit again.

Again, he pushes me back. "Sugar," he breathes. "Just… Let me look at you for a minute. If this is the last time, I want to memorize every stroke of the masterpiece you are."

For a long minute, I lay there feeling intensely, terrifyingly vulnerable while he watches his cum leak out of me onto his leather seat. I can feel the burning heat of his eyes, the adoration in his sweeping lust, and ache in his yearning. Warmth begins to build between my thighs, as if he's touching me with more than his weighted gaze. Just being admired in this way brings my own desire to the surface. As if my womanhood has a mind of its own; or as if he awakened it and now it obeys and responds to his every desire without him saying a word. Whatever the reason, that part of me revels in his admiration, adores his adoration. Longing coils around my core, and I tilt my hips and spread my thighs wider, wanting his touch to ease the ache his gaze has created.

"Oh god," Devlin groans. "I'm already ready to fuck you again."

"Me, too," I breathe, so relieved that I'm not alone in this raging need for him. "I don't think the last time was enough."

"I don't think it'll ever be enough," Devlin says. "I'll never get enough of you, Crystal."

# seven

*Crystal*

We're still in the backseat when I hear a screen door slam.

"Devlin," calls a trilling voice from his back porch, which is just across a small stretch of gravel. "Tootle-oo. You're home early. Why don't you come inside, darling?"

Devlin curses, holding out a hand to stop me when I try to sit. "Stay in the car until I get inside," he says. "I'll make sure she doesn't see you."

He hops out of the car without opening the door, and I lie there, my heart hammering as I listen to his footsteps crunch across the gravel drive to his house.

Shit. His mother was home the whole time. And we're just parked in the driveway with the top down, fucking like bunnies, out in the open where anyone could see us. Hell, someone on the top floor of my house could see us. Thank god my brothers are all at school. Still, I can't help but cringe at the thought that his mother might have heard me. She probably knows exactly what he was doing. But she doesn't know who he was doing it with, and he obviously wants to keep it that way.

Well, that wasn't the goodbye I wanted. But then, if I'm honest with myself, there's never going to be a good way to say goodbye to Devlin. The truth is, I don't want to say goodbye. I want the impossible. Something that can never happen.

When he's gone, I put myself together as best as I can and climb out of the car, running across the lawn to our house and creeping in the back door like a thief into my own home. I'm halfway up the stairs when Daddy appears at the top.

Shit shit shit.

"Crystal," he says, coming down a few steps until he's almost even with me. "What are you doing home so early?"

"I… Don't feel good," I say, trying to calm my racing thoughts. I'm not sure what to do, or how long he's been home, and oh my god, if he heard me, or looked out the window and saw us, I'll just die. "And I was going to practice my cheer for tonight."

"Oh," he says. "Well, why don't you go lie down for a while?"

Is he acting weird? I can't tell. My panic is raging too hard to know if it's him or my own paranoia.

"Okay," I say, taking another step up. "Why are you home?"

"Construction's been halted while they investigate the murder," he says. "But they've found some new evidence, and I think they have a pretty good idea of who's behind the attacks. It's just a matter of making an arrest."

"What attacks?" I ask, barely able to breathe through the tightness gripping my chest and throat.

"A couple more of our guys were attacked this week," Daddy says. "And there's one person who wants the construction of my new operation stopped. One person who benefits most if they succeed."

I know who he means. Preston Darling's father disputed Daddy's claim on that land.

But I also know what I heard at dinner after they found a guy murdered at the site. I know how my sweet old granddad laughed in a way I'd never heard before after basically confessing. He must have fooled the detective since they let him go home. I'm not surprised. He's fooled me all my life. And I'm betting it's not the first time he's lied to the police, either.

Suddenly, I feel a little bad for Preston. He has no idea what's coming his way. My family, they don't play around. No, they go straight for the murder-and-frame-the-enemy approach.

My father starts down the steps, and I turn to watch him descend past me. I see him as a stranger might—the broad shoulders, dark hair, and olive skin; the good looks he passed on to my brothers. He's the same man he's always been, the man who coddled and sheltered me from the truth all those years. But now that I know what he was doing, something has changed. He's not my daddy anymore, the man whose attention and approval I crave above all else. The man whose time I sought so desperately, as if I had to prove myself worthy of my own father's love.

He's not the one who's changed. I am.

"Dad," I say, feeling the funny way the word stops on my tongue when I don't add the last syllable, as I always have.

"Yeah, sweetheart?" he asks, stopping at the bottom of the stairs and turning to look up at me, a hand on the railing and a foot on the hardwood floor, already halfway gone.

"How involved are we, exactly?" I ask. "With the families, I mean. King told me who Mom is. Who her uncle is." What is a parent's uncle, really? Most people probably never even meet their parents' uncles and cousins. It's possible that Mom left the life when she married Dad, an outsider.

"If you're thinking I'm some kind of gangster, I'm not," Dad says. "I'm not a member of any family but my own."

"Oh," I say, letting out a small, relieved laugh. "But... Then why is King going to work for the Valentis?"

"You know, you're a real smart kid," he says. "You and your brother both. I tried to keep you out of it. Thought maybe you could go to college like the other rich kids do these days."

"Uncle Vinny went to law school," I point out.

"That's true," Dad says. "You know, it's hard to keep secrets in your own house. As you kids got older, you overheard things. Maybe it was inevitable that you'd all want to dip your toes in the life. And once you dip your toes in the concrete, Crystal, it's hard not to sink in."

"I thought you said you weren't in it."

Dad squints at me like he's trying to decide how much to tell. "I'm not a made guy," he says. "Uncle Al thought I was better positioned where I am. He was happy to get your mother out of any kind of direct danger, but he wanted to keep her close enough to keep an eye on her."

I nod. "And what if I've had enough now that I got my feet wet?"

"You got a few years before you graduate," he says. "We'll talk about the future then."

"King doesn't have a few years."

"King, he stepped in the concrete a long time ago," Dad says. "He's up to his knees already."

"And you?" I ask, swallowing hard. "If you're not in the mafia, why are you letting King work for them? How deep are you?"

Dad sighs, looking resigned. "Sweetheart, the rest of us are neck deep if not up to our eyeballs in it."

I nod, not sure what else to say. He gave me the answer I wanted, and yet, I didn't want it. Some cowardly part of me wishes I'd never asked, that I didn't know. The part that loved when he sheltered me, that never asked even though I could have all those years. The part that liked being the spoiled little daughter of a rich guy with a candy empire, not one that sold chocolate for blood.

As I lie in bed, unable to fall asleep, I think about that thing my parents always said—our blood is thicker than chocolate. It probably always meant more than I let it mean. It meant that her family loyalties, her mob ties, came before business. As hard as my father worked for his company, he always had to remember that the mafia came first. I'm sure they've been taking their cut ever since they handed him his first loan, the one Mr. Darling never wanted him to take.

Because, when I let myself admit it, Mr. Darling has never been anything but kind to us. Not exactly friendly and welcoming, but how could I expect him to be after Dad took his idea and ran with it. He was guarded when he came over to talk to Dad, but he wasn't rude or angry or hateful. No one has ever said a bad thing about him except my own family. Dolly swears up and down he's a great guy. Devlin would go to jail for him, and even I don't really believe he had anything to do with Royal's kidnapping.

What if the Darlings were right about everything? Can I blame them for not wanting our family to come rolling into town with the big guns out, ready to take down the founders of this sweet little southern town? Can I blame them for not wanting to pollute and corrupt their idyllic little community with blood money?

What if, all along, we were the bad guys?

\*

"Oh my god, I can't believe we're doing this," Dixie says, waving her hands in front of her face like she's about to faint. We're in the bathroom at the football game later that night, getting ready for our routine, which has morphed from a complicated cheer into more of a dance routine. But hey, WHPA doesn't have a dance team, so we're making up for it tonight.

"You'll be great," I say. "We've been working on it all week."

It's been more than a week, but this week, we've practiced it every day, and all of us committed to working at home for a few hours a night. It's been a welcome distraction from wondering what happened to Royal, dealing with his outbursts, watching my extended family leave and realizing I never really knew them anyway, pretending things are normal, and telling myself that I don't miss Devlin or regret what I did.

"I know all the moves," Dixie says, her eyes widening. "It's not about that."

"You look amazing," I assure her.

"You really think so?" she asks, looking from me to Dolly with such hope in her eyes it nearly kills me. I don't think she'll ever be less transparent, and I've grown to appreciate that about her. I've had enough fake bitches to last me my whole life. Still, her need for approval holds up an uncomfortable mirror at times.

Dolly scrutinizes her step-cousin and shakes her head. "You could use some more glitter."

"Okay, let's not glitter-bomb everyone," I say, intersecting the bottle of spray glitter after a prolonged blast coats Dixie's chest and shoulders. "Are you both ready to show those bitches what they could do with their bodies if they'd take the stick out of their asses?"

"Are you sure these aren't too short?" Dixie asks, tugging at her cutoffs. "What if everyone laughs at us?"

"They won't laugh," I say.

"I've been waiting for this moment since they said I was too big for the squad," Dolly says. "I think they were really just pissed that I dumped one of their gods."

"Wait, you dumped Devlin?" I ask.

"Yeah," she says, leaning close to the mirror to swipe under her lower lip and make sure her gloss isn't running.

*"Why?"* I ask, gaping at her.

"I know, right?" Dixie say. "I'd give anything if Colt would ask me out."

"I thought you had a date after class the other day," I remind her, giving her a playful poke.

"I know," she says with a giggle. "I should be grateful. I mean, I am grateful, don't get me wrong. But to go on a real date…" She sighs and clasps her hands in front of her chest like some starry-eyed preteen. It's hard not to laugh at her, even though I know she's seriously that lovestruck. And honestly, who am I to judge?

In the stands, the thunder of stomping feet draws our attention. My nerves surge, and I know it's time to use them to energize our routine.

"Alright, ladies, it's halftime," I say. "Now or never. If you're in, tighten up your ponies and let's show 'em how it's done."

"Oh, I'm so in," Dolly says.

"I'm in, but oh my god, I might faint when I'm out there. Group hug?" Dixie asks, holding out her arms.

We step in and cling together one moment before we do this crazy thing. I know Dolly won't get in trouble—she's the mayor's daughter for fuck's sake—but Dixie's and my fate is still to be determined.

"Just think about all the times Lacey and Carmen and their bitch squad have called you names," I say. "You won't faint. Your muscle memory will do it for you, even if you're too nervous to remember it later."

"I'll be too busy thinking about Colt," Dixie says.

"Well, don't," I say, my heart flipping when I think of Devlin watching me do the routine I choreographed. But this isn't about him, so I push the thought away. I could have done this in New York, even at our fancy school, but let's just say things are a lot more old-fashioned here. There's a reason we're not trying out for Coach Snow in the gym like we should have. This isn't a try-out. It's a fuck-you to the squad who doesn't want us.

"Alright, ladies," I say, checking my phone when a text come through. "Baron's in the sound booth. Let's do this shit."

# eight

*Devlin*

The halftime meeting ends, and I return to the bench with Preston, where I've been the whole game. I miss the game, but in truth, it's a relief to have the pressure off me. I love this town, but it's pushed me to fill my father's shoes since I was old enough to walk. Preston's got it so much worse than I do. His future is uncertain, and while mine is too, in a different way, I have faith in the justice system to clear me and Dad of the crime we didn't commit.

Still, the coach can't exactly put me on the field after what I confessed to. So, I warm the bench with my cousin, who's nursing his broken arm and fading dreams of football glory while the asshole who did it gets to take his place on the field. Nobody ever said life was fair.

The cheerleaders are doing their thing, shaking their pompoms in our faces and trying to catch our eye, but I don't pay them any attention until Preston elbows me and nods in the direction of the entrance. Three figures come striding onto the field, led by this chick looking so badass I don't recognize her for a second. They've all got black Knights ballcaps pulled low over their faces, and I've sure as fuck never seen Crystal wear something like that, never seen her walk like that, like she's about to throw down. But there's no mistaking the two girls flanking her like the trio needs their own slo-mo intro. A pulsing beat thuds from the loudspeakers, rippling across the field.

Everyone in the stands looks around in confusion. The cheerleaders drop their routine mid-cheer, as confused as everyone else. Only Crystal's crew seems to know what's going on. Crystal plucks the pompoms from a couple cheerleaders and tosses them to her partners, forming a line right in front of the squad, forcing them to step back from the sidelines where they do their routines. I glance at the Dolces to see if they have something up their sleeves, but Baron is missing, and King and Duke are watching like the rest of us, waiting to see what's about to happen.

The song kicks into "The Drip," and it's not the edited version, either. The girls hit it—hard. I've sure as fuck never seen Crystal move like that. I don't know if I've ever seen anyone move like that outside of a rap video. In a pair of cutoffs that hug her nice, thick thighs, a WHPA tee tied up to show her tight, flat stomach, and a pair of gold high-tops, she looks like a New York wet dream come to tell the south to wake the fuck up.

For a minute, not one other person in the whole place moves. We're all too busy gaping as they bounce, shake, twerk, and dip.

When Preston whistles under his breath, I want to punch him in the broken arm. But every guy in the bleachers must have a hard-on right now, and I can't punch them all, as much as I'd like to. They're all looking at *my* girl. Imagining *my* girl bouncing on their dicks the way she's bouncing her ass, twirling it like a fucking Tootsie Roll.

A ripple of noise starts as guys in the stands start to hoot and holler, dancing along, humping the air, cheering the girls on, laughing with appreciation, not just at the hot-as-fuck way those girls are moving but at the sheer, unexpected ballsiness. Crystal usually gives off the sexy librarian vibe. Dolly's flashy as fuck, but not raunchy. And Dixie's just some pathetic little freshman who can't get out of her own way.

They all bend at the waist, lifting off their ballcaps and letting their hair tumble out, then popping back up and flinging it around like a bunch of strippers. If Crystal is trying to show me what I'll be missing out on, she's doing a real fucking good job of it. If she's showing me what I'll never get to touch again, that I'll never put my hands on those curves, never run my palms over her velvet skin and my fingers through her thick, dark chocolate locks, well, she's doing that, too. She's showing a whole lot more of her body than she's ever shown at school, like she wants every guy here to know what I had—and what I can't have anymore.

I regret telling her this afternoon would be the last time. As she whips her hair around, shaking the pompoms next to her shimmying hips, all I want to do is get up, go over there, and cover her up. I don't want any other guy to see her like that. To want her like that. She's mine. Every inch of her is mine and mine alone—or it should be. It was. And now it's not.

And the fucked up part is, I can't blame her for it. What did I do with all that while I had it? Did I treat her like the fucking queen she is, like she's the fiercest, classiest, sexiest, softest woman I've ever met?

No. I told her she was nothing.

She's not nothing. She's everything.

And every fucking guy in this town knows it now. There are dudes here who haven't gotten it up in decades who are probably going to go home and fuck their wives like they did in high school.

Crystal ends up down in a squat twerking like she's the Italian version of Cardi B while the other two stand on either side of her, their arms raised in a Y shape as they shake their own asses, pompoms raised. The song ends, and Crystal turns and tosses her hat straight into my lap. Before I can even react, she spins back the other way, throws her pompoms in Kaylee's face, and marches out of there like she knows exactly how much of a point she just made.

Everyone is instantly freaking the fuck out. The crowd is about to storm the field and riot, coaches are running around, someone is yelling through the loudspeaker that the event we just saw was not sanctioned. The football team is jumping up and down and howling like we just won the state championship. Colt comes bounding over and throws himself onto the bench beside me and Preston.

"Dude, what are you doing still sitting here?" he asks, grinning ear to ear. "That was the sickest thing I've ever seen in my *life*."

I glance at Preston. I told them she was mine. But I also told them what she did after that—that I'm not hers. That she didn't want me. That it was all a lie for her, a game. After what her family did to ours, to mine and Preston's, to this town, how can I walk away from them? These are my boys—forever.

"If you're not balls deep in one of those bitches tonight, you might as well cut off your dick and toss it in the river, because you don't deserve to call yourself a man," Preston says.

I check him to make sure. But Preston doesn't say shit unless he means it. I don't know what else to do, so I grab his shoulder in a quick squeeze.

"Get your horny ass off your cousin and go get her," Colt says. "He's right. There's only one reason a girl shakes the booty like that. She wants a dick in it bad, dude. Go wreck that ass."

"Thanks," I say to him and Preston both, standing and adjusting my cock, which won't relax for anything.

"You got one chance to make that shit right," Colt says, clasping a hand over my shoulder. "If you haven't busted a nut inside that juicy ass of hers by tomorrow morning, I'm doing it for you."

I throw his hand off. I know he's kidding, but it's not funny. Not with her. "Touch her, and you'll be eating your nuts for breakfast," I warn him.

"Quit talking shit and go, or I will," Preston says. "If my bitch was that thirsty, I'd have her on her knees choking down eight inches right now."

"No, man," I say. "Crystal wouldn't choke on something that small."

I turn and jog toward the gate without waiting for a response. I've got bigger things to worry about than my trash-talking cousins. Like how I'm going to convince a girl who hates everything about me except my dick that I've got something else to offer her.

# nine

*Crystal*

"Oh my god, you're a genius," Dixie shrieks, doing some kind of happy dance that makes her look more like a hamster than the ass shaking queen she is. "Did you see Colt's face? Was he looking at me?"

"Don't be silly," Dolly says. "Every guy in Faulkner was looking at us. We just played a nasty rap song with all their kids in attendance. They're going to be coming after us with pitchforks."

Just then, Baron ducks under the bleachers to meet us as agreed.

"You did it," I cry, throwing my arms up.

Baron runs over, sweeps me off my feet and spins me around once. "Nice job," he says before depositing me carelessly in Dixie's face. He grabs up Dolly and shoves his tongue down her throat, his hands roaming over her curves like he owns them. She doesn't seem to mind, though.

Dixie giggles. "I thought she was seeing Duke."

Dolly pulls away and looks up at Baron with mock surprise. "You're not Duke?"

He laughs and grabs her ass with both hands, grinding his hips into hers. "Baby, I'll be whoever you want me to be," he says. "As long as you keep right on being you."

I shrug at Dixie. "The twins come as a packaged deal. If you can't handle them both, you don't sign up for that ride."

"What?" she squeals.

"It was a well-known fact in our old school."

"They just look so much alike," Dolly says, twisting around to face us and batting her long, false lashes. "I can't tell which one is which. I never knew there were two of them at all."

I laugh and shake my head, and Baron nuzzles into her neck, his arms still wrapped around her from behind. The twins went to great lengths to distinguish themselves from each other here. Sure, Baron has contacts in right now because he's playing football, but his hair is still noticeably shorter, and his jersey bears his first initial as well as his last name.

"Wow," Dixie says, her eyes like saucers beneath her smoky makeup. "New York sounds so different. I can't believe you used to dance like that, either—in front of the school."

"Parents there were a lot more… Permissive," I say. "I mean, it's New York. Even the rich kids have seen it all by the time they're in high school."

"I better go," Baron says, kissing Dolly's neck. "Halftime's about over. You better go, too, before they haul your ass in to the headmaster. And baby, tonight this ass is all mine." He drags out the last two words, rolling his hips to press his dick into her ass.

"Get out of here and stop mauling my friend," I say.

He laughs and releases her at last, giving us a wave as he jogs toward the field. "Oh, you two did good, too," he calls back over his shoulder.

"You, too," I yell. "Thank you!"

It feels a little weird to be an afterthought to one of my brothers. Not that they weren't always horndogs, but it was usually for a night, a week at most. Now, I think Dolly actually means something to them, though they'd never admit it. I'm glad for them, and for her, and even for myself. While it feels a little strange not to have them breathing down my neck every second of the day, it's also… Freeing. It's a relief not to have to worry that they're right around the corner, ready to clock a guy if I speak to him.

"Where'd you learn to dance like that?" Dolly asks as we leave the shelter of the bleachers. Most of the crowd has returned to their seats to watch the second half, which means we can escape without too much attention. "You're both so good. I felt like such a white girl up there next to y'all."

I laugh and shake my head. It's true that she's a bit awkward in her moves, but with her body, it's not like anyone noticed. "You did great," I say. "It takes a lot of practice."

"You practice that a lot?"

"Well, there was usually a little twerking in our halftime routines," I admit. "We were more of a dance-cheer squad combo. And I took lessons. The real question is, where'd *you* learn to shake that booty like a pro?" I ask, turning to our freshman friend. "Who knew our sweet little Dixie had it in her?"

Dixie's face turns scarlet. "I just like dancing," she mumbles. "I watch videos and do the moves at home. Like you did with cheering. But my parents didn't know. Oh my god, they're here!" Her hands fly up to cover her mouth, and she gives a muffled wail. "They're going to kill me!"

We're almost to the parking lot when someone whistles. Dread clamps around my belly, but I keep going. Dixie, however, turns around.

"Oh my god," she says. "It's Chase London. I think he just whistled at us."

I stop and turn around, a smile breaking across my face before I can stop myself. "Chase," I say, seeing the familiar boy who rescued me from the bad part of town. "Shouldn't you be at your own game? Preston didn't fuck up your hand, did he?"

"Nah," Chase says, gesturing to his jeans and hoodie. "It's our bye week. I came to scope out the competition. You were lying about your brothers."

"Just wait," I say. "The best one is injured right now, and the twins are only freshmen."

"Guess I can kiss my state championship goodbye," he says. "Hey, Dixie. And Dolly. How y'all doin'?"

"Chase!" A tiny blonde girl appears from behind the bathrooms, a hand planted on her hip. She gestures impatiently for him to join her.

"Hey, come here, babe," he says, calling her over.

Great. The Darling girl he's dating.

"This is the damsel in distress I told you about," he says, sliding an arm around her waist and winking at me. "The one who's hot for your brother."

She gives me a forced smile. "Hi. I'm Lindsey Darling."

"I gathered that," I say. "Nice to meet you. Thanks for sparing your boyfriend to help me out that day. He's quite the gentleman."

"Why, thank you, ma'am," Chase says, tipping an imaginary hat at me and smiling in a way that says he clearly adores the flattery.

"Don't even mention it," Lindsey says, clinging possessively to his arm. "Oh, hi, Dolly. That was quite a performance. I didn't know majorettes danced like that."

"Oh, it wasn't for majorettes," Dolly says. "That was for my own personal satisfaction."

"I think it brought some other people satisfaction, too," Chase says with a crooked smile.

"Chase," Lindsey scolds, looking scandalized.

"What?" he says. "The cops are gonna charge y'all with murder if they catch you."

"We should probably get out of here," Dixie agrees, glancing around nervously.

"Murder?" I ask, laughing. "Isn't that a bit excessive?"

"Not really," Chase says. "Pretty sure at least one guy dropped dead of a heart attack when he saw y'all twerking like that. That must be illegal in this town because I've sure as hell never seen a girl move that way around here."

I laugh, my own face warming with pleasure at his admiration. "I might be a bad influence," I admit.

"I bet you are," he says with an appreciative smile. "When you asked for advice about the Darlings, you should have started with the fact that you can do that. I'd have had some different advice for you about landing Preston."

"Chase," Lindsey scolds, pinching his arm so hard he winces.

"What?" he says.

"Come on," she says. "We need to get back to the game. It was nice meeting y'all."

She drags Chase off without another word, though I hear him protesting as she drags him away, "I didn't say she should do it on his dick."

"Well, that was awkward," I say, glancing nervously at Officer Gunn, who's appeared behind the bleachers. He's engrossed in his police radio for the moment, and I don't want to change that.

"Let's get out of here," I say, grabbing a hand of both of my companions and hurrying across the parking lot towards Dolly's huge pink truck. "We can deal with the consequences on Monday. I want to celebrate tonight."

"Yeah," Dixie says as we pile into the cab. "I can't believe we went through with it!"

Dolly starts up the truck and guns it out of the parking lot. "Where to, ladies?"

"Ice cream," I say, still high on the adrenaline and feeling invincible. Even calories can't stop me now. "This definitely calls for ice cream."

"Shouldn't we go home and change first?" Dixie asks, adjusting her shorts.

"Girl, you look hot as fuck," I say. "If anyone says otherwise, they can come talk to me."

She giggles from the back seat. "You are so crazy, Crystal. Next thing I know, you're going to shank someone."

I laugh. "Not my style. I prefer to operate with more subtlety."

"I don't think what we just did was very subtle."

"True," I say. "Some bitches are too dumb to understand the subtle approach, so you're forced to do something drastic. But you gotta use that shit sparingly, or it won't have the desired effect."

Dixie sighs and leans back in her seat. "I want to be you when I grow up."

I laugh at that and turn to Dolly. "You okay? You're awfully quiet over there."

"I thought you liked Devlin," she says quietly, frowning at the road ahead.

I swallow hard. Even though I've been with him, I've never said I liked him. But I do, and these aren't the kind of friends I want to lie to. "I do," I admit at last, feeling as vulnerable as if I were telling Devlin himself.

"Then why did Chase say you were after Preston?" she asks. "Don't fuck with that boy's head, Crystal. He deserves better."

"Oh, that," I say, laughing. "It's a long story, but basically a misunderstanding. Don't worry. Preston is all yours."

"What?" she says, sounding startled.

"Oh, right," I say. "We're not supposed to talk about that. But trust me, I have zero interest in anyone but Devlin. And if there were something going on, your secret would be safe with me."

"There's not," she says, pulling up outside a tiny shop. There's a big sign in the shape of an ice cream cone with the words *Two Scoops of Love* painted on it. Dolly shuts off the engine and turns to me. "I'm with your brothers. I wouldn't do that to them. They deserve better than that, too."

"Okay," I say. "Your past is your business. My lips are sealed."

She nods and climbs out of the car. "Now, as far as what Dixie said, I have to agree," she says as we make our way inside. "You're really something, Crystal. I'd never have done something like that if you hadn't come along. You opened my eyes to things I'd always just taken at face value. Like taking the cheer squad's word that I wasn't cut out to be a cheerleader."

"You know they're all jealous as fuck," I say. "Look at you, Dolly. You're a bombshell. If you were on the field with them, not one guy would look at any one of them. They'd all be looking at you."

"I think it's more that they hated me for being the only girl to ever date Devlin," she says, giving me a quick glance, like I'll be pissed to find out they used to date.

We take a minute to order off the chalkboard menu above the counter, ignoring the curious glances of the couple working tonight. We have the place to ourselves courtesy of the football game, so we don't even have to worry about other people staring. I get my two scoops, a raspberry with white chocolate chunks and a chocolate with dark chocolate chips, and take the booth in the corner with my friends.

"I just have to say one more thing about those bitches," Dolly says, setting her bowl of bubblegum and cotton candy on the table. "Then I won't speak of them again tonight. You have no idea how much shit I took for breaking up with Devlin. It's not like I was the Darling Dog or a pariah or anything. But all my friends basically told me I was too stupid to live. I got pissed at them, and told them that if they wouldn't support me, we didn't need to be friends. So, we weren't. I used to be on cheer in middle school, but after that… I think mostly they were all hoping they'd get to date Devlin now that he was single, and who wants to be friends with your boyfriend's ex?"

It takes about ten seconds of silence for me to look up from my ice cream. She and Dixie are both staring at me.

I set down my spoon. "I do," I say. "I mean, I won't lie, it's hard as hell sometimes. I'm so jealous I want to die when I think about you and him, so I try not to think about it. Yeah, you did that, but it's not who you are. But knowing you were his first time, and his first love, and probably his first kiss… You're childhood sweethearts. You have all this history with him that I'll never have."

"Crystal," she says. "It's not like that. I mean, it is, but not the way you think. Yeah, we did that stuff, but Devlin and me, we were never that romantic fantasy everyone wanted us to be. Even when we were together."

"What do you mean?"

I don't want to know, but my mouth opens and it pops out before I can stop it. Maybe I've held onto denial long enough. I was always the girl who could block out anything I didn't want to hear, who could overlook anything I didn't want to see, even when it was right in front of my face. I didn't get to use girls and parties and fighting like my brothers, so I created a forcefield out of my own mind to avoid dealing with life's painful truths. But now, the part of me I've shut off for so long, the curious part that wants to know, to experience, even when it hurts… That part is bursting from its cocoon and demanding that I acknowledge the beauty in every bit of life, even the raw, ugly parts.

"I loved Devlin," Dolly says. "I bought into all of it. The fantasy, the romance, our parents' plan to push us together. I mean, you know Devlin. How could I not love that boy? I saw him go through some tough times, and I wanted to love him enough to make him my little boy again. But he wasn't. I don't think I really realized that until this year, until I saw what he was doing to y'all. He's flat-out mean sometimes."

"I'm sorry," I say. "I never meant to swoop in and steal your man. I guess you're the one who's a bigger person for being friends with me."

"Oh, no," she says. "You didn't steal him from me, Crystal. We'd been broken up for a year already. I guess I was just so caught up in the game, in the whole school's game, the town's game, that I forgot it was a game. It seemed like if I couldn't get him to love me, then I'd just die. But I don't think he ever loved me that way. We've always been friends, and he's protective of me, but I don't think it was ever more than that to him. I mean, I know you don't want to hear about us hookin' up, but the first time we did it, I said I loved him, and he just got up and walked out of the room."

I press the heel of my hand to my forehead. Oh, god, I really don't want to hear about this. But at least it's not just me. At least he treats everyone like that. I don't know if that makes me feel better or worse. I just know I wish she'd stop talking.

"If you loved him, and he didn't love you that way, then how come you're the one who broke up with him?" Dixie asks.

Dolly takes a bite of her ice cream. "I gave him an ultimatum, hoping he'd see what he was losing. But that's a gamble I lost. I just didn't see how he could feel different than me. We grew up together, playing dress-up, and having pretend weddings in the back yard with our friends."

I push my ice cream away, suddenly wishing I'd never asked, wishing we hadn't come here. I don't want ice cream to be ruined by the memory of this conversation. It churns in my stomach the way her words churn in my head, threatening to make me sick. I don't want to hear this. It's like living my nightmare, my worst fears being confirmed.

"What was the ultimatum?" Dixie asks, leaning forward, her eyes bright with excitement at the prospect of such insider gossip.

"He was my best friend, but I wasn't his," Dolly says. "He always had his cousins. He had his family, and football, and them. I didn't want to be just an afterthought. I didn't want to be a doll he only played with when he felt like it, when he had time. I was more like a dog, like you said, Crystal. There's really no difference between the two. I'd beg for scraps of attention, and sometimes, he'd throw me a bone. But I didn't want to be his last priority."

"You shouldn't be," I say. "*You* deserve better, Dolly."

"I know," she says. "And I guess even then some part of me knew because I broke up with him. I was hoping he'd chase me down and claim me for his own, wanting me enough to put me before anything. But he didn't. I was the one who broke down and went running back, saying I made a mistake and making a fool of myself. But he wouldn't have me back. He's got too much pride for that."

She glances at me, and I know he's told her what I did. They're still friends, after all.

"I know," I say, swallowing hard.

"Under all that meanness, Devlin must still have a heart, though," Dolly says. "Because I've seen the way he looks at you, Crystal. And I can promise you this. He never looked at me that way."

My heart skips at her words, and I don't want to show how selfishly, ridiculously happy that makes me. But I can't think about that right now. Because thinking about that makes me think about how he said some things were more important than football. How he risked his family's wrath to help me find Royal. And then I have to remember that even though he may look at me differently, even though he may have chased me down, though he claimed me in front of the whole school, it's all meaningless now. I told him I didn't want him.

And even if he forgave me, and I forgave him for all he did, our families would never allow it. My family would straight up murder him if they knew what we did this afternoon. And I don't want anything to ruin this night, not even thoughts of my family.

"Well," I say, picking up my spoon again. "Whatever you felt for each other, it doesn't change the fact that you're an awesome person. What kind of dumb bitch would I be if I hated you because of something you did, something that has nothing to do with me and you had every right to do, instead of liking you for being a genuinely badass, amazing friend?"

"I think it's a genuinely badass, amazing friend who would talk me into shaking my ass like a fool in front of the whole town," she says, and the momentarily serious mood lifts as we all break into laughter at the audacity of what we did tonight.

"Well, thanks for being my friend," I say. "I'm sure it's not that easy for you, either."

"I tell you what," she says. "When y'all came along, it was like I'd been living in this room made of mirrors, so I couldn't see that there was a world beyond it. And y'all busted right through that glass, and I saw the world out there beyond Faulkner city limits. I love this town, and I might come back here some day, but I gotta step out of the house of mirrors for a while and see what's out there first. So, I applied to UCLA. And I got in! I'm going to California, girls."

"Oh my god," Dixie squeals. "Maybe you'll meet a movie star and fall in love!"

"Maybe you'll become a movie star," I say.

"I can start as a backup dancer," Dolly says with a giggle. "I can look back and say it all started with y'all."

"I can't believe it was even real," Dixie says with a sigh, licking her strawberry cone. "I mean, how can this be me? My parents would kill me for eating ice cream on a normal day. And I don't even care. Because you know what? I just did something so much worse than eating ice cream!"

"Well, I'm glad I came along to push you out of your comfort zone," I say with a grin.

"You've really made waves at Willow Heights," Dolly says. "And that's not something that's easy to do."

I remember Lacey's warning on my very first day of school, that if I wanted to survive, I wouldn't make waves. Guess I proved her wrong. Here I am, making waves and having ice cream with two of the baddest chicks I've ever met. I'm doing more than surviving. I'm having the best fucking time right now.

Sure, things at home suck. My dad is definitely funneling money to the mob, my mother is the niece of a mafia kingpin, and my grandpa probably killed a guy while he was here. King is planning a life of criminality, the twins are probably going to make the mayor want to run us out of town when he finds out they're double-teaming his daughter, and Royal is fucked up in ways no one is talking about. And me? I'm in love with a boy whose family hates me, a boy I can never have without putting us both in danger—and probably both our families as well.

But I realize as we sit there laughing about the night, reliving the reckless, stupid stunt we just pulled, stuffing our faces with way too many calories to count, that I'm happy. For the first time in as long as I can remember, I wouldn't change a thing about this moment. Because in this moment, I'm not a mafia daughter or a girl who intentionally broke the heart of the boy she loved; I'm not the Darling Dog, a Dolce Daughter, or the Whore of Faulkner. I'm just a normal sixteen-year-old girl hanging out with her besties, laughing, and consuming obscene amount of sugar. And because I know the moment can't last, because I know it's not real, that it's just a tiny bubble of joy and not my reality, every bite tastes that much sweeter.

# ten

*Crystal*

*When girls say they only have guy friends, or they don't get along with other girls, I feel so incredibly sad for them. Sure, my brothers are some of the best friends a girl could have, friends who protect me and have my back. But there's a magic in female friendships, something indescribably intoxicating, a secret ingredient that even we can't name. When we're together, we become powerful, unstoppable. We become magic.*
*I feel sad for girls who miss out on that because they're too busy trying to prove they're better than everyone. Who would want to be different from other girls, when other girls are such amazing, badass people?*

I get home a few hours later, realizing as I wave goodbye to Dolly and make my way along the front walk to the house that my life feels almost normal. Not perfect, but I have friends who drop me off after a night of hanging out with the girls while my brothers party it up after the game. I even sort of cheered at halftime. It's the first time since I left New York that I want that kind of life again. I made mistakes, yes, but I liked having friends, brothers who played football, and even King checking in a couple times to make sure I was okay. Maybe, just maybe, I can still make a better life for myself here. Keep the good parts and learn from the bad.

It's only a little after eleven when I open the door and step inside. Dad's a bit of a night owl, so I'm not surprised to find a few lights on. The house is spotless, thanks to the staff Mom hired while she was here. I'm halfway to the stairs when a voice stops me.

"Where have you been?"

My hand flies to my heart, and I spin to see my brother sitting alone in the darkened living room.

"What the hell, Royal?" I say. "You scared me to death."

Light filters in from the next room, but he's not watching TV or doing anything, just sitting in the dark like a creeper. "Answer the question," he says.

"I was out with Dolly and Dixie," I say. "I told King that, and that I was safe. I thought you were with him. Why aren't you at the postgame party?"

"I don't want to party," Royal says, standing and prowling toward me. "I want to know why my sister's still fucking the guy who did this to me."

"What?" I ask, taking a step back, my heart beating faster in my chest.

"You and Devlin," he says, stopping in front of me, his dark eyes ferocious. "Tell me you're not still fucking him, Crystal."

"I'm not," I say, my throat tightening.

His gaze bores into mine, and I force myself not to look away. But Royal's my twin. He's always been able to tell when I'm lying.

"Bull. Shit." He grits out the two words, glaring back at me. But I'm his twin, too. I can read him as well as he reads me. And it's not the anger in his eyes that breaks my heart. It's the hurt he hides beneath it.

"What did he do to you, Royal?" I whisper, my heart still hammering. "Tell me."

Royal's hands ball into fists, and he steps even closer, his voice menacing. "Tell me why you left school with him today if it wasn't to fuck?"

"It wasn't," I snap. My own anger rises, and I welcome it. I know why he's pissed. It's so much easier, so much safer, than pain. "I left school because you and King were being assholes, and I needed to get away. I'm so sick of being told what to do, and how to dress, and who to be. I just want to be myself, Royal. The same as you get to."

He laughs, but it's not the laugh I know and love. It's a horrible, twisted, black thing snaking out of him like a barbed tentacle. "You think anyone in this family gets to do whatever the fuck they want?" he says. "You think I went through all this because I fucking wanted to?" His voice rises as he speaks until he's shouting, his eyes furious, his fists shaking with rage.

"No, but—"

"You're the only person in this family who thinks she can do whatever the fuck she wants," he yells. "And here I was, thinking I was protecting you. I went through that shit for *you*, Crystal. So you wouldn't have to. So they couldn't get to you. And all along, you were spreading your legs for him—willingly. It was all for fucking nothing!"

His fist shoots out so fast I barely have time to duck. An involuntarily little scream escapes me as I cower away from my brother, my twin, my better half. The boy who has protected and sheltered me with his presence, who would hold his umbrella over me when it rained so I'd stay dry, even if it meant he'd get soaked. The boy who anchored me and grounded me and made me feel safe and calm when no one else could.

But I couldn't do the same for him.

And now this boy is someone else. He's not a boy who has never tried to hurt me in his life, a boy who has never made me feel scared or unsafe.

He's breathing hard as he yanks his hand back. A puff of plaster dust sinks to the floor.

"What's going on out here, you two?" Dad asks, his footsteps thudding in the hall as he approaches.

Royal and I stare at each other, neither of us moving. My heart is racing as he looks from me to the hole he put in the wall as if he can't comprehend how it got there.

"Nothing," I say, and I turn and run upstairs, away. I don't want to see the look on my brother's face.

I stand in the hot shower and let it wash the tears away. They don't hurt as much with the water stinging my eyes. I hardly feel them.

When I get out and crawl into bed, I can hear Royal and Daddy yelling at each other downstairs. I pull the pillow over my head and try to block them out, try to go back to hiding the way I always did, as if that can make things go back to the way they always were. I try to think about tonight, to get back the feeling of triumph and exhilaration that lasted the whole time I was with my friends eating ice cream and hanging out at Dolly's house, as if I could live suspended in her little pink bubble with her.

But you can't un-pop a bubble once it breaks.

I wish for Devlin's incessant football throwing that used to drive me so insane. I'd welcome it tonight, and not just because I know he's not home, that he's at some party doing who knows what to whatever girl will do it. I don't care. Any distraction would be better than listening to my family implode.

*

I wake later, my heart pounding. The house is quiet, and no light filters in through my window. I hear a scuffing sound and sit up, my hands fumbling for the light. Images flash through my mind—that imposing older man I saw on the Darling's porch, a rusty old pickup full of hooting rednecks, Grampa Dolce laughing about killing a man.

Hands close around my legs, groping me through the blankets before I can hit the light. I stifle a scream.

"Shhh," he whispers. "It's me, Crystal."

"Devlin?" I hiss. "You scared the fuck out of me."

"I hope not," he says, sliding onto the bed next to me. His arm slides over my body, and he pushes closer, nuzzling

145

my neck. "Because I'm here to fuck that tight cunt until you scream my name like you did earlier."

"Devlin," I say, pushing at his chest. All I can think about is that Royal is in the room next door. "You can't be here."

"I know," Devlin says, inhaling deeply, his nose pressed to the nook of my shoulder. "But I can't be anywhere else. Don't you think I've tried?"

I reach over him to switch on the lamp and catch the scent of alcohol on his breath. Suddenly I'm furious. He wants to come over here drunk and horny, knowing that I can't say no to him. He doesn't care what it'll do to my family, who it will hurt. But I care.

"What do you mean, you tried?" I demand. "What'd you do, Devlin? Fuck some random Darling Doll at your party, get up and walk out? I guess that's your M.O. Right? And when it turned out she wasn't me, you came here looking for the real thing because let me guess, I'm so fucking special?"

"Is that what you did tonight?" he asks, sitting up and glaring at me. "Is that where you've been? You sure looked like you were ready to get fucked nice and deep when you were shaking that ass around on the field. So if you're not getting it from me, who'd you get it from?"

"Fuck you, Devlin," I say. "That had nothing to do with you."

"Yeah, then why'd you throw your hat in my face?" he asks. "If you weren't thinking about me when you were rolling your ass like you were taking a dick, then who were you thinking about? If it had nothing to do with me, then who was it about?"

"No one," I say, turning away.

Devlin's fingers wrap around my chin, and he turns my face to his. "Or maybe you just like an audience, like we had in the locker room," he says. "Is that it, Sugar? Is that why you got so wet when I was fucking you in front of the team? You liked it, didn't you? You're a little tease. You get off on thinking about all those guys dying to bust you open and fuck you until they can't think straight. You think you're so above it all, but you want them to beg, just like I do."

"You're disgusting, Devlin," I say, shoving his shoulder. "Get out of my room."

He grabs my hand, pulling it down to his lap and holding it there while he grips my chin with his other hand. His cock is thick and hard inside his jeans, and my pulse flutters when my fingers wrap around it. "I'll let you in on a little secret, Sugar," he purrs. "You can fantasize all you want, but no one can fuck you like I do. You can push me away and go fuck that asshole from Faulkner I heard you were talking to after the show, but you'll never find a man who can wreck that cunt and make you scream like I can."

"I wasn't fucking Chase," I whisper, heat pulsing between my thighs at his words.

"Good," he says, his hand sliding from my chin and down to my throat, where he grips me gently this time, the pressure so light it feels more like a caress—or a warning. "I wouldn't want to have to kill someone I respect. But if he put his dick in you, I'd do it. If I have to follow you around putting a bullet in every guy you talk to until I'm the only guy left, I'll fucking do it, Crystal. You're mine, and the sooner you admit that, the easier we'll both have it."

"You're fucking crazy," I say, yanking my hand from where he's still holding it in his lap. "You can't just threaten any guy I talk to."

He grips my throat tighter, his blue eyes piercing into mine. "I told you, I don't sleep around," he says. "I'm not fucking anyone else, Crystal. I haven't even looked at a girl since I first set eyes on you. So forgive me if the thought of some other guy tasting that sweet cunt, fucking it raw like I do, makes me a little crazy. Consider this a warning. If you're going to play that game, then yeah, there will be casualties."

"What the fuck, Devlin," I ask, jerking back and shoving his hand from my throat. "Why are you doing this? Let me off the fucking game board. You've already won. You had me, you broke me, my family is in ruins. We agreed this was over. Now you're telling me you'll murder any other guy I go out with?"

"Yeah," he says. "That's what I'm saying."

We sit there looking at each other for a minute. My head is swirling with conflicting emotions. It's true that I wanted him to fuck me in that locker room. Not for the reasons he said, not because it made me hot, but because they would all know he cared, that he wanted me, that he'd claimed me. He might have shattered me into a million pieces to get there, but I rose from the ashes like a phoenix that day. I triumphed.

I triumphed because he laid claim to me in front of everyone, told the world I was his and no one else could touch me, not even his cousins. I thought I ruined it forever when I told him I didn't want him. I've been aching to take it back, for another chance. And now he's giving me just that. Claiming me to insane extremes.

But that was a game, and this… This isn't. Is it?

"Are you fucking with me?" I ask. "Is this your revenge for what I did to you? Or why are you here, Devlin?"

"You're the one playing games with my head," he says. "First you can't get enough of me, and then you don't want anything to do with me. Then you want me to make you cum, but you tell me it's goodbye. Then you turn around and do what you did tonight, making me want you. And you tossed me your hat like I'm your man. So what is it, Crystal? What do you want?"

"I want… You," I admit, my throat aching with unshed tears. "But I can't have that. So just… Just go."

"And I want you," Devlin says quietly, taking my face and turning it toward him again. This time, his grip is tender, his gaze soft but intense. "I don't fuck around, and there's a reason for that. It means something to me. More than it should. I know you kept coming back for more because that was your game, that you wanted to make me fall for you. And you did. You're the one who won, Crystal. You wanted me, and you got me, and here I am. I'm not going anywhere. You can't tell me it was all a game and be rid of me. It's not that easy."

"Devlin," I whisper, closing my eyes. His lips meet mine, gentle but firm, commanding mine to open for him so he can taste my mouth, his tongue searching it as if for the hidden clues that go deeper than my words. Is he as fucked up about this as I am? Is it as hard for him to trust my motives as it is for me to trust his?

His tongue caresses mine as he lays me back on the bed, his hand cradling my head. Without breaking the kiss, he pushes my blankets down, settling his body between my thighs. Need builds inside me at the contact, and I tug at the fabric of his shirt, pulling it up his body and over his shoulders. He lifts up for a second to let me peel it off, then grabs my shirt and pulls it over my head. He gazes down at my body, clad only in a pair of white cotton underpants, like I'm more beautiful than anything he's ever imagined.

"My god, Crystal," he says, his voice low and rough. "Look at you. Can you blame me for being so fucking crazy?"

Before I can answer, he lowers himself onto me, his warm skin meeting mine. Relief and pleasure wash over me, and I wrap myself around him, greedy for the comfort of his body on mine. He devours my mouth, rocking his hips against mine with every swipe of his tongue. We kiss, and kiss, and kiss, until I'm drunk with it. He rocks slowly against me, the ridge of his cock pulsing against me with steady, dizzying pressure until I can't hold back. I cry out into his mouth as I cum, ashamed at my inability to hold back.

Devlin moans in response, grinding me deeper into the bed. When at last he pulls away, my lips feel swollen and hot.

I arch up against him, my nails digging into his shoulders. I need more, even as my breath is still coming quick and hot.

"Devlin," I whisper, throwing my head back as his heated lips trace my jawline and move down the column of my throat. "Are you drunk?"

"No," he says, leaning up on his elbows to look down at me. "I had a couple beers, but I know what I'm saying. I'm one hundred percent yours—heart, body, and soul. And you're mine, Crystal Dolce. I don't care who knows it or what happens next. I just know I have to be with you."

I pull him back down, kissing him like it's the only thing I'll ever need. How can he say those things to me, such perfect things, after all he's done? How can I believe them, or even want to believe them? I only know that I do. That I feel the same about him. In this moment, nothing else matters. There's just us, and it's enough, and more than enough. It's perfect.

He kisses me more forcefully this time, sweeping me up in his consuming passion, thrusting his tongue roughly against mine, sucking and biting at my lips, my chin, my neck. His tongue swirls over my skin as his hands roam over me with possessive roughness. I drink in the desperation in his touch, the thoroughness of his hands as they rake over me, squeezing my breasts, my hips, my ass, pushing between my legs.

I open for him, craving all of it and more. He pulls my panties aside and sinks his fingers into me, groaning against my throat and sending shivers through me. Knowing he feels the same, that he's as hungry for me as I am for him, electrifies me. I reach for the button of his jeans, undoing it and pushing them down.

Devlin's ready for me, pressing his hardness into my hand and rasping my name against my neck, sending tremors of desire spiraling through my entire body. I suck in a breath, my knees clenching as I squirm for relief against his hand. I stroke along his length, wanting it so badly I could weep even as I tremble at the sheer size of him, the heat, the way he feels so wild and raw against my small fingers. I can feel his vein pulsing against my palm, but I stop at the ridge around the head, running my thumb over the tip.

"Put it in," he orders, his voice rough and commanding.

"I'm still sore from today," I say, my thighs trembling around his hips.

"Get used to it."

He grabs my hips and rolls us over, so I'm straddling him. His rigid shaft is hot as a fever against my tender flesh. "Lift for me, baby," he says, guiding my hips up. "Now sink that tight cunt down over my tip nice and slow. I want to feel you take me balls deep in your grip. I'm all yours, Sugar. Every inch."

I swallow hard and guide him to my entrance, feeling my bruised flesh tighten in protest at the invasion. I press past it, to the ache inside me that wants this, needs it, despite the pain. When I look up, Devlin is watching me take him in, his eyes hooded and glazed with that look of pure, blissful oblivion I love so much. I watch, too, biting my lip to keep from panting at the sight of his cock stretching me open so far, sliding deeper and deeper. Taking my hand away, I sink onto him to the hilt, my thighs tensing at the familiar ache when he reaches my depth.

His hands tighten on my hips, and his gaze meets mine, his eyes burning like the blue edge of a flame. "Ride me, baby," he says, his voice hoarse with lust.

"I…I don't know how," I admit. I feel cold and vulnerable and exposed sitting here on him where he can see me fully. He feels so far away.

Devlin's eyes darken with something else, and he sits up, pressing his warm chest to mine. It was just what I needed, and at the same time, so horribly intimate that I wish he was lying down again. This is Devlin Darling. Whatever he says, it's a lie, a trap. I've been here, and I know what comes after.

"It's okay, Crys," he murmurs, stroking my hair back and circling the back of my head with his big hand. "I'm here for you, baby. Always. I'll show you. I just need to be inside you again, to feel you like I did before. I want to watch you fall apart, go to pieces for me. It's the only thing keeping me from falling apart."

A little thrill goes through me at his words. Because he *needs* me. Devlin Darling needs me. And it's not just another ploy. Even if he says so later, I'll know the truth. I can see it all over his face, in the desperation in his eyes. I can feel it all through his body, in the desperation in his touch. In the way he's trembling with holding back; in the tenderness in his arms as they cradle me against him.

"What about what you said before?" I ask, my own voice almost cracking with the effort of being still with him now, like this, while he's inside me. I want to move, want to feel the friction between our bodies build until we both combust.

"What did I say? You should know by now I'm full of shit, Crystal. Don't believe half of what I say."

"That I'm better off without you," I say. "It's not true. I'm only good with you."

"That one was true," he says, lacing his fingers through my hair and cradling my head. "You're better off without me and you know it, Sugar. I'm no good for you. But I can't live without you. I tried, and I don't know how."

"You'll never have to," I whisper, leaning in to kiss him. "I promise."

"You'll never leave again?" he asks, his eyes searching mine. His gaze is so vulnerable it tears my heart open along the scars left from the last time, when I broke my own heart by walking away from him. This is the real Devlin Darling, the one only I know, the one who doesn't want to hurt me any more than I want to hurt him.

"Never," I whisper, sliding my arms around his neck.

"Good," he says, stroking my cheek with his thumb. "Because even if you try, you'll never get rid of me. You can break my heart into a thousand pieces a thousand times over, and I'll still love you just as much."

He breaks off, looking as startled as I feel, like he didn't know he was about to say those words until they were already out. Suddenly, my heart is hammering so hard I can barely breathe. I wanted to make him fall for me, but I never imagined a boy telling me he loved me. It seemed like something that happens in movies.

"You love me?" I ask, my voice choked with emotion.

I expect him to deny it, to shove me off and disappear the way he likes to do when shit gets real. For a second, his eyes get that unreadable look, and I'm sure he will. I tense, ready to lift off him, but he slides both arms around me and squeezes me against him, not letting me go. "I've never stopped for even a second, not even when you told me I was just a pawn," he says, his voice soft and smooth, sure of himself. "I'll never stop. You're not just my heart, Crystal Dolce. You're my soul."

"I love you, too, Devlin," I whisper. I link my hands behind his neck, and our eyes meet, and it's the most intimate, intense connection I've ever felt. He grips my hips as I begin to move, never breaking the connection. It's different this time, something else mixed in with the frantic desperation to claim each other. Now, we've been claimed. I am his, and he is mine. I know in that moment that nothing will break us apart again. Not his family, and not mine. He broke me, and I broke him, but nothing will break *us*.

Because now there is an us. Now, we're fighting for the same thing. We're on the same side. I'm no longer trying to pick up all the shattered pieces of myself, the ones Devlin broke and chipped away, and put them all back together somehow. Without him, it's impossible. Our broken pieces have blended together, mixing until I can't tell what belongs to me and what belongs to him. They'll never be separated again. Even if I managed to build myself back up into something close to what I was, there would still be parts of Devlin always with me, little shards of him buried in my flesh, in my soul.

And in truth, I don't want to be the girl I was. I don't want to separate our broken pieces, to look at Devlin's damage and hand it back to him. I want to take those parts and treasure them, nurture them, fit them together with mine. I want to take all our broken pieces and form something new with all of them, both his and mine. I want to form something beautiful, something uniquely ours. I want to put them all back together and build *us*.

# eleven

*Crystal*

*Our love is impossible. It's impossible that I could love a boy who's done the things Devlin has done to me. It's impossible that he could love a girl who hurt him in the callous way I did. Somehow, though, we've found a way. And if we can find a way to love each other, to forgive each other, despite those things, shouldn't our families be able to do the same? How can they hate each other more than we've hated each other? Could our love bring them together? Or will it splinter them from within?*

"Where's that from?" Royal demands on Monday when I open my locker before school. A cookies-and-cream cappuccino sits in the front, a variation on the drink that's been here every day since I came back. I already knew it was Devlin, even when he pretended to hate me. But now I know for sure. This is the drink I told him was the perfect blend of sugar, caffeine, and chocolate.

"Uh, Dixie got it for me," I lie.

Because how can I tell him otherwise? How can I tell him that I love the boy he blames for hurting him? That on Friday night, while he slept in the next room, plagued by nightmares, his sweet little sister let a boy into her room, into her body. And I didn't just *let* Devlin put his dick in me. I wanted it. I put it in and rode it hard and didn't let him stop until he came so deep inside me that it hurt. I didn't think about my family, or how it would reflect on the Dolces, or if it fit the image of a Dolce daughter. I didn't give Royal a single thought. I took something just for me, and I loved every second of it.

How can I tell my brother that his twin is that kind of monster?

"Ooh, coffee," Dixie says, tromping up to join us in her goth boots and black outfit. "What'd you get?"

Fuck.

Royal's eyes narrow. "Dixie got you that?" he growls at me.

"I did?" Dixie asks, totally missing the frantic eye movements I'm making as I try to convey that she needs to go along with this, all smooth like Dolly would. But Dixie isn't practiced in the art of artifice.

Royal snatches the coffee from my hand, his face darkening with anger. "Why the fuck is someone getting you coffee?" he asks, his dark eyes boring into mine.

"I don't know," I say, my heart hammering and my mind racing. I don't know how to talk Royal down anymore, not like I used to. He's a stranger now, the brother I no longer know, separated from me by a week missing and a million moments I'll never experience with him.

"Who's leaving these in your locker, Crystal," he asks, his voice low and cold.

I shake my head. "No one's said anything about them."

"Who?" he demands, stopping in the middle of the hall, letting the crowd flow around us.

Dixie hangs back, her eyes wide as she chews at her lip with a guilty look on her face now that she's caught on. I shake my head at her, not wanting her to witness whatever's about to happen. Royal is seriously unhinged right now, and

I finally understand the need my family has to keep it together, to keep up appearances. Because the thought of him blowing apart in the middle of the hall is humiliating, and I have this irresistible compulsion to calm him before Dixie or anyone else sees.

Dixie mouths an apology at me and scurries off, leaving me to face my twin alone. It shouldn't be hard. I've fought with my brothers a million times. But this Royal, Royal 2.0, isn't a boy I know how to fight.

He shakes the cup at me, looming over me with anger pulsing in his temple. "You said you weren't seeing him anymore."

I don't want to lie to him, but the truth will hurt him too much. There's nothing I can do that won't hurt him more, and I've already done enough. So I don't say anything. My hands begin to shake. My palms are clammy, my nerves are frayed, and anxiety crawls along the inside of my skin like a disease. I try to breathe, but Royal's the boy who could always bring me back from the edge of panic, the boy who tethered me to reality. But he's not that boy anymore. The rope has been severed, setting me adrift.

"Answer me," Royal barks.

I shake my head, tears threatening behind my eyes. "Royal, don't."

People begin to slow, to linger, to watch a situation that shows signs of combustibility.

"Every fucking day one of these has been in your locker," he says, his voice rising with anger. "It's been him all along?"

"Royal," I hiss. "You're making a scene."

"Do you think I give a fuck?" he growls, his fist clenching around the coffee. The plastic lid pops off, and the cardboard crumples in his grip. Brown coffee splatters onto his arm and the floor, leaving blobs of whipped cream dribbling over his knuckles. "You've been fucking him all along, haven't you? Is this your payment? I'm gone for a week and you turn into a cheap whore who spreads her legs for a cup of coffee?"

My eyes sting with the pain of his words, but my throat closes, and I can't speak. Royal is supposed to be my brother, my best friend, my better half.

Before I can force out a word, he slams the cup into my chest, his palm flattening it against me. I stumble backward at the impact, the remainder of the coffee leaking down my front, soaking into my shirt. Strong arms catch me from behind at the same moment that Devlin pushes through the crowd behind Royal.

"Did you just hit her?" he asks, his voice low and deadly.

"Aww, shit," Colt says behind me. "Ain't it too early for brawling?"

It's never too early for my brothers. I lurch forward, out of Colt's arms, as Royal turns to Devlin, his fists already up.

"He has a concussion," I scream at Devlin, who looks like he's ready to commit murder. "Don't hit him!"

Devlin's eyes dart from me to my brother. Royal uses that moment to swing. He's not quick enough, though, and Devlin dances back, out of the way.

"Stop," I scream at Royal, jumping onto his back. I don't know what else to do. He's always fought like he had a death wish, but this time is different. He's already injured. I don't know what would happen if Devlin hit him in the head. Royal swings at Devlin again, and this time, Devlin isn't ready, probably thinking Royal will stop now that I've attached myself like a barnacle to his back. Royal's fist slams into Devlin's face, and he stumbles back against the lockers, cursing and spitting blood.

"You want to touch my sister again?" Royal asks, barreling forward. "Try it, asshole. See where you end up."

"Don't you dare hit him," I say over his shoulder to Devlin, who still has his hands up but isn't swinging. His eyes blaze with fury, but I can't tell if he's pissed at me or at my brother. When Royal swings again, he sidesteps him, and Royal's fist glances off the locker. It catches on the metal edge, and he swears as blood runs down his fist.

"Stop," I order, trying to wrestle Royal's hands down.

But he's not done. He grabs my hands and wrenches them apart, swinging my arm over his head and twisting sideways, dislodging me from his back and spinning me away. He lets my hands loose too late, when the full momentum of his turn is still with me. I go reeling sideways and hit the floor on my ass, about as ungraceful as a fall can be.

"What the fuck do you think you're doing, treating Crystal that way?" Devlin asks, grabbing my hands and pulling me to my feet, wrapping his arms around me.

"Now you wanna tell me how to treat my sister?" Royal thunders, lunging at us.

Devlin pushes me behind him, backing away from Royal with me pressed up tight to his back. "Whatever you got going on in your family, keep that shit at home," Devlin says. "It doesn't belong in the halls of this school."

"You have about two seconds to get your hands off my sister," Royal snarls.

I know I have to get them apart before this escalates. At the same time, I'm terrified Devlin is going to run his dirty mouth about where his hands have already been, which might be hot when we're hooking up, but I don't really want him saying those things to my family—especially not in front of a bunch of random people in the hall.

"Devlin, it's fine," I say. "Just go. I'll deal with it."

"You sure?" he asks, his voice so quiet only I can hear in the buzz of excitement in the hall.

"Yes, go," I say, ducking around him and putting both hands on Royal's chest, shoving him backwards.

"Run away like the pussy you are," Royal yells over my head at Devlin, who must be leaving. I don't look. I'm too busy trying to keep Royal from losing his shit again. "You don't deserve my sister. You better hope I never see you speak to her again!"

"Royal," I hiss under my breath. "Chill the fuck out."

"Get your hands off me," he says, jerking away from me. "Keep fucking him and see what happens, Crystal. I dare you."

After a second of staring at each other, both of us breathing hard, Royal turns and shoves past the other students. And I notice something different. They cringe back from him now. It's not the way they look at the Darlings, with awe and respect and a little dose of fear thrown in for good measure. This is straight up scared, as if they don't know what he'll do next, who he'll explode on. I don't blame them.

It's a different respect from what they show the Darling cousins. They're scared of Royal, and not in the uneasy way they were when Colt was on the move with a dog collar in hand, searching for a target. I duck my head and hurry to the restroom to clean up, grateful that I'm wearing black today so the coffee stain can be washed out easily.

When I walk into my next class and take my seat next to Colt, people whisper, but it's different. They look curious and excited rather than disgusted by the school slut.

"What's going on?" I whisper to Colt, ducking my head and turning it his way so no one else will hear us.

"Everyone's trying to figure you out, Crystal Sweet," he says with a grin. "You caused quite a stir this morning."

"I wasn't the one fighting."

"You kinda were," he says. "And even if you hadn't been there, everybody in this school knows you were the cause of that fight. They can't figure out what you are, where you fit."

"Probably doesn't help that you took the Dog label off me."

"Nope," he says with a grin. "Took us a while to figure you out, too. Now I'm just having fun watching you drive them all crazy while they try to guess where you'll land."

I cross my arms and smirk at him. "So, you've figured me out?"

"I know where you belong," he says, leaning forward on his desk so he's looking up at me with that adorable grin.

"Where's that?" I ask, arching a brow.

"With us, baby," he says. "You belong with us."

"That'll never happen," I say, trying to picture a scene where I sit with the Darlings instead of my brothers.

"Oh, it'll happen," Colt says. "Trust me, Crystal Sweet. When my cousin wants something, he gets it. And he wants you."

I shake my head and turn my attention to the teacher. But my mind returns to his words.

If Devlin and I love each other, if he really meant all those things he said to me on Friday night...

Maybe we could make it happen. Maybe we can bring our families together. Maybe we can all share the spotlight, the throne. My brothers can have the popularity and power they want, and the Darlings won't have to give up their place. And Devlin and I will be in the middle.

Then I think of how angry and broken Royal is. Could I convince him to join the Darlings without him thinking I'm a traitor? After all we've done to each other, if I can forgive Devlin, does that make me a horrible person, or a bigger person? And if I could convince my family, could Devlin convince his?

The Darlings have something going at this school. They've achieved a delicate balance, something different from what my brothers had in New York. My brothers were popular, but the Darlings are more than popular. They're untouchable. And for the most part, they're benevolent kings, despite what I've experienced. I have to remember that I was the only person facing that kind of abuse. They made an example of me. And like Dixie said, they did worse to me because I didn't just accept it like she did. I didn't understand it. She's always known it was more than being a target. She's known it holds its own strange prestige.

People know that the Darlings might bestow favor upon them—and they're here for it. The cousins might pull a nobody into their circle of exclusivity, elevate them to their dream for no other reason than that they can. They might give a girl a necklace and tell her she's worthy. They might tell a guy he's good enough to join their prestigious secret society and learn their secrets. They might invite someone like Dixie, who's heard of their legendary parties and dreamed of them for so long, to come along.

Or they might not.

Most people at this school adore the Darlings. They admire them. They want to land a Darling boy as a point of pride, or because they know they could be set through the whole of high school if they get a necklace. And yes, there's a little sliver of fear—just enough to make them remember that although they might join the Darlings for a night or a month of debauchery, they are never their equals. With one word, the Darlings can take it all away, like they did to Lacey. They revel in their favor, glory in it, because they know it might not last.

I can't help but think how hard they must have worked for that. And here we came waltzing in like a bunch of entitled punks, thinking we'd grab the respect and adoration and fear of the entire school for no other reason than we wanted it. No wonder the Darlings fucking hate us. This isn't just some throne their grandfather put them on when they were in diapers. It's a carefully crafted empire, one they built together and maintain every day with artful care and attention.

Sure, a name means a lot. But Dolly has a name in this town. Even Dixie is related to the mayor. Lacey has a name and look what happened to her. A name isn't enough. The Darling cousins did this. Their name doesn't hurt, and their fathers' and grandfathers' reputations in the town doesn't hurt. But these boys, they've done something special here, something unique, something even my brothers didn't have in New York. My brothers were football gods, party boys, fuck boys. This is more than popularity. It's worship.

Besides my brothers—before them—the Darlings had no enemies. No one challenged their rule, no one defied them. And it's not because people fear them. Mostly, it's the opposite.

So yeah, they've fought my brothers, but they have every right to defend their place at this school, one they've held for as long as they've been here. They've created an environment, and atmosphere, that benefits them. Why would they give that up?

It's not all good, and I don't agree with all of it. In some sick way, I have to admire the genius of it. There's a reason the Darlings have a whole table full of Dolls and only one Dog. Girls want to be their Dolls. Guys want to be their friends. Everyone wants to be absorbed into their orbit. But there's a limited number of spots at their table, and at the next one, and the next. That makes it even more special when a girl is chosen, honored, brought to their table and told she's something special. It makes every girl want it, and more, it makes her think she might attain it.

But the Dog, she's the reminder of what could happen. She's the whipping boy. The hint of danger, the dark side of the Darlings that hides in ancient caverns under the library, the threat that it's not all revelry and merriment. The reminder that if they get out of line, if they go too far, the Darlings only have to order it, and they could be the next one on a leash.

This system governs the halls of Willow Heights far more than money or names, more than the staff and administration. The Dolces came along, thinking we'd topple this thing that's as organized as the mob, a tiny little gang with a hierarchy and unspoken rules we didn't even bother trying to learn. So yeah, we deserved to be put in our place.

But now… Now I have a chance to do something about it. To sway things. And I won't waste that opportunity, even if my brothers are too arrogant and proud to see it. I swore I'd get rid of the Darling Dog, and now I'm in a position to do it. I finally have influence, though it's the furthest thing from the way I'd envisioned it happening. I don't have influence with the other students, but I have influence with Devlin. And he makes the rules.

I didn't take down the Darlings. But maybe I was never meant to destroy them. I can get more done from within than I ever could from the outside. Now I just have to convince my brothers that they can slide into the best spots on the game board, not as competitors, but as a team. If someone had told me a month ago that my brothers would be the ones I was most worried about convincing, I would have laughed. But here I am, more caught between our families than I've ever been. I just need to find the way out.

# twelve

*Crystal*

*Finally, I understand. Colt was wrong about us being Romeo and Juliet. But he was right about one thing. My place is with them. My family's place is with theirs. Somehow, I'll convince them. I'll convince them that even though they hate the Darlings, that they aren't the enemy. If the Capulets and Montagues had known how it would end, would they have done things differently? Or sacrificed their children for their pride?*

I stop at the door to the gym, my heart racing in my chest. Inside, I can hear a single basketball bouncing against the hardwood. I swallow hard, trying not to lose my lunch. It's the end of the day, and I can hear the football team on the field behind the huge building, the whistles and grunts and thuds. I squeeze my eyes closed and try to push away the memories of the last time Coach Snow called me here.

I shove open the door and step inside, blinking in the dim interior, my eyes trying to adjust after the bright, November sun outside. When I blink my vision clear, I wish I hadn't. A blond boy with a cast on one arm stands across the gym, slowly dribbling the ball with his good hand.

The door slams behind me, and I jump, swallowing a shriek of surprise.

Preston turns toward me. I step back, my hand fumbling for the bar to open the door.

"Wait."

I stand frozen as he walks toward me. I should run. I should turn and get the hell out. But I see Coach Snow in her office, a pair of glasses perched on her nose, looking at something on her computer. Does that mean I'm safe?

I remember the coach who walked away from me that day when I begged for help. I remember what Coach Snow said to me that day—that you can do what they want you to do, or be who they want you to be.

No. I'm not safe.

I turn, throw the door open, and bolt. I hear Preston call my name, but I don't stop. I'm halfway around the side of the gym when he grabs my arm from behind and spins me around, pushing me against the gym wall. Damn, he's fast.

"I'll scream," I warn. "Devlin will fucking kill you."

It strikes me how ironic that statement is. That just a few weeks ago, I would have threatened him with my brothers. But he doesn't care about pissing them off. Now I have his cousin on my side. And he cares what Devlin thinks.

Preston's piercing blue eyes skate over my face, and he has the nerve to look surprised when his gaze meets mine and he sees my pupils dilated with fear and the wild look in my eyes.

"You're scared of me," he says.

"Of course I'm fucking scared of you," I snap. "You assaulted me, threatened me with a knife, tied me up, and told me your football team was going to gang rape me. Am I supposed to think you're a harmless little bunny rabbit after that?"

"You know," he drawls slowly, his gaze sliding to my lips. "I think you're a honey badger after all."

"And you're a snake," I say, jerking my arm away from him.

A smirk tugs at the corner of his lips. "You know who wins that one, don't you?"

"What do you want?" I demand.

Preston's eyes search mine for a long moment, and then he lets out a little scoff. "I want my arm back," he says. "Can you fix that for me, Honey Badger?"

"No more than you can undo what you did to me in that locker room."

"I'd say it worked out pretty well for you," he says. "You got my cousin out of the deal, didn't you?"

"So now you're going to make me pay for that?"

He works his jaw back and forth for a second. "Do you love him?"

"None of your fucking business," I snap.

"Oh, but it is my business," he says, leaning in, his voice lowering as he stares into my eyes. "He's so fucking smitten he can't see straight. But I can. So either you love him, or you're fucking with his head. Which one is it, Honey Badger?"

I swallow hard, my heart hammering in my chest. This time not because I'm scared of what he'll do to me, but because I'm scared of being vulnerable in front of this demon boy. "I love him," I say, my voice steady enough to give me strength. "What about it?"

"Good," he says, reaching out and taking my hand. His hold is firm but not painful as he drags me back toward the gym doors.

I balk, digging my heels in. "Let me go, Preston."

"I'm not going to hurt you," he says. "Just go to your meeting. We'll talk after."

He leads me through the door of the gym and releases my hand. With a nod toward Coach Snow, he picks up the ball and walks slowly down the court, dribbling the ball. The noise echoes around the room, but this time, my legs are steadier as I make my way over to the office where Coach Snow sits behind a wall of glass. I glance back at Preston, wondering what his psychotic brain is cooking up for me after this. I wish he'd just gotten it over with.

"Crystal, come in," Coach Snow says, taking off her glasses and setting them on the desk when I walk in.

I step inside and close the glass door before taking a seat. "You wanted to see me?"

"I did," she says. "I'm afraid I have some not-so-good news."

"Let me guess," I say. "Arkansas's not ready for this jelly?"

She laughs. "That's a very good way to put it."

"Thanks," I say. "I knew I wouldn't make it. That's why I didn't come try out. You can't put a girl on the squad when all the other girls hate her."

"Well," she says, leaning back in her chair. "I'm glad you understand."

"I do," I say. "And I think I made my point at the game. So, if that's all…"

She nods, then sits up straight again. "Actually, before you go… Are you okay?"

"Yeah," I say. "Why?"

She glances at the basketball court where Preston is shooting a one-handed basket. "Well, I'm sure I only hear a fraction of what goes on with the students here, but I did hear some disturbing things about an incident that may have occurred after our last meeting."

Oh my god. My face burns, and I think I'm going to die on the spot. Not only has the rumor gotten around the whole school, but even the teachers heard about the supposed gangbang in the locker room. Lovely.

"Nothing happened," I mumble.

She sighs. "Okay. But if you need to say anything, I'm here. No judgments."

At least it's better than a crusty old administrator talking to me about this, but holy hell, I'm so not telling a teacher about what happened that day. Especially not when I can barely admit to myself what happened. That I'd go to those lengths, tell Devlin to fuck me like that, just to get him to fall for me. That's the moment he told everyone I was his. That's the moment when he was forced to admit his own feelings for me—to his cousins, to me, and maybe even to himself. So yeah, maybe I really am a whore. Not for the reason everyone thinks, but because I used my body to get what I wanted, what I needed. And it fucking worked, didn't it?

He helped me get Royal back. That was what I was after.

"Thank you," I say to Coach Snow. "I appreciate it. But you should know better than to believe the rumor mill around here."

"I do," she assures me.

"Good," I say, standing. "Then if we're all done here…"

I think about what my family would say if they knew I'd wasted this opportunity to ruin the Darling name. But I'm well beyond that. It strikes me that I'm now protecting Devlin. For the first time in my life, I'm lying not to protect my family, but to protect someone else from my family. I've protected the Dolces from scrutiny, rumors, and themselves. For the first time in my life, I have something for myself, and I won't let my family ruin it. This lie isn't about my family. It's protecting something that is mine and mine alone.

I'm about to step out of the office when I pause. What if Devlin had been absent that day? What if it had been some other girl he didn't care about? Part of me wants to turn in

Preston, but I know better than to start shit with him again. Not to mention what Devlin did in the hall for me when Royal hit him. I know how much that hurt Devlin's pride to walk away, to leave me with my brother. I know he did it for me, that he wanted to hit Royal but didn't. If he's willing to put aside our family feud for me, I should do the same for him. Not only that, but I don't exactly hate Preston, though I should. Some part of me feels for him. He lost everything when he lost football.

But there is someone else who was there that day. The adult in the situation should have stopped it before it even started. That should never have fallen on Devlin's shoulders.

I turn back. "You know, something almost happened," I say to Coach Snow. "Devlin stopped it, but one of your football coaches walked away when he saw it going down. I asked him for help, and he turned around and left."

Coach Snow nods slowly. "Do you remember which one?"

"I don't know his name," I admit. "But he's one of the football coaches."

Coach Snow taps on her keyboard for a few seconds, then turns the screen to me. The coaches school pictures all smile back at me. I point to the one who refused to help me that day. She thanks me, says I might have to come talk to her and the admin again, and then I'm free to go. I feel light as I step out of the office. But then I stop, my pulse quickening when I see Preston there, playing his sad solo basketball game.

I could walk back into Coach Snow's office like a coward, but I'm going to have to face him eventually. I keep my feet planted and wait for him to notice me. After one more shot, he tucks the ball under his arm and walks toward me. With every step, my heart thuds louder in my chest. "Come on," he says, taking my hand and pulling me toward a door I know all too well.

"No," I say, yanking at my hand. "Let me go, Preston."

He sighs and releases my hand, reaches into his pocket, and hands me his knife, handle first. "Take that if it makes you feel better. I just want to show you something."

"How dumb do you think I am?"

"Come on, Crystal," he says, sounding genuinely frustrated. "Devlin's my boy. I would never hurt his girl."

"You already did."

He rubs between his brows with his thumb. "You're right," he says at last, lifting his head and meeting my eyes. "There's no excuse for what I did to you. I'm the worst of all the pieces of shit you've ever encountered, and I know it. But I told you I'm not a liar, and I'm not a liar."

"Sounds like something a liar would say."

"Look, Devlin didn't say you were his girl until he did," Preston says. "And now you're his girl, which means you're one of us. Which means, whether I like it or not, I'd take a fucking bullet for you, Crystal."

"I thought you and Colt turned your back on him when he went to jail."

Preston's jaw tenses. "Where'd you hear that?"

"From Devlin."

"Then keep it to yourself," he says. "That's between us. We don't need that shit getting out."

Interesting. So Devlin told me something they don't want the school to know. I treasure that little piece of information more than I should. Devlin doesn't just love me. He trusts me.

"Okay," I say, flicking the blade of his knife out. "Then tell me what happened, and I'll go in there with you."

"You know what happened," he says. "Devlin's dad ratted out Grampa Darling. Devlin knew he'd be in serious trouble for that, so he tried to take the fall for his dad. They were both arrested. We were supposed to shun him except at school."

"You're just faking it?" I ask. "Does he know that?"

"We're not faking anything," Preston says. "Devlin did right by his dad. The dude's too fucking noble for his own good. Colt and I aren't holding shit against him because he didn't do shit wrong. So, did I answer all your questions?"

"Walk in front of me," I say after a second's hesitation.

"Want me to put my hands above my head?" he asks sarcastically, shoving the door of the locker room open and stalking in.

I step in behind him. My heart lurches into my throat. Preston walks back to the shower where he dragged me that day and stops, turning to the stall. I can't look. My breath is coming fast, and my mind spins so wildly I can't hold a thought. It's just a blur of images, of raw emotion choking through me like it did in those moments, that horrible, endless stream of minutes where I hung here alone, waiting for every woman's worst nightmare to come true.

"Why are you doing this?" I ask Preston, my voice strangled.

"Look," he orders. "It's just a shower stall, Crystal. It can't hurt you."

I squeeze my eyes shut. He's wrong. It hurts too much.

I hear him shift, and his arm slides around me. I jump, shock hammering into me. But his grip is comforting as he stands next to me, not pinning my arms but holding my waist; not trapping me but supporting me.

I didn't know the whole world would shift when Devlin said he loved me.

"I know I'm the last fucking person on this earth who needs to be giving advice," Preston says, his voice a soft murmur. "But even evil people get it right sometimes. As my old man likes to say, every action you take is letting the world know who you are. You can stand there and cry about it like a little bitch, or you can suck it up and show no fear, like a man."

"I'm not a man," I say through numb lips.

"Open your eyes, Crystal," he says. "You're stronger than this."

He's right. There's only one thing in this room that can hurt me, and it's not a shower stall. I open my eyes. It's so unremarkable, that shower stall. The floor and walls are just tile. The showerhead is just stainless steel. No rope. No blood. No hair.

No echoes of my screams.

I remember hanging there, so filled with terror that it knocked me over the edge. I went numb, not just my arms but my soul. I gave up. There was nothing left, not even hope.

But Preston doesn't get to write this narrative. Because it didn't end with him.

There was nothing for me here until Devlin walked in and brought meaning. When he stood in front of me and blocked me from their sight, I knew in that moment that he would protect me, that he wouldn't let anything bad happen to me, no matter what Preston had said. That was the moment my heart beat again, the moment that hope bloomed in my soul again. When his hands touched me, I remembered that I could feel again, no matter how numb I'd been up until that moment. He hadn't just proven that I was his in that moment. He'd proven that he was mine.

He had made a move that changed the whole game. He proved I could trust him. I didn't just win some stupid, meaningless game. He truly cared. I used it against him, and he still cares. More than I even realized until this moment, when it sinks in all over again.

"Preston," I say slowly, not moving away from him but tensing, ready for the other shoe to drop. "Why are you being nice to me?"

"Don't sound so shocked," he says, dropping his arm from around me. "I'm a nice guy." Without waiting for an answer, he lets out a snort of laughter.

"What's so funny?"

"I told you I'm not the liar. I can't even keep a straight face to sell you that bullshit."

"So?" I press. "Why are you suddenly being nice to me?"

He turns to me, his expression calm and his voice matter of fact. "Like I said, you're Devlin's girl now. Besides that, I respect you in your own right. I've got to hand it to you, Dolce. You played the game, and you played it well enough to hook my boy, and that's not easily done."

"And you're not going to try to ruin my life to get back at me for that?"

He shrugs and says to me what Devlin always says. "All's fair in love and war."

"What about this?" I ask. "Is this part of the game? Part of the war?"

Preston shakes his head. "Nah. You did him wrong, but if he chose to forgive you, that's between y'all. I got no beef with you, Honey Badger. As far as I'm concerned, you're solid. You didn't rat me out when you could have with the cops, and you didn't just now. I won't even ask for forgiveness, but at least I can tell you there won't be anything else to forgive."

"You don't have to deserve forgiveness," I say, turning to the Darling boy I know least, the one who scares me most. I force myself to let go of the fear that wants to sink its teeth into me when I meet his piercing gaze. He might not be a nice guy, but he did me a solid just now. "I can give it, anyway. That probably makes me the biggest fool in Faulkner, but I can't hate you for something that brought me Devlin. Just like I can't hate him for what he did to me. I get it. We came in here like a bunch of punks trying to tear down the kingdom you so meticulously built. Of course you defended your turf."

Preston gives me a long, searching look before shaking his head. "Forgetting what any of us did would make you a fool. Forgiving it makes you a better person than anyone in either of our families deserves."

"I don't know about that," I say, Royal's haunted eyes flashing in my mind. He deserves better than me for a sister.

"I do," Preston says. "Well, except maybe my uncle. God must have been picking the parental lottery winner the day that guy fucked Devlin's mom."

"Lovely image," I say with a tight smile. I cross my arms and squint up at him. "So, are we friends now or something?"

"Don't go getting all sentimental on me now, Dolce," he says. "I don't do friends. I got room for three things in my life. Family, football, and fucking. If you ain't any of that, you ain't shit to me."

"What about Dolly?" I challenge.

For the briefest moment, a flash of a second, something crosses his eyes. It's such a fleeting glimpse, like the one I saw when I called him his grampa's little bitch. I may never figure this boy out, but I know when I hit a nerve.

"What about her?" he asks, crossing his arms to mirror my position, his head back while he looks down his nose at me in that superior asshole pose he likes so much. The one I like so much, too, damn it. He may be straight psycho, but he's still hot as fuck, just like Devlin.

"Nothing," I say, strolling toward the door.

Preston follows, and though my heart does an instinctual lurch against my ribcage at the sound of his footsteps behind me, I know he's not going to hurt me now.

Devlin told them I was his, and now the whole world knows it. Even my brother, after this morning.

I stop just outside the locker room door and hand back the knife. "Thank you."

"Don't mention it," he says, closing his knife and pocketing it.

"Not just for the knife," I say.

"I know what you're thanking me for, Crystal," he says. "Give me some fucking credit."

"Okay." I nod, tightening my arms across my chest. "Then tell me this. The night Royal disappeared, who took him?"

Preston narrows his eyes. "I told you that."

"Give me some credit, too," I say. "I'm not a dumb bitch, Preston. You said you know every car at Willow Heights, and yet, you described that car as a shitty pickup."

"Those kids didn't go to Willow Heights."

"Uh huh," I say. "But I bet you know what kind of truck it was. I bet, if they go to Faulkner, you know exactly who they are."

Preston curses under his breath, giving me a dark look. "So what if I do? If I can figure it out, so can the cops, if they want to. So could you."

"How?" I ask. "Go around looking for every shitty pickup in this redneck town, and then go knocking on the door asking if they ambushed my brother? You saw it. You could recognize it."

Preston lays a hand on my shoulder, his grip firm and his eyes hard as they bore into mine. "It doesn't matter who they are," he says. "And trust me, you don't want the cops to find them, either. Because if they do, they'll question them, and you won't like the answers they give."

I swallow hard, a funny flutter catching in my throat. "What does that mean?"

"It means they're just a bunch of punks who have no money and no better options for earning it," he says. "They're not the players in this game. They're the pawn you sacrifice on your first move."

"Stop talking metaphors and tell me straight."

"Learn to ask better questions."

We stare at each other for a long moment. I know the question he wants me to ask, the one I need to ask, but I can't. I can't, because he'll give me an answer I don't want, an answer I'll have to think about, and I've been refusing to think about it every second of every day since Royal woke up. And the fucked up part is, I might believe him. I don't want to believe him, but I might.

Some part of me already knows what he'll say. Some part of me already suspects a truth so horrible I can't let myself think it, let alone hear it spoken aloud.

"I thought you said you weren't a liar," I whisper, my heart pounding in my chest, my throat, my ears. I can barely speak.

"And I thought you said you weren't a dumb bitch."

"Then I guess we're both wrong," I say, and I turn and walk away. My heels echo inside the cavernous gymnasium, but it's the only sound. This time, Preston lets me go. He doesn't follow. He doesn't have to. The damage has been done.

# thirteen

*Devlin*

"Come on, my dudes, let's party it up!" Colt slides over the door and into the back seat of the Ferrari, tossing boxes of condoms to me and Preston as he goes. "I've been saving up all week. I'm gonna bust a nut in some blondies tonight."

"Actually, I'm a little bruised up," I say, shifting the car into gear and gunning it. "I might skip the party tonight."

"You mean you're going to a party of two," Preston says, slugging my shoulder as we pull out of the convenience store lot.

"Devlin's in lo-ove," Colt hollers, jumping up and grabbing me and the seat in a headlock, trying to give me noogies like we're eight years old again.

"Knock it off," I say, shoving him off.

Colt collapses back into his seat, laughing his ass off.

I don't say anything for a few minutes. I know they're just doing their thing. But when we turn onto the street to my neighborhood, I come clean. These guys might give me shit, but they're still my boys.

"Yeah, I'm going to be with Crystal," I say. "It's the only time her family doesn't have her under lock and key. And to be honest, getting drunk with you assholes doesn't measure up."

"Okay, lover boy," Colt says, still chuckling.

"And yeah, I fucking love her," I say. "Get used to it."

"Damn," Preston says, shaking his head. "I hope you know what you're getting into."

"I'm not getting into anything," I say. "I'm already in it."

"Gramps will never let it happen."

"He's not going to ruin my life like he tried to do with my parents."

"That's exactly what he's going to do," Preston says. He has some special insight into Grampa Darling. Not only is he the favorite, but his mind works the same way. I wish I could have done more to get him out from under our grandfather's thumb, but what was I supposed to do? I was a kid just like him when Grampa singled him out, and his dad was a hundred fucking percent on board with grooming Preston to take over the business.

"We'll figure something out," I mutter, pulling up beside the Benz in the garage.

"More pussy for me," Colt sings, hopping out of the car without using the door, as usual. "Let me go give my second mom a kiss, and then I'll hit the party with you, Pres."

Colt has a strange bond with the woman who should have been his mom, the woman who's not actually related to either of us, though you'd never know by the way she smothers us.

"Slip her some tongue for me," Preston calls after him as Colt goes bounding into my house, his middle finger held high for us.

"The only guy who can talk about getting pussy and kissing his mother in the same breath," I say, shaking my head.

"You sure you know what you're doing?" Preston asks.

"No fucking clue," I admit, throwing the brake and getting out of the car. "I just know I can't stop doing it. And I don't want to."

"Then don't," Preston says, getting out of the car and taking my keys. He rests a hand on my shoulder and squeezes. "Just know where it ends, Dev. You got one semester left. High school is ours. We can do whatever the fuck we want. Once it ends, that's the real world, and no one gets to do what they want out there."

"This is Darling country," I say. "We should be able to do what we want."

"If every Darling did whatever the fuck they wanted, it wouldn't be Darling country anymore," Preston says. "There's a system. You follow the system, and things stay the way they are. That's what keeps us at the top. You buck the system, and it all falls apart."

"I know," I say, slumping against the car. "But don't you ever question why it is the way it is? Why it needs to stay that way? If maybe it's time the system changed?"

"No," Preston says, dropping his hand from my shoulder. "There's no point."

Colt emerges from the house, jogging down the back steps and striding over.

"Have fun at the party," I say, pushing off the Ferrari.

"Enjoy it while you can," Preston says, circling the front end to climb into the driver's seat. "You got a few months left."

I wave and head for the house. He's right. We all play our parts. If this thing our parents built is a house of cards, then we're each essential. Take one card out, and the whole castle falls. I don't want that for my family. They've worked hard to build this, and it would be selfish to knock the whole thing down. My job is to marry the daughter of the mayor, and one day become the mayor—not to fall for the seductive curves and pit bull heart of the sexy little mobster's daughter next door.

But I already know it's too late.

In the house, I find my parents in the kitchen where we eat, Mom sitting sideways across Dad's lap with her arms around his neck.

"I'm home," I call, heading for the fridge. I grab a couple ice packs and the plate of food Lucinda left me, which I toss in the microwave to heat up. Crystal's on her way, but it'll take her a few minutes to get away from her family and get a ride home. Just one more thing that frustrates the hell out of me. I want to be the one to take her home at night. But word would get back to her brothers, and I don't want her to get any more shit from her family than she already does. If my family is controlling, hers is a fucking prison.

"How's your arm?" Dad asks as I sit down with them a minute later.

"Fine," I say, tearing into my food. "Just need to ice it for a few minutes."

"Skipping the postgame party?" Mom asks.

I shrug. "Didn't feel like it tonight."

"Mm?" she says noncommittally, but I don't miss the raised eyebrows as she and Dad exchange a look.

"Anything on your mind, son?" Dad asks.

"No," I say, biting off a mouthful of chicken. "Some things are more important than partying."

"Well, I think it's good that you're not drinking so much lately," Mom says. "That's not healthy for anyone, especially at your age." She pulls a face, and I know she's holding back what she wants to say, some more scathing words about my real mom's permissiveness.

My phone chimes with a text, and I glance down at Crystal's message.

*Unsweet Dolce: OMW.*

Those three little letters get my head all turned around and my dick stirring.

"I'm going to head up and get some rest," I say, pushing back from the table without finishing my food.

"Sure, Dev," Dad says. "We're turning in ourselves, but I'll leave the back door unlocked for your guest. I hope you'll bring her through the front and introduce her to us soon."

"I will."

We stare at each other a second. I wonder if he knows who I'm bringing up to my room. He's not stupid—he knows I'm acting shady because I'm bringing a girl home—so he probably knows who. He's seen her here before, but that was before we both got arrested because of her family. Knowing Dad, he's happy for me and doesn't blame her a bit. The man is a fucking saint. It's kind of disgusting.

"Dad," I say slowly, rethinking my exit. I grip the back of my chair, staring at my hands, the same big hands he has. I'm like a carbon copy of him on the outside, but inside, he's good through and through, while I'm lucky to be called anything less than a monster. "How do you manage to live in this town and be your own man?"

Dad clears his throat and wraps an arm around Mom's trim middle, shifting her weight onto one knee. "I wouldn't say I've been able to be my own man," he says. "And if I am now, it took more sacrifices than it was worth to get here."

Mom wraps her arms around him, snuggling tighter against his chest. She's one of the sacrifices he made, one he was forced to make when Grampa Darling chose who Dad married the first time around.

"There's no way to change his mind?" I ask.

"He doesn't see what he did as a mistake," Mom says. "He thinks we made the mistake."

"There is a way," Dad says quietly, frowning down at the table in front of him. I can read the pain etched into the lines on his face, lines caused by worry, years of court battles, the loss of two of his brothers. Lines caused by my grandfather. I don't know how he had a father like that and turned out so good, while I had him and turned out so bad.

"A way that doesn't involve giving up our whole family and living destitute in the trailer park across town because no one will hire me?" I ask. It's one thing to leave my name, but Colt and Preston are part of me like my limbs. Who else in the world will ever know the ins and outs of our family, understand the intricacies of our fates? Who else would be able to know without a word what I needed, what I meant by some obscure remark because they know my life like it's their own, the same way I know theirs?

"In this town, with this name?" Dad says, leaning back in his chair. "I know I'm supposed to give you a pep talk, but... I can't think of a way."

"You could do worse than Dolly Beckett," Mom says. She always loved Dolly. Hell, the girl is a copycat of Mom—magnified tenfold. Maybe that's part of the reason I could never feel what I was supposed to feel for her.

"It's not just that," I say, kicking my toe against the leg of the chair I'm leaning on. I admit, it's a big part of it. But I want the freedom to live like anyone else, to make a name for myself instead of bearing the burden of someone else's. I know that's impossible, but for a moment, I think about it. I can't run away from who I am.

"What is it, honey?" Mom asks, bringing me back to earth.

"Nothing," I say. "Thanks for coming to the game. I hope y'all enjoyed it."

"We did," Mom says. "You were brilliant, as always. Don't forget your ice packs."

I pick them up, say goodnight, and head up to my room to wait for Crystal. This is reality. Like Preston said, I better enjoy it while I can. Four months. That's how long I have until graduation. The longest I can possibly hope to have with the girl I love.

I try to imagine a life outside Faulkner, but I can't. I couldn't leave my cousins, anyway. It's no different than being disowned. It doesn't matter if I'm across town in the trailer park or in New York City with Crystal. If I broke from the Darlings, I'd never see them again. And not only that, but they'd hurt because of it. If I took us off the game board, if I pulled my card from the crazy card house, it might free me, but it would send everyone else tumbling down. I could leave behind my name, my inheritance, all of it—if it only affected me. But I can't make anyone else pay for my sins.

As if in answer, my phone chimes. Crystal's here. Now it's time to pay for my sins like I do every time I'm with her, every time I have to remember what I did to her, and know that she's a big enough person to forgive what no person should have to—a bigger person than I am.

When does that end? When can I stop paying? And what exactly is the total cost of my sin?

# fourteen

*Crystal*

*Life in limbo. There is no fighting, but there's no peace, either. Weeks pass, and even though Devlin very publicly stood up for me at school, I can't sit with him. I am a Dolce girl, not a Darling Doll. People stare and speculate. They're still waiting to see what I'll do. Or maybe they're waiting for the Darlings to tell them where I belong.*

*Even I'm not sure of the answer to that. At home, I am a good Dolce daughter. At school, I'm a curiosity, a mystery that no one can solve. Only on Friday nights can I sneak away and be a Darling girl—Devlin's darling. I love my family, but I live for our Friday nights together. I can get through each week only by counting down to the time when I can be with him again. When I can be myself again. A few hours stolen each week is all I get. I take it greedily, wallow in it, glut myself with enough genuine*

*acceptance to last me for six more days. Funny how what
started as a game has become the only real thing in my life.*

As I'm waiting with Dixie next to Dolly's pink monstrosity
of a truck after the game a few weeks later, a dark green
mustang slides up in front of us. The window lowers silently,
and Preston leans down from the driver's side to see us.
"Hop in if you're going to Dev's tonight."

"Wait, *you're* giving me a ride?" I ask, balking. We
hashed things out, but I'm not sure I entirely trust the guy.

"'Fraid so," he says. "Hop in or not."

I check my phone, where I see a message from Devlin
telling me as much. When I look at Dixie, she smiles and
nods eagerly, a yearning look in her eyes that tells me she
wishes she could be in my shoes right now, going off to see
the guy she loves. "You'll be okay?"

"Dolly's just changing," she says. "She'll be out any sec.
Go, before your brothers see you."

"Okay," I say, giving her a wave and diving into
Preston's leather seat, my heart thudding at the thought of
my brothers catching me. As far as they know, I leave after

the games to go hang out with the girls—not their sworn enemy.

"I didn't know you had a car," I say to Preston, buckling up as he peels out of the parking lot.

He laughs. "It's not New York, Honey Badger. Everyone has a car."

"Not everyone," I mutter. I haven't been able to get away for more than a couple more driving lessons with Devlin, and I'm far from being ready to get my own car. We ride in silence.

"You know, I underestimated you," Preston says after a bit, laying an arm along the back of my seat. "You seem all quiet and meek. I thought you'd be easy to break."

I shrug. "Sorry to disappoint you."

"Oh, I wasn't disappointed," he says. "You were easy. I just didn't expect you to break Devlin, too."

I smile and turn to the window. "I didn't break Devlin. I fixed him."

Preston chuckles. "See, that's what I mean. I expect the type of girl who would be proud to brag that she broke him. You know, one of those bitches who can't stop boasting about how badass she is, when really she's just a little brat who needs to be put in her place. But you…"

He takes a strand of my hair and winds it around his finger, a slow smile spreading over his lips. I think it's the first time I've ever seen him smile, and even though it's a small one, it matters. To me it does.

He raises my hair to his nose and inhales. "I think you always were in your place," he says. "We tried to knock you down, but we couldn't. Because you were always where you belonged. At the top, with us."

"Wow," I say. "Did the untouchable Preston Darling just admit he was wrong?"

"I'm not too proud to admit when I make a mistake," he says. "I mean, it's never happened before, so I can't be totally sure, but I like to think I'm pretty self-aware."

"So, you know you're a complete psycho?"

He smiles again, this time even bigger, a real smile with teeth showing and everything. "Yeah, baby," he says quietly. "I know."

He turns to the road, and we ride the rest of the way in companionable silence. When we arrive, he drops his arm from the seat and turns back to me. "You know why I call you a honey badger?"

"Because it's nicer than calling me a bitch?"

Preston's mouth twitches with a smile, but it's his eyes that get me. They're so flinty, such a steely blue, but the smile reaches right to the center of them. Knowing I put that smile there feels like winning. "You're small, you don't look that intimidating, but mess with you, and damn."

Before I can answer, he slides out of the car, coming around to open the door and holding out a hand to help me up. I hesitate to take it, to take any kindness from him. With him, everything feels like a trap. At last, though, I let him take my hand and pull me up. When I step out of the car, we're standing face to face, his blue eyes so bright the color jumps out of the night.

He reaches up and tucks my hair behind my ears. "You know, I kinda wish I'd realized it before Devlin did." He leans down, his fingers lingering below my ear as his lips skim mine.

I lay a hand on his chest and push him back. "Preston."

He offers no resistance, stepping back from me until my hand falls away from him. He shrugs and says, "I had to do it once, Manhattan. I've never kissed a New York girl before."

"I thought that was your sex bucket list."

"Never kissed a girl I didn't fuck."

"Well, then I guess tonight will be a first," I say. "I'm all Devlin's."

*

"I've been thinking about this all fucking week," Devlin murmurs into my sweaty hair as he collapses on top of me an hour later. We skipped the postgame party again—the last one of the season—so we can be together. It's quiet at Devlin's, and I can be as loud as he makes me. I hate that he's missing his party, but it's the only time we can really be together. This, and science class, which doesn't include quite the same perks.

"Me, too," I admit, cradling his head against my chest and running my fingertips over the tattooed skin of his forearm. "What do these mean?"

"Different things," he says, pulling the blankets over us without moving from his position on top of me. "Why, you want me to put your name in ink so everyone knows I'm yours?"

"No," I say, laughing. "What if I changed my name or something?"

"Don't worry," he says. "I'll make it say *Crystal Darling*."

My heart does a little flip. "Devlin…"

"Kidding," he says. "I'll just have them write *Sugar*. But we'll both know what it means."

"You're not going to tell me what they mean, are you?"

"Some of them mean something," he says. "Some of them don't mean anything." He turns his arm over, letting me see the morning glory vine winding up the back of his arm, blooming on his tricep. "This is my biggest one, and I just got it because a guy from Faulkner High wanted to practice on someone."

"Wow," I say. "That's brave."

"Not really," he says with a chuckle. "I was drunk off my ass. Good thing he was actually really fucking good. I could have ended up with a cartoon animal."

"What about this one?" I ask, rubbing my thumb over the one I saw the first time I met him, when he was standing in the parking lot with his arms crossed, and I could see the ink on the back of his forearm. It's a Latin phrase written in fancy script.

"It's the Swan's motto."

"Oh," I say, swallowing hard. He never talks about that with me. "They make you tattoo that on yourself?"

"I like ink," he says. "It's addictive."

"Hm," I say. "Maybe I'll get one."

"I don't think so."

I pull back and look down at him. "You don't think I'm brave enough to get a tattoo?"

Devlin leans up on his elbows, his eyes darkening as he looks down at me. I can feel him hardening inside me again. "I like your virgin skin," he says. "I want to be the only one to leave marks on you."

"Me, too," I whisper. "I love the marks you leave. They help me know it's real even though I can't even talk to you all week. I wait for it all week, every week, Devlin."

I know we're digging our own grave, that there's no way for this to end except in disaster. Every time we're together, it's as precious and bittersweet as if it were the last time. Each time, it could be. We're both willing to risk it for now, even knowing it can't end any other way. We're a toxic, doomed, beautiful disaster waiting to happen. But it will happen. There's no way around that, no matter how hard we pretend.

He tightens his arms around me, scooting down and pressing his lips to my hammering heart again. "It kills me that we can't be together at school."

"Me, too."

Since the day he refused to fight Royal, the day he stepped in to defend me to my own brother, Royal has barely spoken to me. As far as I can tell, he hasn't ratted me out to anyone else in the family, but he must know what that meant. At school, my brothers rarely leave my side, escorting me like bodyguards and refusing to let me so much as speak to a Darling. With the way my family talks, I've been too afraid to let Devlin even climb through my window. I might make noise, and if they came in and saw him fucking me, they'd shoot him while he was still inside me.

"You can't talk your brothers into giving me even one chance?" Devlin asks, pushing himself up on his elbows and leaning down to kiss me. "I can prove to them that I'm going to do right by you. I'll keep trying until the day I die, Crystal. One day, I'll show you I'm worthy."

"I know you're worthy," I say lightly. "But I don't mind you proving it. Especially with jewelry."

Devlin smiles. "You're one of those girls?"

"Every girl likes shiny, expensive things."

"Noted," he says, rubbing his nose back and forth against mine. "And you know my family's cool with you already. It's just your brothers we have to convince now."

"So, you're the liar in the family," I say, rolling us onto our sides, my legs still locked around his hips. "I would have thought it was Colt."

"What?"

"Preston said he wasn't the liar in the family," I say. "I thought Colt was. But it must be you."

"You really have to talk about my cousins while I'm still inside you?" he asks. "I was getting hard again."

"You talked about my brothers when we were hooking up."

"That's different."

"How?" I ask. "Because they're my family, not yours?"

"Because they're not girls who want to fuck me."

I snort and roll away from him, sitting up to arrange his blankets over my legs while Devlin disposes of the condom in the trashcan beside his bed. "Preston does not want to fuck me," I say. "He hates me. He wants to hurt me, so yeah, he'd probably rape me because he knows how badly that fucks a person up, but he doesn't actually want to fuck me."

"He hates you because he can't have you," Devlin says, pulling me back down beside him. "Because you're the only girl who doesn't cream her jeans when he starts talking shit. Because you never bowed down to him. It kills him that you weren't interested."

"In a guy who basically sexually harassed me from the second I walked into this school? Gee, that's a real shocker. How could I resist that?"

Devlin smiles a little. "I'm glad you resisted," he says, tucking an arm around me and pulling me back to him. "I want to be the only man you can't resist."

"You are," I say, leaning in to kiss him. "But don't tell me your family loves me. Your dad got arrested because of me."

"Not because of you," Devlin says, folding his arm under his head and staring at me with those intense blue eyes. "I promise he'll love you if you'll give him a chance."

"You hid me from your mom," I remind him.

"That was before this," he says, squeezing my hip. "That was when it was goodbye."

"So… What? You want to introduce me as your girlfriend now?"

"Mom loves us," he says. "She might be upset about your family getting us arrested, but she'll come around. And my dad doesn't hate you. The guy helped name you, Crystal. You should get to know him."

"Okay, I gotta hear this," I say. "I know you think your family is omnipotent in this town, but my parents didn't even live here when they had me."

"That was the idea for the first candy," Devlin says. "The one my dad came up with."

I lean up on my elbow. "That's not true. My dad named the first candy after me."

Devlin holds up both hands. "Okay. Not trying to argue."

"I mean, the first one that was his," I say. "Obviously, he got the store from my grandpa, so the first ones were his recipes, and then Dolce Drops put him on the radar, but Dolce Crystals came out the year I was born…"

Devlin doesn't answer.

I flop back on the bed and pull a pillow over my face. "Which means he probably named them a long time ago," I groan. "He'd been working on that recipe for years. Oh my god. He didn't name his signature candy after me. I'm named after a stupid hard candy."

"Hey," Devlin says, pulling me close again and pressing his nose against my neck. "It's not so bad. If that's the worst you can say about your dad, that's nothing."

"You know that's not the worst I can say about him," I say, uncovering my face. "And what would you know? From what I hear, your dad's a regular saint."

Devlin arranges the pillows to lie on his back, an arm under his head. "He really is," he says, sounding pretty damn smug.

"But he cheated on your mom," I say, laying a hand on his chest. I remember what Dolly said, and suddenly I'm glad she wouldn't tell me. I want him to tell me this, to tell me everything. Talking to him is as addictive as touching him.

Devlin's face tenses, and his muscles tighten under my fingers. "Who told you that?" he asks, his voice edged with the coldness I remember too well.

"Your mom did," I remind him. "At that party where you led me around on a leash. Remember?"

He swallows, the muscle in his jaw standing out with tension. He plucks my hand from his chest and pushes it away. "Why do you want to know about my family?" he asks.

"Because I want to know everything about you," I say, trying to hide the hurt from my voice. "And I want you to be the one who tells me. Don't shut me out, Devlin."

He clenches his jaw, his eyes fixed on the ceiling. "How am I supposed to believe you love me, Crystal?" he asks, his voice low and edged with bitterness.

"You?" I ask, drawing back. "How am I supposed to believe it, after everything you did?"

"Exactly," he says, sitting up and staring down at me. "After everything I did to you, how can you love me? If you just need me to fuck you like I did in the car that day, I can understand that. I can make you cum, screaming my name, every Friday night. But let's stop pretending this is more than that to you."

"Devlin." I sit up and wrap my arms around him, even though he's still tense, his muscles straining with anger under my touch. He turns his face away, but I know this boy now. I can see the pain under that anger.

"Look at me," I whisper. I take his chin and turn his face to me, like he's done so many times to me. "I don't know where you got the idea that I just want you for sex. As much as I love your penis, it's not why I'm with you."

My attempt at a joke falls flat. Devlin pulls my arms off him and turns away, sitting on the edge of the bed with his back to me and his head in his hands. He's so fucking beautiful, a god of a man, with every inch of his glorious body on display, all those muscles in all the right places. I do know where he got that idea. Because he looks how he does, and he has money, and a name, and every girl in this town wants him. Probably a hundred different girls are all over him at every party, thinking that's what he wants. And now he thinks it's what all girls want from him. He said as much on the lawn one night, that he couldn't give me money, and if I didn't want sex, he had nothing else to offer me. But he's wrong.

"Devlin," I say, crawling over and wrapping my arms around him. "You have everything I could ever want. Just let me have it. I want to know you, inside and out. But I can't do that if you won't talk to me."

"Telling you about my fucked up family is somehow going to make you love me?"

"I already love you," I say, stroking his smooth, bronzed skin. "Please talk to me."

He sighs and runs a hand through his hair. "Yeah," he says. "My dad cheated on my mom. There. Are you happy?"

"Are you?" I ask.

"No," he says. "Now you think my dad's an asshole, and you probably think that I'll cheat on you."

"So, convince me otherwise," I say, lifting his arm and pulling it around me. I snuggle into his side, resting my head against his shoulder.

Devlin pauses. "No," he says, shaking his head. "If you believe that, then you believe it. If you trust me, then you trust me."

"Then why don't you trust me with your family secrets?"

"I trust you," he says, turning and laying me down on the bed. He lies beside me, so we're facing each other. "And they're not secrets. The whole town knows. If you really want to know, ask anybody." He pauses, running the back of his knuckles up my arm, sending chills dancing through me. His gaze is intense and heated as he watches goosebumps rise under his touch.

"I don't want to ask anybody," I whisper. "I want to ask you."

"Okay," he says slowly. "My grandfather arranged my parents' marriage, and they weren't happy. If you want to know all the drama, you can ask. But I love that when you look at me, you don't see the entire fucked up family saga of my name dragging around behind me. That's not me, Crystal. This is me."

I understand his words so much it hurts. With him, I can just be myself, not the Dolce daughter, and I love that. I also love that he feels the same about me. His family history is just that—history. I want his future. I wrap my arms around his neck and press a kiss to his lips. "Okay," I say. "Don't tell me, then. It doesn't matter. What matters is right here."

Devlin's hand falls on my waist, pulling me to him. "Agreed," he says.

"Just tell me one thing," I say, pulling back. "How come you never told me you had a sister?"

"She's not my sister."

"Your... Stepsister?"

"And cousin," he says with a grimace. "It is Arkansas, after all."

"You don't like her," I say, noticing the change in his tone since we started talking about Mabel.

"It's not that," he says. "She hates all of us. I think the divorce fucked her up more than all of us—or in a different way, anyway."

"That bad?" I ask, thinking about the impending situation in my house. Knowing my parents, though, they'll just run away from it, pretend it doesn't exist, and stay married forever.

Devlin shrugs. "A never-ending clusterfuck that took up most of my childhood. Mabel's got Darling blood, but she doesn't want to be a Darling. She hates what we do at school. She doesn't play into any of it. I'd bet money that the day she graduates, she'll ditch Faulkner and never look back."

"I thought she was Grampa Darling's favorite."

Devlin scoffs. "His favorite to manipulate."

We're quiet for a moment, and then I take my shot. I've wanted this since the day I walked into Faulkner and saw Dixie on her knees in front of Devlin. I didn't imagine this was how it would end, but it's time that it does.

"I don't like what you do at school, either," I say quietly, keeping my gaze steady on his.

Devlin draws back, a frown pulling together between his brows. "Is someone still messing with you?"

"No," I say. "Not since the day you got into it with Royal and defended me in front of the whole school."

"Good." He laces his fingers through mine and kisses the back of my hand.

I speak before he can change the subject. "Devlin, I want to be with you, but I won't lie. I hate what you guys do at school. I hate the whole Doll and Dog thing. Why can't everyone just be who they are? Like we are here."

"It's not that easy," he says, trying to roll away. I hold tighter, throwing a leg over his hip.

"Why not?"

"It's not my decision," he says.

"You made me the Dog," I point out. "And you undid it. I think it's that easy if you want it to be."

He's quiet for a long moment. "Okay," he says at last, nodding. "I'll make it happen. For you."

"Really?"

"I don't give out those necklaces," he says. "I gave one to Dolly when we were freshmen. That's it, Crystal. It's not my deal. I'll talk to my cousins, but you'll probably have to let us each keep one Doll."

I swallow hard, trying not to feel the blow of that one word—*us*. He wants to keep one Darling Doll, too.

Which is fair, I remind myself. He can't take Dolly's necklace. She's the original Darling Doll, the one the rest are named for. But even knowing he doesn't love her that way, the fact that he wants to let her wear that label forever still stings.

"Okay," I say. "But no more Darling Dog."

"That was around before us," he says. "If we didn't pick one…"

"Then the Midnight Swans would," I fill in.

He doesn't answer, but he doesn't have to. When he avoids my eyes, it's enough of an answer.

"I know about your secret society," I say, squeezing his hand. "I was in that basement. That's where they meet, right?"

"I don't want to lie to you," he says. "So don't ask me about it. All I can tell you is that I didn't know Royal was there, and I had no idea my family had anything to do with it. You found out when I did."

"Okay," I say, nodding. "I believe you." I run my hand up his, pressing our palms together. Devlin searches my eyes a moment as if he can't believe I'd let him off that easy. But some things are not my business. I'm not going to force him to tell me what he doesn't want to tell me. We're our own people, with our own pasts, and that's okay. I'd rather leave my shameful past where he never has to see it, and I respect him enough to afford him the same privacy.

"Crystal…" he says slowly, then clears his throat before continuing. "I'm not telling you what to do, or how your dad should run your family, but maybe your brother needs more help than he's getting. Like, mental help."

He tenses, as if expecting me to get angry and pull away. Instead, I swallow hard, tightening my fingers in his, never wanting to let go. "I know," I admit. "My dad would never allow it, though. The men in my family don't go to therapy. Talking about your feelings is like a weakness in their eyes."

"I think it goes beyond talking about feelings. He was fucking kidnapped. I mean, I'm surprised there's not some kind of court-mandated therapy after that."

"Well, he didn't go to court," I say slowly. "He didn't do anything wrong. I'm sure someone told Dad he needed to see someone, but he's not going to talk."

Devlin moves his thumb across the back of my hand in gentle strokes. "I'm sorry. I wasn't trying to upset you. I know it's not easy for you."

"For me? Nothing happened to me. My brother—I can't imagine." I break off, shaking my head and forcing back the ache in my throat.

"I know," Devlin says, winding a strand of hair behind my ear. "But you're my girl, and he's not. So I'm more worried how it's affecting you."

"What about you?" I ask, forcing myself to face this truth at last. We've avoided this topic up until now. I don't want to think about him being the boy who confessed to destroying my brother's life. "Do you have a court date?"

"No," Devlin says, sighing. "They ended up letting me go without a charge. They had no evidence against me."

"Really?" I ask, pushing up on an elbow. "I didn't know that."

"I would have told you, but when I asked to talk to you when I got home, you dumped me."

I wince at the callous way he says that—because it's true. "I'm sorry, Devlin," I whisper. "You know I didn't want to."

He squeezes me against him. "I know, Sugar."

"So, they only had your confession as evidence for the arrest?"

"Yeah," he says. "The fact that I got that text and then took you to the school looking for him convinced them I didn't know where he was."

"When did you find out?" I ask, my heart suddenly thudding in my chest. It's another question I've been scared to ask, but one I know I need the answer to.

"Where he was?" Devlin asks. "I got it when we were here that evening, but I saw the text about the body first. When you were talking to your dad at the construction site, I saw the other text that said he was at the school."

"Why didn't you tell me right then?"

"I didn't want to scare you," he said. "I should never have run down to the site. It was stupid to upset you like that, and I didn't want to upset you again if we didn't find anything up at the school."

"So you tried to keep me out," I said. "You should have known I'd just follow."

"I should have," Devlin says with a small, sad smile. "And I shouldn't have wanted to protect someone else. You come first, Crystal. From now until always."

My heart melts, and a swell of emotion rises in my chest. I'm deliriously happy, and yet my heart breaks for every moment we won't get, every kiss we won't share. These beautiful, stolen moments are all we get.

"Devlin," I whisper, pressing my heart to his, so he can feel it racing just for him. "Don't talk like that."

He smooths my hair back and kisses my forehead. "I was protecting something that doesn't matter. The Swans don't matter. You matter. Only you."

"You know your family won't let us be together any more than mine will."

"You're wrong," Devlin says. "My dad would never want me to repeat his mistake."

"Your family is not just your dad," I point out.

He nods. "My granddad doesn't listen to anyone who doesn't tell him what he wants to hear. But we'll make it, Crystal. We will."

We lay there in silence for a minute, clinging to each other while the hand of time moves silently, inexorably, towards the end of *us*. The future and the past are inching closer and closer, ready to collide, to trap us between two impossible choices and crush us under their slow, agonizing weight.

I try not to think about the fact that his life is planned out the same way his dad's was. What if Grampa Darling forces him to marry Dolly? What will he do to Dolly if she refuses? To Devlin? Could I stand in the way, refusing to let it happen, if I knew one or both of them would be hurt?

"What if they won't let us be together?" I ask, anguish gripping me at the thought.

"Don't worry," Devlin says, cradling me in his arms, his voice brimming with the conviction of a desperate man. "Things will be different for us, Crystal. I promise."

"How?" I ask, my throat thick. "What if this is all we get—clandestine evenings when no one is around? Is that enough for you?"

"It won't be all," he says fiercely. "I promise you, Crystal. We'll find a way to be together. If I have to go against my family, be disowned, and leave my name behind, then that's what I'll do."

I swallow hard, searching his eyes. "You'd do that?"

"For you I would," he whispers, cupping my soft cheek in his rough palm. "Would you?"

# fifteen

*Crystal*

*How can I choose between my family and my lover? Between everyone I've ever known and loved, the brothers who have protected me, cared for me, fought with me, teased me, picked me up when I fell, and a boy who tormented, teased, and callously hurt me? How can I choose between my own twin, a boy who has been by my side since we swam together in the darkness of our mother's womb, and one I just met? And how can it be this hard to choose?*

When I walk into lunch the next Monday, my eyes are drawn to the Darling's table, the way they always are. I immediately spot some drama going on, and nosy bitch that I am, I want to stop and watch, see why three of the Dolls are openly sobbing and clinging to each other. A dart of panic goes through me, and my gaze skips over the group until it lands on Devlin.

*He's okay.*

He smiles, and my heart skips for a new reason. But I tear my eyes away and glance over to my table. Royal is already there, watching me. I hurry over, pretending not to notice Devlin's smile, or that Colt is standing in front of the table where the girls are crying.

"Did you see what's happening at the Darling table?" Dixie asks, nearly bouncing out of her seat in her excitement.

"Calm down there, Dixie," I say. "You're about to pop out a boob."

"Dude, you're such a buzz-kill," Duke says, tearing his gaze from my friend's bouncing chest and aiming a pout at me.

"Sorry, not sorry," I say, rolling my eyes. "You're not supposed to hit on my friends, remember?"

"Hey, I'm not hitting on her," he says. "That doesn't mean I can't look at her tits."

"Um, yeah," I say. "It does. She has a face."

"Yeah, but why would I look at that when her tits are bouncing like they need a dick between them?"

"I don't think that would stop the bouncing," Baron says.

"Only one way to find out," Duke says with a grin.

King and Dolly join us, scooting in at their usual places.

"That deal's off, anyway," Royal snaps at me.

Oh, right. They didn't fuck my friends because I didn't fuck anyone. Now that I'm with Devlin, I guess my friends are fair game. They're already dating Dolly, anyway.

"Anything good happening today?" Dolly asks the table.

I shrug. "Looks like Colt's dumping the cheer squad."

"Oh my god," Dixie squeals. "Do you think he'll ask me out?"

"Are you stupid enough to go?" Royal asks.

"Stop being rude to my friends," I say, glaring at him. "Dixie didn't do shit to you."

Royal glares daggers back at me. "When you stop being the Darlings' cum dumpster, I'll be nice to your friends again."

238

My face flushes, but I can't tell if it's embarrassment that he'd talk to me that way—in front of my friends, no less—or anger.

"Whoa," King says, putting an arm around Royal. I can tell it's not the friendly type of hold. It's his silent way of communicating when other people are around and he can't say, "Get yourself together or I'll pretend to be supportive while really crushing your ribs with my bare hands." I've never been more glad to have him for an older brother.

"No offense, but I think you could really use someone to talk to," Dolly says in her sugary Southern twang. She unsnaps her suitcase-sized pink sequin purse and pulls out a Dr. Pepper. "My whole family went when my dad got remarried. I'd be happy to pass along my doctor's number. He's real sweet."

"I don't need a fucking therapist," Royal says, slamming his fist down on the table.

I jump, and so does Dixie, who shrinks closer to me like I can protect her.

"What do you need?" I ask my brother quietly.

Royal just stares at me, breathing hard, his dark eyes full of such turmoil that I don't think even he can answer that question. He needs a new family. A father who doesn't use him like a pawn, a mother who isn't so busy pretending her life is perfect that she doesn't even notice, and a sister who doesn't run off and fall in love with his mortal enemy. He needs us to understand.

But how can I understand when he won't talk to me? I can't. All I can do is be there for him, support him, and love him. And I haven't been doing any of that. I've been selfishly concerned with my own needs, with my own heart.

"I need you to start acting like my sister again," Royal says at last. "We're not the bad guys here, Crystal."

I stare at him, my fingers shaking. I don't know how to say this without hurting him. "What if we are?"

"Then you're on the wrong side," he says slowly.

"Maybe we shouldn't take sides," I say. "Maybe we should all be on the same team."

"But we're not," he says.

"The Darlings aren't the problem," I say, squeezing my hands around my knees to hold myself steady.

"What are you saying, Crystal?" King asks, his brows lowering and his expression turning ominous.

"I'm saying, maybe it's time to put all this behind us," I say. "The Darlings might listen if you just talk to them. I think they're ready to make peace."

"And how do you know this?" King asks.

I tick the reasons off on my fingers, trying to sound more rational than I feel. I'm terrified of his reaction. Royal is unpredictable and moody, but King is steady. He'll listen to reason. "They're not fighting you anymore," I say. "Devlin refused to fight Royal. And you made the team. You're on. Why keep attacking them? You got what you wanted. Plus, they're not bothering me anymore."

"That asshole still hasn't given us our parking spot," Duke says.

It's all I can do not to slap my palm against my forehead. "Are you really that petty?" I ask instead. "It's a fucking parking spot. Who even cares? Park in the one beside it!"

"It's not the parking spot," King says quietly. "It's what it represents."

"That part's true," Dolly says. "The Darlings have always had that spot. It's tradition. Their great grandfather got that spot when his family paid to have the lot paved."

"And it belongs to the top donor," Baron says. "We're the top donors. They need to accept that and give us our spot back."

"It's not over until they turn over their spot and admit there's a new rule in town," Duke says.

"Or until there are none of them left to admit it," Royal says. "Then everyone will know the Dolce reign has begun."

\*

When I step out of my last class of the day, Dixie is waiting.

"Did you hear what happened?" she asks, her eyes dancing with excitement. It's nice to see her so enthusiastic about something again, like she was when I met her. After Colt betrayed her, she was so glum, but she seems to have bounced back. Even though she's still boy crazy, she's seemed more confident since our dance routine. Being brave looks good on her.

"I heard bits and pieces," I tell her as we head for our lockers.

"They dumped all the Darling Dolls," she says. "Took all their necklaces and everything."

I spot a couple girls from the cheer squad crying at a locker.

"You'd think they lost their boyfriends," I say, a twinge of guilt going through me. "Not some asshole who only drops into their DMs to see if they're down to fuck."

"Being a Darling Doll is better than having a boyfriend," Dixie says, rolling her eyes. "It means you can date anyone you want."

"Except a Darling," I point out. "They don't date, right? They just hook up."

"Well, you got Devlin," she says. "Which means it could happen for someone else."

"Dixie…"

"What?" she asks, a defiant tilt to her head. "You were the Dog, and you got Devlin. I could get Colt."

"I didn't say you couldn't," I say. "It's just… Is he treating you okay?"

"Like Devlin treated you?" she asks. "Listen, I know I won't be the Dog for long. I'm not dumb. Someone more interesting, more challenging will come along. I've got to take what I can get and hope it's enough to make him fall for me like Devlin fell for you."

"Just… Don't let him walk all over you, okay? I don't want to see you get hurt."

We arrive at my locker, and I try to ignore Becca and Kaylee, who are standing nearby, casting ugly glares in our direction.

"She'll get one for sure," Becca says. "I hear she's, like, actually dating Devlin Darling."

"But she was the Dog," Kaylee says, tossing her blonde hair back and making a face at me.

I roll my eyes and turn to my locker.

"No one can go from Dog to Doll," Becca says. "It's impossible."

"They said that didn't count," Carmen says, completing the bitchy trio. "That she wasn't really the Dog."

"But her best friend is still the Dog," Becca says.

"Yeah," Kaylee says. "Why would anyone be friends with that smelly old mutt?"

They giggle in that mean way girls do, and I watch Dixie's face redden.

"Ignore them," I mutter to her. "They're trying to get to us."

"It's just gross," Carmen says. "I can't believe they did that skanky dance in front of all our dads. And some people should seriously know better than to shove themselves into clothes that don't fit."

"I don't get it," Becca says. "What makes her so special?"

"It's just because she's new," Kaylee says. "He'll get bored with her, and then he'll give the necklaces back."

"I don't know," Becca whispers. "Maybe we should try to find out."

I turn, closing my locker and smiling serenely at them. "You want to know how I landed Devlin Darling?"

"No," Kaylee says with a sneer.

Becca glances at her friend, looking annoyed, then turns to me. "Well? How did you?" she asks, lowering her voice to a conspiratorial, excited whisper, like she expects me to tell her some big secret.

"Well, you can start by not being a bunch of catty bitches," I say.

"How do we do that?" Becca asks.

I laugh before I realize she's not joking. "Look, I told you before, if you want to come to the other side, I don't hold grudges," I say. "You can start by apologizing to Dixie, who has more balls than the three of you combined."

"Like we'd risk being your friend," Kaylee says. "You'll probably be the Dog again by tomorrow. I don't want a reputation for picking up strays."

"Yeah," Carmen says. "Like they say. Sleep with the dogs, you wake up with fleas."

"Maybe if you lose her," Becca says, cutting her eyes toward Dixie. "Since you weren't a Dog after all."

"You still don't get it, do you?" I say. "You're so busy jumping when the Darlings tell you to jump that you don't see how silly all this is. The Darlings said I wasn't the Dog, so now you're just going to go along with them, pretending it never happened?"

"Well… Yeah," Becca says.

I shake my head and turn to Dixie. "Let's go."

"Lacey said they're going to pick more Dolls tomorrow," Dixie says as we head for the doors. "They're each going to pick one. Do you think Colt will pick me?"

"I don't know, honestly," I say. "I don't think you should let them label you and tell you what you are. But I know you have a different opinion on that."

"Don't you want Devlin to pick you?" she asks, widening her eyes at me.

"No," I say. "I told him I don't like any of it. He'll give his to Dolly. She's the original Doll, and he cares about her. And I guess whoever Colt and Preston pick will be their girlfriends, basically. I know they don't date, but once they each pick a favorite, that's how everyone's going to see it."

"It could be me," Dixie says.

I sigh, shaking my head. Just because I don't share her obsession with the labeling, that doesn't mean it's not important to her. "Maybe," I concede. "I haven't seen him hanging out with any girl in particular. Maybe they'll just keep them for a while and give them to the girls they ask out when they're ready to date someone. I mean, I don't know why guys would give random girls jewelry, anyway."

"Then I'll never get one," Dixie says glumly. "Colt would never actually date me. I mean, I could maybe be a hookup girl for him, but he'd never be my boyfriend. I wish you hadn't told Devlin to get rid of them."

"Sorry," I say. "I thought it was demeaning. Maybe I should have left it alone."

I remember the girls crying over it, and suddenly, I'm not so sure I did the right thing. It seemed so dehumanizing to me. But these girls liked being labeled. It made them special. And now I took that away from them.

I wish there was an easy answer, but I don't see one. I don't know if I did the right thing, or if I did something cruel. I thought I was on the right side, but now I don't know which side is right. I don't even know which side I'm on.

"Maybe I can still be the Dog," Dixie says.

"You're worth so much more than that," I tell her. "You got up in front of the whole town and shook your ass like a boss."

Dixie sighs. "Which, by the way, I'm still grounded for. I was hoping I could go to the Darlings' New Year's Eve party, but I don't think it'll ever happen now."

"I'm sorry," I say. "It's my fault. But I'm not sorry you did it. You were a rock star."

"I'm not sorry, either," she admits with a sly grin.

"And hey, if it makes you feel any better, I don't think your parents would stop you from going if the Darlings invite you."

"You really think so?"

She's so earnest it hurts me to look at her. I told Devlin I didn't like them having Dolls and Dogs, and he said he'd get rid of them. He's already disbanded the Dolls. As I look at Dixie, though, I wonder if she's right. Is this her only chance to be close to Colt, her only chance to win him over? I don't know if I'm ruining her dream or saving her dignity. And really, is it my place to decide? I thought I was making the school better, but now I'm not so sure. Maybe I should have kept out of it, the same as my brothers should have. Are all my good intentions paving stones on the way to hell?

# sixteen

*Crystal*

*There's a reason I don't want to be a Darling Doll. Not only is it too close to the Dog, but I'm done with people labeling me. I want to choose my own label. I don't want to be a pawn in someone else's game or a toy someone plays with. I'm no one's fangirl. I'm Devlin's equal. He's changing the rules for me, and the whole school has taken notice. I don't need a necklace to prove my worth. I already wear a fucking crown.*

"Royal's got a meeting with the coaches at lunch today," King says to me on Thursday as we head to my locker before school. "I thought I'd go with him."

"But the season's over," I say, hoping they'll split off so I won't have to get my coffee in front of Royal. I swear,

Devlin's needling him on purpose. I asked him to stop with the drinks in my locker, but he said no one was going to tell him he couldn't take care of his girl.

"Season's over, but Royal needs to play next year," King says.

In Devlin's spot. It won't matter then, though. Devlin's graduating. He doesn't have to fight Royal to keep his place. They could all play together if they'd just get over their stubborn pride.

"We've got detention, but we can skip to look out for you," Baron says.

"It's fine," I say. "No one is giving me shit anymore. You know that."

"Yeah," King says slowly.

Duke throws an arm around my shoulders. "Baby sis is the only one of us who's made it to the top. No one messes with you."

"And I don't think she even tried," Baron says, studying me with a look I've never seen before, both impressed and wary. The look of someone who underestimated me. Even my family does that—maybe especially them. It's one thing for the Darlings to do it without knowing me. It's hurts a little that the Dolces still think I'm some fragile, helpless little girl, even when I've proven otherwise.

"You don't think I went through shit to get here?" I ask, lifting my chin and staring back at Baron. "If I'm on top, it's because I fucking earned it. Believe me, I paid my dues."

"She's right," King says. "She did what it took to earn their respect. Not just the Darlings, either."

I'm not sure it's respect that the other girls at Willow Heights are giving me. As we arrive at my locker, I notice other girls watching, their jealousy so apparent its almost palpable. Everyone knows who gets me coffee every morning. Everyone knows that Devlin doesn't do things like that—or he didn't before me. I may not have a ballerina necklace, but I'm the only girl the Darlings are showing favor right now.

"And maybe I'm right about not fighting them," I say, turning the combination on my locker.

"If you can't beat 'em, join 'em," Royal says, but it sounds more like a challenge than a suggestion.

"I didn't join them," I say, relieved to pull open my locker and hide behind the door. "I just accepted the way things are."

That's not exactly true. I'm changing things from the inside. But no one else knows I'm still seeing Devlin, so I can't tell them that. Royal caught me coming in that night, and he obviously doesn't believe it when I deny my relationship with his enemy, but at least he hasn't told the others.

When I open my locker, the coffee is there like always. I can't hide it. I don't know what else to do, so I get out my books and the cup like it's perfectly ordinary, like I don't notice Royal's hands fisting at his sides. I'll have to talk to Devlin again.

"You'll be okay with just the girls at lunch?" King asks.

"Fine," I say, closing my locker and smiling up at my brother.

"Try not to fall on any dicks on the way," Royal grumbles.

"Try not to run into the counselor on the way," I shoot back. "She might actually, you know. Help you."

"If you want to help me, give me back my sister."

"I'm right here," I say, exasperated by this bickering that never ends.

Royal works his jaw back and forth. "Yeah," he says at last. "You are." Then he turns and walks off.

I'm not the only one who's changed the minds of the other students at Willow Heights. Since the day he went ballistic on Devlin in the hall and screamed at me about the coffee, everyone treats him like a ticking time bomb. They move out of his way as he passes, shying away from him and casting wary glances his way.

I sigh and turn to King with a tight smile. "I'll be fine at lunch. He obviously needs you with him. I'll see you after school."

He leans down to plant a quick kiss on top of my head. "Have a good day, Crys."

Guilt flares inside me as I make my way into class. I feel for my oldest brother, stuck in the middle of all this. As the buffer between Royal and me, he bears the brunt of Royal's anger. All he wants is to protect us both, but he can't. He'd let me date a Darling if it meant I was safe at this school, but that would bring Royal's wrath down on me tenfold. I'm the one in the wrong, the one hurting my brother so I can selfishly hold onto something of my own, something that's already doomed.

I'm the problem. I need to just stop before it goes any further, before it all blows up in my face. Before my family decides to kill Devlin.

Because that's what Royal would want, and as I remember their callous laughter about taking the life of some innocent worker at the construction site just to frame Preston's dad, I have no doubt that they'd do it. Devlin's not just working for the wrong person. He's fucking the Dolce Daughter, the girl they still see as sweet and innocent.

I take my seat next to Devlin, and my heart rips slowly down the middle at the knowledge of what I have to do. I don't even know where to begin. Do I do it quick and callous, like I did when he came home from jail? Or do I slowly pull away, making myself unavailable until we've grown apart? Which one will hurt him less?

"Stop putting coffee in my locker, Devlin," I say. "I mean it. Royal can't handle it."

"Okay," Devlin says, his hand finding my thigh under the table.

I want to melt into it, to whimper with pleasure as his warm palm skims over my skirt, grazing along the thick fabric with a jealous familiarity. My skirt rises just an inch, but I can feel the air on the newly bared skin above my knee like a whisper from his hot lips. The dance, the *tease*, makes me yearn for more until it settles into a heavy ache between my thighs. I want his fingers on my skin, under my skirt. I want his rough, possessive touch, his commanding hands that demand my surrender.

How can I tear myself from this boy, the one whose touch brings me to life and makes me blaze like a wildfire? How can I choose to douse that fire instead of letting it run free?

I have to, though. I have to because the fire he's started is burning up my twin, continuing his torture. I've always put my family first, before my own needs. Why should this be any different? What made me think that this time, just once, I could have something for myself?

*

The cafeteria is buzzing with excitement as we settle in at our table at lunch. It feels empty with just the three of us, but kinda nice, too. I like hanging out with just the girls, not having to censor what I say.

"Anything we need to know about?" I ask, nodding to the rest of the room. My back is to them, and though I know Devlin wouldn't hurt me, I don't know if I'll ever stop feeling jumpy when the other Darlings are in a room with me.

"They're making an announcement," Dixie says, leaning across the table toward me, her eyes rounded and brimming with so much excitement I'm surprised they haven't popped out of her head.

"Okay, calm down there," I say. "You're scaring me a little."

"This could be *it*," she whisper-shrieks, grabbing my hand with bruising force. "Colt could be announcing his Doll."

Before I can answer that, a gasp goes up. I turn to watch the Darlings stride in, all three of them walking side by side like some kind of wet-dream team. Dixie sighs, melting back in her chair. I can't blame her. The three of them together like that are almost too much to bear.

Dixie slips around the table to sit with me and Dolly, our backs to our table as we face the rest of the room from our spot in the corner. The whole cafeteria falls silent, as if every girl is stunned speechless by the sight of them, all broad shoulders, taut abs, trim hips, and long legs. Colt grins and tosses his floppy blond bangs off his forehead. Preston smirks. "Well, look at that," he says. "They got themselves all prepped and ready for us. Just the way I like it."

"We've trained them well," Devlin drawls, strolling over and gliding his fingertips along the edge of their usual table. I swear every girl in the cafeteria must be watching those fingers, imagining them on her skin. But only I know how it truly feels.

Well, me and Dolly. My stomach twists, all my smugness that he's mine alone suddenly vanishing. Devlin turns, his eyes sweeping across the room and meeting mine.

A shock goes through me, my pulse racing and my thighs threatening to clench. God, one look and I'm putty for this boy. How am I supposed to exist without him in my life?

"You've probably heard that we took back the necklaces," Preston says. "Today, we'll give them back—but only three. We'll each choose a girl worthy of being a Darling Doll. We might have gotten a little lax with it before, but this time, we're choosing only the best. Girls worthy of the name."

"Oh my god, oh my god, oh my god," Dixie whispers under her breath.

"Calm down," Dolly says, squeezing her arm. "You're still the Dog. You can't be a Doll."

Colt picks up where Preston left off. "I'm sure y'all are burning up with questions, so I'll try to answer them ahead of time. Like before, how long you're a Doll depends on how long we say you are. If we get done playing with you, or you don't play nice, we'll take back the necklace. So you better have it with you at all times."

A little murmur goes up as girls speculate on whether they'll be next. I see Becca getting fanned by her friends like she's about to faint. Kaylee looks smug as she smiles up at the boys, sure she'll get her necklace back. Colt winks at her, egging her on.

I start to roll my eyes at the spectacle. The Darlings love their audiences. But then I realize it's all part of their control, part of their carefully constructed kingdom. The seniors listen, so the freshmen follow suit. They don't have to quiet the room like the headmaster before an assembly. Everyone wants to hear what they have to say. It's never boring, and at any moment, they might announce a winner, and that person's life will change.

"One more thing," Devlin says, his silky voice rippling over the crowd and soothing them into silence before his gaze settles on me. "The Darling Dog is retiring. There will be no new one chosen."

They let that sink in for about ten seconds, just enough time for everyone to comment to their friend, and their friend to make a quick reply. Devlin's eyes never leave mine.

I feel a tiny grin creep across my face, and the smallest smile tugs at the corner of his lips. He slides his hands into his pockets, looking so self-satisfied I can't decide if I want to smack him or eat him. He's such a colossal dick, but the fact that he knows it, that he enjoys wielding so much power, makes him strangely irresistible. He used his power, and he did it for me. And he's damn sure going to make me show my appreciation later.

Damnit, now my thighs really are clenching.

*Fucking Devlin.*

"Do you think he's really going to ask me?" Dixie squeals, pulling me from the trance Devlin's got me in. "Maybe that's why they got rid of the Dog. So they can make me a Doll."

"They're coming this way," Dolly says, nudging me with her jeweled pink heel.

"I'm going to faint," Dixie whispers, clutching the edges of her chair.

"Maybe they're just getting back the collar," I say, not wanting my friend to be disappointed. Hell, I don't want to be disappointed. I know Devlin cares about Dolly, and since the Dolls are named for her and I told him I didn't care about this stuff, I shouldn't even want a necklace. But they made it so exciting that even I got caught up for a minute.

My heartbeat picks up with every step they take until it's racing by the time they stop in front of us. For a second, I think—*maybe*. Maybe I could have Devlin, and Dixie could have Colt, and Dolly could have Preston. Maybe we'd be at the top, like Dixie wants, like the Darlings already are. Could it be this perfect, the three kings with their three queens, all of us best friends? Isn't this every girl's dream? How can I say no to that if they offer?

"I'm sure you came for this," Dolly says, reaching inside her shirt. She pulls out a tiny, diamond ballerina charm. And even though I know what I do, and I said what I did, it still stings that he let her keep it when he took it from all the other girls.

"Dolly," Devlin murmurs, a frown pulling between his brows. "You don't have to give that back."

"I know," she says. "But I've been holding onto it for too long. Holding onto something that hasn't belonged to me in years—maybe it never did. Something I thought I needed. But I don't need it anymore."

Everyone in the cafeteria is dead silent, leaning in, trying to hear, but Devlin and Dolly keep their voices low. She buckles the necklace and holds it up. It hangs suspended in the air between them, but he doesn't reach for it.

"You love ballerinas," he says.

"And you," she says in her sweet, southern drawl, "Don't love me." It's not a question, not bitter or sad, just a fact.

He looks like he's going to speak, but she holds up a hand to stop him, her pointy iridescent nails glimmering in the overhead lights. "I thought you were *end game,* Devlin Darling. But you weren't. Not for me. You were more like… A preseason exhibition game. I got my whole season in front of me, my whole life. I got my own playoffs to win, my own championship ring waiting. And this isn't it."

Devlin swallows before reaching out, a fond half-smile forming on his lips as his hand closes around the thread of white gold. "Go get that ring, Doll."

I see something in that moment, something I know I'm not supposed to see. I see Preston. I'm sure I'm the only one who sees it, but it's there for just a flash. Maybe it's because he's standing in front of me while Devlin stands in front of the girl he wants. Maybe it's because my own shoulders want to slump with relief as much as his when Devlin takes the charm from Dolly, removing his claim from her. Maybe it's because I'm looking for it, because he fascinates me, because I see him in a way no one else does.

He's a boy hurting for what he can never have because her family and his family say they don't belong together. That's something I understand all too well.

Preston's eyes meet mine, and whatever was there slips behind his mask of indifference. He holds my gaze, and suddenly, I can barely breathe. Something passes between us, and I know that he can see it in my eyes. He knows that I saw what he tries so hard to hide.

But it's Colt who speaks next. He turns to the crowd, not keeping this between him and his choice like Devlin, where only a few people overheard.

"There's only one girl at this school who deserves to wear my necklace," he says, holding up a hand. The chain threads through his fingers, the little charm dangling below his fist. "She's the last person I would have expected to be making a Doll, but here I am."

Beside me, Dixie lets out a tiny squeak. She's panting so hard it's a wonder she hasn't passed out from hyperventilation. At the next table over, one full of girls who spend their energy on academics rather than trying to climb the social ladder, I spot Mabel Darling. She's the only girl in the room not hanging onto Colt's every word just about as hard as Dixie is. While even the girls around her watch Colt with stars in their eyes, Mabel continues eating like nothing is happening.

Colt goes on after a pause to let all the girls wonder if he could be talking about them. "This girl took me by surprise," he says. "At first, you might think she's soft, but she's stronger than you know."

Dixie turns red all the way to her ears. I squeeze her hand, and for the briefest moment, my eyes meet Mabel's. She glances up now and then, so it's clear she's not deliberately avoiding the spectacle, but her expression is one of complete disinterest, as if her cousins aren't there at all. Now that's a girl who deserves some kind of honor—not that she'd want it. She refuses to play the game, even though her grandfather is the gamemaster. How does she do it?

I pull my attention back to my friend, who's about to realize her dream.

"This girl stole our hearts without even trying," Colt says. "By being badass but classy as fuck—and by shaking her ass like Nicki fucking Minaj."

He turns around and steps over my lap, sinking down onto my legs so he's straddling me like he's about to give me a fucking lap dance.

"What are you doing?" I grit out through clenched teeth.

"I saw you first," he says, reaching back and buckling the necklace around my neck.

"You know I'm Devlin's," I hiss.

"If things don't work out between y'all," he says with a wink before rising stepping back.

The whole cafeteria is silent. Every person in the room sits frozen, not even breathing.

All except Mabel, who sets down her sandwich and takes a drink of her Evian water like nothing is happening. Beside me, Dixie has gone still, her face pale as she gapes at

Colt. I want to say something to her, but she won't even look at me.

Instead, I have to look at Devlin, my heart thudding with unease. His back is to the room, but I can see his face. His eyes are blazing with fury, his jaw so tight I can see the muscle jerking as he grinds his teeth. But he's not going to confront Colt—not here. Not now, with the whole school watching. Because the school isn't just a bunch of puppets for the Darlings. They keep them in check somehow, too. They have the Darlings on a pedestal, and the Darlings know exactly how precarious that position is. They don't overstep their boundaries, and they never show weakness.

Fighting with Colt here would show weakness. The Darlings won't show a crack in their united front—I know that. Devlin would fuck me in front of the whole team to keep anyone from knowing they're human, that they fight and bicker like brothers. They have to be perfect to the other students, to keep their precarious balance atop the throne. Colt made a move, and now Devlin has to follow. He has to look like he knew that was coming, like it was all part of the plan.

I have to admire how perfectly he plays the part. Without even glancing at Colt, without looking for a girl he can claim now that Colt had collared me for himself, Devlin steps between us, crouching in front of me. He doesn't make a spectacle for everyone else. He keeps his voice quiet, so I know this isn't a show—it's real.

"This is the only necklace I ever gave a girl," he says, his blue eyes holding mine, his gaze strong and sure as the anger melts when our eyes meet. "If you don't want it because it belonged to someone else, I understand that. But I'll never give jewelry to any girl but you. I know you didn't want to wear one of these, but you're already wearing one, and this belongs to you whether or not I put it on you. The only question is, do you want me to?"

I nod, my heart in my throat. If he claimed me in the locker room that day, I ruined it. I told him I didn't want him, and he told everyone I wasn't his after all. I'm not making that mistake again. I want him to know that I'd never even think of another guy, despite what Colt just did. I am his, one hundred percent, and I don't care who knows it. I want them all to know. He is mine.

Devlin leans in, so close I can feel his warm breath against my skin as he slides his hands behind my neck. This time, they're gentle against my throat instead of the demanding chokehold he shows me when he's inside me, but they're every bit as possessive. He buckles the necklace before sitting back on his heel, adjusting it so it lies the way he wants on my chest.

"This is only the beginning," he promises, his fingers brushing across my collarbones. "I'm going to drape you in these before we're through. Because they got your name wrong, Sugar. You're not crystal—you're a fucking diamond."

From the corner of my eye, I see the brainy girls at the next table covering their hearts and swooning over his words. They're not jealous anymore—not now. Devlin has chosen, and jealousy implies they think they deserve it more, that they can get it. They don't. They only want to be in my place, having the most incredible boy in the world saying these words to them. By the end of the day, they'll have their own fifteen minutes in the spotlight when every other girl in school comes to them to ask what Devlin said.

And me? I can't think of a single thing to say back to him. I press my hand over the charm, my heart swelling. I may not have wanted to play into their game, but like he told me before, we're all players whether we want to be or not. I'm not off the gameboard yet. I may not have known I needed it, that my game piece was in jeopardy, but he did. He knew what I needed at this school, how to get the girls off my back, how to make me queen. It's not the necklace that I needed, but what it represents. It's not what it means to me that matters, but what it means to everyone else at Willow Heights.

Instead of words, I wrap my arms around Devlin's neck and kiss him. He presses his lips tenderly to mine, a chaste kiss, but he makes it last a little longer, long enough for any questions in the room to be answered. I belong to him and him alone. After a few seconds, he pulls away and steps back.

Preston watches Devlin, watches me, the same way I do him. He looks back and forth between his cousins, then at Dolly, then back to me.

*Give it to her*, I will him silently. *Tell her how you feel.*

Preston steps forward, one of his legs on either side of my knees, so I'm face to face with his crotch. He runs a hand over the top of my head and down the back until he's cradling the back of my neck, nudging me forward, even closer to the subtle bulge I can see in his slacks.

"My eyes are up here," he says, a taunt in his voice.

I jerk my gaze to his, my cheeks flaming. "Is this some kind of joke?" I ask.

One look at Devlin tells me otherwise. He looks like he's about to blow a fuse. His face is red, and his fists are trembling at his side. But he doesn't move while Preston releases his hold on my head, and without a word of explanation, reaches behind me and buckles his necklace.

# seventeen

*Crystal*

For a second, no one moves. The cafeteria is so quiet I can hear Mabel chewing. Then Devlin turns and storms out, and the whole room erupts in frantic whispers and excited chatter. The Darlings know how to make drama, that's for damn sure.

A strangled noise comes from Dixie, and she jumps up and scurries for the door.

"You guys are assholes," I say to Preston and Colt. I stand, ready to go after her, but Preston hasn't moved from where he stood to put the necklace on me, so I'm flush against him when I stand. I put my hands on his chest to push him back, but he reaches out a finger and tips my chin up.

"Devlin told me what you said about me," he says. "Just so you know, I'd never rape you. I'd make you want it so bad it hurt, and then I'd give it to you until you begged for mercy. And then, Manhattan, I'd make you cum so hard it was agony."

Before I can think better of it, I reach up and slap his face. Preston's eyes flash with that terrifying, psychotic blaze of rage I've seen before. Before he can lift a hand to retaliate, Colt throws an arm around his neck, hooting with laughter as the buzz in the room becomes a roar of excitement.

I'm so grateful for Colt that I could cry, but I don't have time for that.

"Only Devlin gets to talk to me like that," I say to Preston, then shove past them and take off after Dixie or Devlin. I don't know which one I need to talk to first. When I asked for them to get rid of the Darling Dolls, I didn't mean I wanted all the necklaces for myself.

I spot Dixie at the end of the hall when I step out of the cafeteria. I call after her, but she ducks around the corner into another hallway. "Dixie," I call again, jogging after her. My heart aches for her. I have to tell her I had no idea, that I don't want Colt. I have to give her his necklace.

Suddenly, a hard hand wraps around my upper arm, spinning me around and slamming my back against the lockers. "What the fuck was that about?" Devlin demands, his icy eyes burning into me like frostbite.

"I don't know," I say, trying to yank free of his grasp. "They're your cousins. How should I know what sick games your family thinks up?"

"That wasn't my family's doing," he snaps.

"Then take it up with your cousins," I say, trying to push past him. "I need to talk to Dixie."

Devlin grabs my wrist, pinning it to the locker above my head. "You said you weren't fucking Preston. You said he didn't even touch you. And I'm such a fucking fool that I believed you, Crystal. I should have seen through that in a second. What guy could resist getting his dick wet when he saw your body all tied up, every inch of you bare and ready for him?"

"He didn't."

We stare at each other, and I can feel him trying to make me submit with his will alone, trying to make me cave and tell him what he wants to hear. But I won't be the girl to betray him like that. I won't lie to him, and I won't put a wedge between him and Preston.

"I know my cousins," he says slowly, stepping forward until his body pins me against the lockers. "I know they don't give those necklaces to girls they're not fucking."

"You think I'm fucking your cousins behind your back?"

"What else am I supposed to think?" he growls. "Is this all just another part of your game? Some sick plot you cooked up with them while I was in jail?"

"Devlin, no," I say. "There's no game. I didn't know they were going to give me those necklaces any more than you did. If I'd known, don't you think I would have stopped them? At least Colt. You know Dixie's obsessed with him."

Devlin glares at me, his nostrils flared as his gaze burns into mine. "Prove it."

"I will," I say. "Just… Give me a few minutes to talk to Dixie. She's really upset."

He presses forward, grinding the ridge of his cock into me. "Does it feel like I'm going to wait?"

"But—"

"If you don't want me to pull up your skirt and fuck you right here against the lockers, then we'd better take this somewhere private in the next sixty seconds."

"Devlin," I say, my fingers curling around those thick, muscular biceps. I fight to keep my head, not to turn into a quivering puddle of jelly at his touch, not to let lust control me even as he rocks against me and my core melts.

"I put you first above everything, even my family," he says. "Are you telling me I'm less important to you than your silly little friend?"

I realize then that he's right. He's fighting his cousins for me. That's got *him* really upset. He might not show it the way Dixie does, but he's hurt and confused and jealous, maybe even insecure. His whole family turned on him when he confessed to something he didn't even do, to protect *them*. He's patched things up with his cousins, but maybe some doubt, some suspicion and hurt, still lingers. And I've betrayed him in the worst way, luring him in and making him care about me just so I could rip his heart out. I can't blame him for being slow to trust.

I told him nothing happened with Preston, but he'll never have anything but my word to go on. I need to give him this—and I want to. I want him to know with absolute certainty that I'm his girl, just as he told the whole school. That I'm his and only his, and I'll never be anyone else's, no matter what happens. I'm not his mother, who will be cowed into marrying someone I don't love. If I can't have him, I'll have no one.

"Devlin," I say, cradling his face between my hands. "You're the most important person in the world to me."

"Good," he purrs, rocking his hips against mine. "Either I come first, or I don't. But you better tell me which one it is right now because I don't take anyone's sloppy seconds."

"It's you," I whisper. "It's all you, Devlin. I'm all yours. Every part of me."

"Then I'm going to cum inside that tight little cunt you promised was just mine," he says, his hand snaking behind my thigh and pulling me harder against him. "And I'm going to make sure you remember that. Then you can talk to your friend."

I nod, my pulse fluttering in my throat when I see the pure, raw lust in his eyes. I'm not sure we're going to make it sixty seconds before we fuck.

"Take me to your car," I say, wetting my lips with anticipation. My heart is racing with the dizzying combination of excitement and trepidation as his gaze locks on my mouth. Without another word, he grabs my hand and drags me toward the door at the end of the hall. I scramble to keep up and not lose my footing as he barrels through the door and across the parking lot. He barely gets the door open before grabbing me and shoving me roughly inside, plowing in on top of me.

"You better be glad it was me who ended up in that room with you that night," he says, reaching behind him to pull the door closed before pushing on top of me again. "Tell me you never wished it was my cousin who popped that sweet little cherry and made you bleed."

He presses his mouth to mine, but I turn my face away, bracing my hands on his chest. "What does that mean?" I demand.

"We both know Colt wishes he'd ended up in the room with you instead of the Dog," Devlin says. "Does that make you hot, Crystal? Knowing my cousin wants to fuck you as bad as I do?"

"What?" I ask, shoving at him even as he leans down to run his lips along my jawline. "That's not true."

"Yeah," he whispers against my ear while his hand hooks under my thigh, drawing it up to his hip. "It is true, sugar. If Colt had taken you to his room first, he and Preston would be taking turns with you every night, both of them wrecking your sweet cunt instead of just me. Or maybe they already have. Is that what you were doing while I was gone that week?"

"I told you I didn't fuck either of your cousins," I growl, fighting my body's response as he rolls his hips against mine, letting me feel the heart-stopping thickness of what he's about to force inside me. "I don't want to fuck anyone but you, Devlin. So shut up and fucking do it."

"Or maybe you like them both at once," he purrs in my ear, grabbing my ass with both hands and squeezing as he grinds against me until I think I'll burst. "Is that how you like it, you little slut? One in the front and one buried in this tight ass you like to tease us with so much?"

"Get off me," I snap, shoving at him.

Devlin's grin turns feral. "That turns you on, doesn't it? Are you picturing my cousins while I cum inside you, Sugar?"

"You're really pissing me off," I growl through clenched teeth.

"As long as you're not picturing them when you cum," he says, jerking his belt open. "Because I'm about to make you cum so hard you can't walk straight. Are you wet?"

"No, I'm not fucking wet," I say, bucking to get him off. He doesn't give an inch.

"Liar," he says, sliding his hand between my thighs. He smirks at me while he palms my mound, his fingers stroking the wet fabric of my underwear. "Fighting turns you on, doesn't it, you little slut?"

"Don't call me that."

"Slut."

My palm stings across his cheek, and his eyes flash with that terrifying, addictive power. The next second, his mouth is crashing into mine, his shoulders pinning me to the seat while he pulls himself free of his pants and pulls my underwear aside. And then he's inside me, and I cry out, both relief and pain at his sudden entrance crashing over me at once.

"Yeah, Sugar," he says pushing up on his fists and looking down at me, not thrusting again but staying still to feel my walls clench and spasm around the intrusion of his thickness inside me. "Make those sounds for me. I know you like it rough."

"You bastard," I pant out, my body rippling with pleasure as I adjust to his size inside me. "I wasn't ready."

"You feel pretty fucking ready to me," he says with a smirk. "All that talk about my cousins really got you going, didn't it? You're so wet it feels like you came just talking about it."

"Shut up and fuck me," I say, grinding against him, hungry for the friction of movement, wanting him to pound into me until I'm bruised and battered and wholly spent.

Devlin begins to move, agonizingly slow, teasing me with only a taste of what I want. "You know, you could have had Colt," he says. "Grampa Darling didn't give a fuck who wrecked you, as long as one of us destroyed the sweet little Dolce princess."

My heart does a funny little drop in my chest. "What?" I breathe.

"It could just as well have been Colt," Devlin says. "It wouldn't matter to our grandfather. Would it matter to you, Crystal?"

Suddenly, I'm furious, and I shove Devlin hard, but he doesn't budge. "You were just following your grampa's orders?" I demand, the words lashing my tongue as I speak. Maybe I should be relieved knowing that like he said from the beginning, it really wasn't personal. But all I can think is that all along, I was just a job to him—a job that some creepy old man told him to do. He didn't pick me to go to his room that night. I picked him. I'd gone to homecoming with Colt. It should have been Colt. But I wanted Devlin, and so, I'd let myself believe I could have him.

And damn if I didn't get more than I was asking for. He's still fucking me, his cock bare as it sinks into me, his eyes taunting me, daring me to stop him. I want to stop him, to make him walk away aching for this, wanting satisfaction but not able to get it. But as he sinks into me to the hilt, that gloating grin still on his lips, I don't know if I can stop myself, let alone him. He's being an asshole, the kind of asshole that drives me over the edge.

"Get off me," I growl at Devlin, bucking under him. He uses the position to go deeper, grunting as he flexes his muscles, giving me the quick, hard thrust he's been holding back.

"Yeah, fight me, baby," he taunts, his voice like honey as he smiles down at me. "You're sexy when you're mad. It makes seeing you lose control that much hotter."

I pull back to slap him, but he grabs my hands, pinning them to the seat beside my head and fucking me harder, deeper, until I can't breathe. All I can do is squirm and writhe under him as he holds me pinned, his cock pulsing deep in my center until I break apart around him, the orgasm coming quick and sudden, rippling through my limbs and leaving me dizzy and panting.

I don't know how I can still come for this boy, not when he's hurt me like he has. Not when it was all a setup from the start. I seethe under him even as I lie there catching my breath, feeling him fill me and complete me in a way no one else can.

Or maybe it's not that no one else can. It's just that he happens to be here, just like he happened to be there the night he took my virginity.

"Damn, that's hot," Devlin murmurs into my neck, his cock still full and straining inside me. "I love it when you cum on my cock. When I feel your cunt throbbing like that, it sends me over the edge."

He pulls out and finishes on my stomach, his hot cum burning into my skin like a brand, claiming me as his own. He sinks onto me and cradles me in his arms, laying his head on my chest like he always does, like nothing happened.

I don't say anything. I'm too angry and hurt, and I'm afraid I'll cry if he looks at me.

"Guess I know how to make you feisty now," he says, his breath still coming fast.

"Your grandfather set this all up?" I ask at last, when I can't bear him holding me like a treasure when I know the truth now. That it's all a lie.

"You knew that," he says, not bothering to lift his head.

"No, I fucking didn't," I snap. "I didn't know, you asshole. I didn't know this was a fucking lie."

"This isn't a lie," he says, drawing back to look down at me. "You knew it wasn't real at first. I told you that morning. That doesn't have anything to do with *this,* Crystal."

"I didn't know you didn't even want to fuck me," I shoot back. "At least you could have wanted that."

"I do," he says, giving me a funny look. "I just dragged you out of school because I couldn't wait two minutes to fuck you. That's how crazy you make me, Sugar."

"Get off me," I say, shoving him again.

This time, he obeys, sitting up and tucking himself into his pants. "Why are you doing this?" he asks. "You knew from the start that I only took your virginity to break you—and your family. That doesn't mean I didn't want it."

"I thought it was *your* plan," I say. "I didn't know someone else told you to do that. I didn't know you didn't even want to get in my pants, that you only did it because someone was forcing you to."

He doesn't say anything, and I know it's true. He already told me that he doesn't sleep around, so why would I think he'd fuck me when I was barely more than a stranger? It's not because I was special to him, not because he knew even when he wouldn't admit it to himself, or even because he was so attracted to me that he got carried away. No, it's because someone made him do it.

I turn to the door, but Devlin grabs my hand. "Crystal, what's this about?" he asks. "What does it matter if it was my plan or someone else's? No, I didn't plan to fuck you that day. I was pissed at myself when I woke up and couldn't remember if I'd done something stupid while I was drunk. I don't fuck around. You know that. But I wanted you so bad I couldn't help myself."

"Great. So I only got you because you happened to wake up horny, and I happened to be there."

"No, Crystal," he says, taking my hand. "You got me because when I woke up in that room with you, it was fate. I've been yours from the moment I made you cum for the first time. I never knew I could make a girl feel that good. But I knew I never wanted to stop."

"Well, I'm glad I make you feel so fucking special," I snap.

"You knew the truth," he insists. "I'm sorry I did that to you, God, I'm so fucking sorry. You have no idea how much I wish I could go back and do it over, make it different for you. Make it special."

"Well, you can't," I say. "And now I have to know that not only did it mean nothing to you, but you didn't even want to do it in the first place. You were just going along with some creepy old man who apparently thought fucking me would ruin my family. So maybe before you obey him next time, you should think about what kind of sixty-year-old man goes around picking high school girls he wants his grandkids to fuck."

"I have," Devlin says, his voice harder now. "You know we broke with him when we got arrested."

"He broke with you," I correct. "And did you tell them it was him all along, that he's the one who fucked up my brother so bad I don't think he'll ever be the same? Did you rat him out, Devlin? Or did you try to take the fall for him, too?"

"I told them what I knew," he says quietly. "About my family and about yours."

"Don't bring my family into this," I growl. "That had nothing to do with them."

"Then tell me this," he says. "Why would my grandfather put Royal in his own house first, where anyone knows to search if they suspect him, when he could have put him in that basement all along? Why would he take him out of there and put him in my father's attic? How could one sixty-year-old man get a guy Royal's size up a ladder?"

I glare at him, my heart hammering in my chest. I don't want to hear this. I can't. I can't think about what he's saying, can't let him convince me they make sense. "Why don't you tell me?" I grit out at last.

"You can't hide from the truth about your family forever, Crystal," he says, taking my hand and lacing his fingers through mine.

"Yes, I can," I whisper, my throat tight. "I've been doing it all my life."

"So I'm supposed to tell you all my fucked up family drama, supposed to cut ties with them and paint them as the bad guys in all this, and you're just going to go on pretending your family is perfect. And I'm supposed to go along with that?"

"Yes," I say again.

"Okay," he says after a long pause. "If that's what it takes to be with you, I'll do it."

"No," I say, a tear forming on my lashes. "That's not fair. And this isn't fair, either, Devlin. We can't keep doing this. You knew it had to end, so we might as well do it now. It was all based on a lie, anyway."

"I'm not letting you go again," he says. "Whatever I have to do to convince you this is real, whatever I have to believe, I'll do it. I love you, Crystal. I'm not walking away from this."

"You don't have to," I say, taking a deep breath, sucking up the tears and the feeling that my insides are being turned inside out. I reach for the door, but Devlin grabs my other hand.

We stare at each other, both our hands linked. Devlin swallows, his ocean eyes searching mine. I know what's below the frozen surface now. I know the boy with all the confusion and conflicting feelings and loyalties, the hurt from a messy past and the name that promises him an exalted future in this town. And I know that if I stay with him, he's going to lose that. That's the only thing that gives me the strength to speak.

"You have to let me go," I whisper.

"If you can honestly tell me that you'll find someone who can love you like I do, I'll go."

I can't tell him that. But I don't need someone to love me like he does. Our love is poison. There's a reason everyone wants to keep us apart. They're right to. We're destroying each other, and if I'm the only one strong enough to walk away, then that's what I'll do. That's what Dolces are best at. Running when things get too hard.

I pull my hands from Devlin's, open the door, and step out of the car. He says my name, but I close the door before he can say more. I'm not strong this time. My legs are shaking, my breath coming in hiccupping gasps as I take a step, every fiber of my being telling me to stop, to turn around, to dive back into the safety of his arms where the pain doesn't grip my veins as if my blood has died without his oxygen to fuel it.

I take another step, and another. Each step doesn't hurt less, but by the time I reach the walkway, I've grown accustomed to the pain. That's when I feel eyes on me. I pause, glancing around. At first, I don't see anything. Then the door to Baron's Tesla swings open, and Royal steps out.

# eighteen

*Crystal*

"Get in the car."

Royal's voice is hard and flat, so cold I might be scared if I had anything left to feel right now. I don't have the energy to fight with him, so I walk over to the Tesla, parked in the front row where Devlin used to park. Royal's lip is swollen and bleeding a little, and when I get to the car, I see King in the driver's seat. He looks a little banged up, too. I climb in without a word of protest. Royal climbs back in the passenger seat, and we take off.

"What happened?" I ask when we're on the road. "Did you get into another fight?"

"Don't worry about it," King says.

"Where are we going?"

"Did you think you were the only one who could skip school?" Royal asks.

"We got worried," King says. "We heard what happened at lunch. So we came to find you."

"Did you…" I swallow hard, shame washing over me. "When did you…?"

"If you don't want people seeing Devlin fucking you, don't do it in front of the whole world," Royal snaps.

"You were watching me have sex?" I ask, anger and humiliation raging inside me. "What the fuck is wrong with you?"

"Nobody wants to see his enemy nailing his sister," King says. "Or… anyone nailing his sister. Trust me on that."

"Where are you taking me?" I ask.

"We're going to go talk to Dad, see what he wants to do about this."

"I ended it," I say. "I just told Devlin we couldn't see each other anymore."

"Was that before or after his dick was inside you?" Royal asks, twisting around to glare at me in the back seat.

I cross my arms over my chest and raise my chin, staring him down. "After."

He gives an incredulous snort, his eyes raking over me with disdain. "Is that cum on your shirt?"

"Listen, Crystal," King says. "Dad is going to destroy that family. You really don't want to be mixed up with them."

"Or what?" I ask. "He'll kill me, too?"

"Nobody's going to kill you," King says. "We don't want to see you get hurt. And if you care about any of the Darlings, that's going to happen."

"It's already happened," I say. "And I know it was stupid and wrong to keep seeing Devlin, so I broke it off. Now, can we go back to school?"

"Since when are you so worried about your education?" King asks, glancing at me in the rearview mirror. The scrape under his eye is swelling. "It's half a day. Dad will get you excused."

"She's not worried about her grades," Royal mutters.

"Don't talk about me like I'm not here," I growl. "If you have something to say, say it to my face."

"Alright," Royal says, turning in his seat again. "How many class periods are you spending on your back in Devlin's backseat? You know who fucks in cars? Trashy whores."

"Well, I'm sure all of you would know, considering how many girls have seen your backseats."

"How many backseats have you seen?" Royal shoots back. "I heard you took a necklace from all three of those pieces of human filth. Are they passing you around now? One's not enough for our baby sister?"

"I'm not a baby," I snap. "And I need to get back to school to talk to my friend."

"Which one are you pretending is your 'friend'?" Royal asks. "Isn't that what you called Colt when he took you to homecoming?"

"Dixie," I say through clenched teeth.

"You can talk to her later," King says as we pull into our driveway. "Right now, we need to talk to Dad about this."

"Why?" I ask. "It's none of Dad's business who I'm with. For that matter, it's none of yours."

"Stop pretending to be naïve," Royal says, climbing out of the car. "You said you weren't a baby."

He slams the door and stalks into the house before I can answer.

I climb out of the car at the same time as King. His eyes drop to my stained shirt. He looks away and clears his throat. "Go change your clothes. Then we'll talk to Dad."

I've never felt so dirty and disgusting, not even the first time, when Devlin told me he'd used me, and it wasn't personal. I walk up the stairs, my entire body heavy with shame. I change my clothes and smooth my hair, but when I look in the mirror, I don't know this girl. This isn't me, and my brothers know it. They know I'm a whore who fucks in parking lots. Why are we all still pretending?

I toss my school clothes back into the closet and pull on a pair of yoga pants and a baggy cheer tee from my old school. I've just finished running my fingers through my hair, shaking it out and messing it up, then tossing it into a messy bun, when a knock sounds. Before I can answer, the door opens, and my brothers and father swarm in like an invading army.

"What's this your brothers tell me about you still seeing that son of a bitch?" Dad asks, his brows drawn together in anger.

I wish I hadn't changed, that I'd just gone downstairs. Now they're in my space, and I feel even more vulnerable and defensive. I edge onto my bed and wrap my arms around a fat lilac pillow, holding it in front of me as if it can shield me from their accusations.

"I was still seeing him," I admit. "But I'm not anymore."

Dad's eyes narrow, and he studies me like I'm not his daughter but some conniving stranger who might be tricking him into giving up mafia secrets I can later use against him. I remember Devlin's words, and I hate that he planted those seeds of doubt in my mind, but now I can't help the suspicions that creep in, whispering in the back of my mind.

Memories sneak in unbidden—Royal waking up and asking for Dad, saying he didn't want to be moved again. Dad asking what Royal said when he woke up in the hospital. Royal saying he went through that to protect me somehow. What did they do?

"That whole family is out to destroy us," Dad says. "They turned my building site into a crime scene. I've just now been cleared to go ahead with it. What are you doing messing with them behind our backs, Crystal? Your loyalty is to this family and this family alone."

I nod. He's right. It shouldn't matter what he did. Devlin's family is just as bad, and they're trying to destroy ours. They've both done shady, horrible things. Why am I holding my family to a standard that his doesn't meet? I have an obligation to protect my family, not let the Darlings infiltrate my family, my heart.

"And all this time, for months, you've been sleeping with that piece of shit," Royal says. "You don't even care what they did to me, do you? As long as you can have your little fuck buddy."

"He's not a fuck buddy," I snap. "It wasn't like that. I care about him."

"Well, stop it," King says. "You can't be seeing a Darling. Not when our families are at war."

"They drove us out of town twenty years ago," Dad says. "Now, we're going to drive them out. When we're done with them, there won't be a single Darling left in Faulkner. They've hurt our family long enough. Look what they did to Royal. I'm not going to let them hurt my little girl, too."

"Their reign is over, Crystal," King says, his dark eyes locked on mine. "Do you want to go down with them, or do you want to be standing with the victors at the end?"

I don't care about victory or taking anyone down, but they're right about my betrayal. Their accusations are the truth. I risked my family's wrath by continuing to see Devlin. I knew what was at stake. I knew the consequences. Now it's time to face them.

"I'm sorry," I say. "I'm sorry I kept seeing him, and I'm so sorry for what happened to you, Royal. I don't want to make it worse, and if me seeing Devlin hurts you, then I'm so fucking sorry. I should never have risked that. I just... I didn't know what to do. You've always been my rock, and I wanted to be that for you, but you kept pushing me away."

"You're saying it's my fault?" Royal asks. "That I pushed you into his arms?"

"No," I say sharply. "I just didn't know where to turn. And he was there, and he makes me feel good. I'm sorry, but that's the truth."

"I was here," King says quietly. "Why didn't you come to me?"

"Because you shouldn't have to hold us all up," I say. "You shouldn't have to hold us together, and you take on so much already. I know you're dealing with what happened to Royal. I'm sorry. I should have just gone to you. But how was I supposed to tell you that I want to be with Devlin?"

"You want to be with him?"

"No," I say, shaking my head. "I mean, I do, but I don't want to hurt anyone."

"And I want a flying unicorn that farts out kittens," Royal says. "Grow the fuck up, Crystal."

"It doesn't matter what you want," Dad says to me. "You can't see him anymore, Crystal. Do you understand?"

I nod, a lump in my throat. "I know."

"Good," he says. "Because he's doomed along with the rest of that family. They've all signed their own death warrants, and we won't stop until every last one of them is six feet under—or wishes they were."

That's when I realize how stupid I've been. I may love Devlin, but I've put him in danger, and not just from his grandfather. It's my family that's the problem, like he said all along. My grandfather killed an innocent man to frame Preston's dad. My mother is a mafia princess. My dad admitted they were all involved. He's not just saying these things. He fully intends to end lives.

I sit up, dropping my pillow. "Don't hurt them," I say, my heart racing. "Not Devlin. I get that you want revenge for them running you out of town when you were younger, but the Darling cousins weren't even alive then."

"I thought you didn't like him anymore," Royal says, his eyes narrowing.

"I won't see him anymore," I say to Dad. "I promise, Daddy. I'll never see him again if you leave him alone. If you don't hurt Devlin."

He blows out a breath, a frown creasing his brow. "Fine," he says after a pause. "I suppose there's no harm in leaving a kid or two around. They won't have any power once their parents are gone. We'll be running this town by then."

"Exactly," I say, nodding frantically, terrified he'll change his mind. "Please don't hurt Devlin. Or his cousins. It's not fair to go after people who never hurt you. None of them deserve that."

Royal snorts, but he doesn't say anything. He only glares at Dad with a sullen expression, waiting for his answer. I think about adding Devlin's dad, but I know Dad would never let go of his grudge against him. If I can keep Devlin safe, that's enough. The cousins are a bonus.

Dad sighs. "I'll leave them out of it. But if you're lying…"

"I'm not," I say, swallowing hard. I can't lie about this. If I do, and Devlin gets hurt—or worse—there's no going back from that. It might kill me to stay away from him, but there's no other option now. If I don't stay away, he'll literally be killed. Our relationship always existed on borrowed time, and that time has run out. One beautiful month is all we'll ever get.

"I'll know if you're lying," Royal says.

"I know," I admit. "Now, if you guys are done, I'm going to take a nap," I say, leaning back on my pillows.

"Sleep well, Sweetheart," Dad says, turning away. "You know we're only trying to protect what's ours."

Right. He's trying to protect his business, his construction site, his new plant. And I'm just lumped in with that because I'm just another thing Daddy owns, something he has that the Darlings don't.

Royal gives me one long, suspicious look before turning to follow.

King's been relatively quiet during all this, but he's watching me. "Want me to send you up something to eat?" he asks.

"I'm not hungry," I say. "But thanks."

He lingers in the doorway. "I'll wake you for dinner."

"Okay."

He pauses another moment before pulling the door closed. I want to feel bad for him. I know he wants to make sure I'm okay, that he's trying to take care of me, but he's part of all this. He agrees with Dad, with Royal. He will always take the side of the Dolce family, which means when I don't, he's the enemy.

I open the window a crack so the damp December air can come in, and then I slide down under the blankets and try to sleep. But I keep coming back to one thing. Devlin was right about my family all along. We really are the bad guys. And if I go along with them, then I'm the bad guy, too.

# nineteen

*Crystal*

*I guess what they say is true. Every villain is the hero of their own story.*

It's dark outside. I haven't moved since they left my room. I faked sleep when it was time for dinner, and now I lie in bed, digging my fingers into the bruises Devlin left on my thighs, craving the ache. It doesn't come. I feel nothing. I stare at the rain outside my window, wishing I could sink into the bed and let it suffocate me.

A knock sounds at the door, but I don't answer. I don't want to see them. They're all liars and hypocrites and worse. Just like me.

King sticks his head in the door. "Crys, sweetheart? You up?"

"No," I mutter, turning my face away.

King comes in anyway. He sinks onto the edge of the bed, switches on my lamp, and sets a bowl on my chest. "I brought you ice cream."

I want to scream at him. Ice cream can't fix this, can't even make it better.

"It's rocky road," he coaxes.

"I don't care," I mutter.

"You can't wallow forever, sis. Even if you hate us, you still gotta eat."

I can't stay mad at King. I can't. Because he's the only one who's come to my room to talk to me. He's the only one who is trying, and even if he can never make it better, he loves me enough to try, even knowing this paltry little gesture is wasted on me. He knows ice cream isn't enough. But it's all he has, so he's giving it to me.

I sigh and push myself up to sitting. "I don't hate you," I say, setting the ice cream in my lap. "You're a good brother, King. Better than any of us deserve."

"Shut up and eat your ice cream," he says, but I can tell he's pleased. I know, even if he doesn't show it. That's the only thing King has ever wanted to be—a protector, a savior, a hero. But even he can't solve this impossible equation, where the only solution involves everyone getting hurt.

For a minute, I eat my ice cream, and he watches like a mother hen, always taking care of me, making sure I'm fed even when I skip dinner, making sure I'm here and safe even when I'd rather climb out my window and run across the lawn to the boy I love and hate with all my heart. Just thinking about him makes pain twist tight inside me.

"How do you do it?" I ask after a while.

"Do what?" King asks.

"How do you fall in love and then just get over it and move on?"

"Dolces don't fall in love," he says. "Love makes you weak."

"Then I guess I'm weak."

"You're not in love," he says sharply. "It's just a little crush, Crystal. An infatuation. You'll get over it. I promise."

But he's wrong. If he's never been in love, how would he know? He doesn't know what it's like to live for a glimpse of someone's true self, a genuine laugh, a smile that reaches the eyes and sinks in until you're seeing not just their soul, but your own soul reflected back at you.

He doesn't know what it's like to lie in someone's arms and feel like every word he says is a treasure, to have to tear yourself from him with anguish when it's time to go home and you have to stop the flow of ideas that move between your two minds as if they're connected by more than just words but the most fascinating notions ever spoken.

He's never gasped at the strength of the ache gripping his heart, or those little moments of truth when two people are nothing but themselves, and the outside world with all its expectations and pressures is stripped away. Everything is laid bare, like even our skin is peeled back, and our raw hearts are pressed together in the most terrifying, beautiful, painful joining of souls.

"You'll change your mind when you feel it," I say.

"I won't feel it," King says. "Love is a luxury that people like us can't afford."

"People like us," I repeat.

"Crys, I told you what I'm doing when I graduate. There's no room for weakness or love in that life."

"Our parents are married," I point out. "All the uncles, too."

King hesitates, shifting on the bed. "Yeah," he concedes. "But I don't want to put anyone in that position. A family is a liability in that profession. If I loved a girl, I wouldn't want to put her in danger like that."

I think of Devlin across the lawn, in his bedroom. I wonder if he's hurting. I'm selfishly glad he won't be out throwing the football tonight since it's raining. I wonder what else he does when he hurts. Does he fight like Royal? Drink and hook up like the twins? Or is he like King, too busy trying to moderate everyone else's pain to allow himself to feel anything?

I shake the thought away and return my attention to my brother. "But... I mean... Don't you want kids? You'd make a great dad."

He gives a little smile and snags my spoon. "I've got you guys."

"You don't want kids of your own?" I ask, half-heartedly swiping for the spoon.

"No," he says, scooping a bite of ice cream from the bowl. "I mean, if something happened, if I made a mistake and knocked up some chick, then yeah, I'd do the right thing by her. But even then, I wouldn't let her love me."

"King," I say, accepting the spoon when he hands it back. "Are you really sure this is the life you want? It sounds like you're giving up a lot."

"We all make sacrifices."

"But why go to work and make money if you're not going to use it to create the life you want for yourself? I know you, King. You take care of people. You've basically raised us. You're both our mom and our dad. I don't believe you don't want that for yourself."

"I've got it," he says, throwing an arm around me and rubbing his knuckles into my head. "I've got you to take care of. Now, take back that thing about me being a mom or I'll rub a knot in your hair you'll never get out."

"Okay, okay," I say, laughing and squirming to free myself. "You're one hundred percent tough guy. Not even a bit nurturing."

"Good enough," he says, releasing me and picking up the bowl that tipped over in our tussle.

"Look what you did," I scold, pushing my mussed hair off my face. "You got chocolate on my blanket."

King plucks the errant spoon from my bed and puts it back in the bowl. "I'll get it cleaned," he says, setting the ice cream on the nightstand. "But first, promise me you'll be okay."

I don't want to lie to my brother, even though I know he needs it.

"What if…" I swallow hard, running my hand down my flat stomach and letting it settle there. "What if we forced them to let us be together?"

"You better not be saying what I think you're saying."

My heart hammers in my chest, but I have to ask. I have to know if it's possible. King is the only one I can ask. Even if he cares more about our family name, our image, than anyone else, he also cares about my happiness. He cares

311

about more of us getting hurt. If he could stop it, he would, no matter what it took.

"I'm just asking," I say, forcing myself to sound casual. "What if we could bring our families together?"

"You can't," he says firmly. "If you had a baby, the Darlings would take it. They've done it before. Hell, Mabel's dad took her from her mom. Why do you think she lives with her dad? Because he's a Darling, and her mom wasn't— at least not by birth. And they were fucking married at the time. She wasn't some irresponsible teenage mom. The Darling still got custody. They always will."

"Devlin wouldn't fight me for custody. He'd stand by me."

King shrugs. "Doesn't matter. Grampa Darling would lawyer up and start digging into our family history, trying to get the kid from both of you. They'd find out what kind of people we are, and you'd never see that baby again."

"But… I mean, Uncle Vinny could take our side," I say, grasping at straws.

"Uncle Vinny's not that kind of lawyer," King reminds me. "And yeah, he got us out of a few scrapes. But these custody lawyers, they dig a hell of a lot deeper than someone picking up Duke for getting drunk and loud. Our family might have some sway in New York, but there's a reason Dad didn't want the FBI sniffing around when Royal disappeared. People go digging, they find things."

"Devlin wouldn't let them," I insist, holding desperately to my last hope.

King snorts. "Crystal, Devlin would be dead long before that baby came. The day our dad found out, to be exact. And I'm not being dramatic here, baby sis. He'll order a hit on him."

My fingers are shaking as I stare at my brother, so calmly telling me that our father would kill the boy I love to keep us apart. "He'd do that, even knowing it would kill me, too?"

King sighs. "Listen to me, baby sis. If you really do love that boy, or even if you just like him, you need to leave him alone. You're not going to change Dad's mind, and you're not going to change Mr. Darling's. You got two options. Let him go live his life, or keep fucking around with him, and he doesn't make it to see twenty. I'm sorry it has to be this way, but that's the way it is for us. Think about that next time you want to do something crazy like fall in love."

But I don't have to think about that because I know that day will never come. I already know I'll never fall in love again. Devlin is my one shot, my one love. I'll never love anyone else. Even if I could, I've learned my lesson, and I won't let it happen. Like King said, love is a liability. I'd never take that risk again.

That doesn't change the fact that I've already fallen, and there's nothing I can do about it. It's too late for me. I love Devlin, and there's no going back from that. But if loving him means making sure he stays far away from me so he can live a long and happy life with someone else, then that's what I'll do.

# twenty

*Crystal*

*I remember Christmas break last year. Three weeks of freedom—from stares, whispers, girls cattily speculating on what it would take to knock me and Veronica from the throne. A break meant I could stay home with my family and just be myself. Was that only a year ago? A year and another life, another world, another girl. Now, those three weeks fill me with dread. Three exhausting weeks of faking it, of pretending to be the girl they want, the Dolce daughter. Knowing that no matter how hard I try, I'll only disappoint them because the harder I fake it, the further away she gets.*

The next day is Friday, the last day before holiday break. I'm glad I won't have to face the Darlings for the next few weeks. Distance from Devlin will help. I've done it before. I can do it again.

I walk in with my brothers, ignoring the way people are looking at me, like I'm some kind of mysterious rarity they'd like to put under a microscope. I guess the Darlings have put me there. I open my locker, already knowing the emptiness will knock a hole in my heart. Even though I'm expecting it, the missing coffee still hurts more than I want to admit. It's been there every single day since Devlin got out of jail, even when we weren't speaking to each other. Today, it's gone. I guess it's really over.

I feel numb and sick as I let my brothers escort me to class. Once they're gone, I pivot and head to the nurse's office to beg out of first period. I can't face a whole class of Devlin Darling.

I wait until the next class has been going for five minutes before I head to my locker, relieved for the empty hallway. No stares or whispers from girls about the Darling Doll spectacle the day before. I can't believe that for one moment, I let myself believe I'd be Devlin's queen.

"Hey, Juliet," comes a slow, southern drawl from behind me.

Damn it.

"Skipping class?" I ask, twisting my locker combination without looking up.

"I got bored," Colt says, stopping to lean on the lockers beside mine. "My favorite source of entertainment wasn't there today."

"Well, I hope you're happy," I say, gritting my teeth. "You got what you wanted. Devlin and I are done."

"What makes you think I wanted that?"

"You gave me the necklace," I say. "So did Preston. What else could you be doing but trying to cause drama?"

"Alright," Colt says with a grin. "So, how about it, Juliet? Your balcony, eleven o'clock. Wear next to nothing. I know I will be."

I turn to him, a lump in my throat. "I mean it."

"So do I," he says, the smile dropping away. "I always thought I'd be your Romeo."

"Colt…"

"You won't even give it a shot?" he asks, taking my hand and giving me those puppy dog eyes that even now are hard not to meet with a smile and reluctant surrender.

I squeeze his hand. "I hope you find your Juliet," I say, giving him a gentle smile before drawing my fingers from his. "But it's not me."

"Yeah, okay," he says, slouching back against the lockers. "I just thought maybe this time I'd be the best. But once again, I'm the fuck-up."

"How are you the fuck-up?" I ask, remembering the way he moved on that football field. It reminds me of the way my quiet, soft-spoken uncle Vinny turns from a lamb into a vicious wolf in the courtroom.

"Devlin's the favorite here," he says, gesturing vaguely to our surroundings. "And Preston's the favorite at home. I was supposed to get you, Juliet. I took you to homecoming. But then you took off with my cousin…"

I roll my eyes. "Devlin told me you were supposed to fuck me to destroy me. I know none of you actually wanted me."

Colt grins and shakes his head. "You really think that? Trust me, Devlin's no whore. He wouldn't fuck a girl he didn't want for all the money in the world. Not even his own inheritance."

"But you would?" I ask with a smirk.

"I'd totally fuck you, Crystal Sweet," he says, raking his blond hair off his forehead and offering me a roguish grin.

"So, how are you the fuck-up?" I ask. "Because you ended up with Dixie instead of me?"

"I'm not *with* Dixie," he says, making a face. "But yeah, it should have been me in that room with you that day."

"That would have left Devlin with Dixie," I say. "She's a little young for him."

"Nah, I would have nailed you both," Colt says with an arrogant tilt to his chin.

"You really know how to charm a girl."

Colt's smile slips away, and he shrugs. "I've been a fuck-up since the day I was born," he says, "And they found out I wasn't Devlin's brother."

"Why would you be Devlin's brother?"

"We have the same mom," he says, looking at me strangely, like I should know this.

"You're half-brothers?"

"And cousins. It *is* Arkansas." He adds a wink, but I mull over his words. That's exactly what Devlin said. It strikes me how close these boys are—more than cousins. More than brothers, even. In truth, I envy their closeness. I wish I was part of something like that, facing the world with my brothers, as equals, as ourselves, against any threat. Devlin and Colt went through that long, messy divorce and custody war that Devlin said took up most of his childhood. They formed a united front, right down to the line they recite when people bring up their family drama.

"I didn't know that," I mutter, feeling stupidly jealous and hurt that Devlin didn't tell me that.

"Devlin doesn't like people remembering that," he says with a shrug. "Not that he's got anything to be ashamed of. I'm the bastard child."

"I'm sorry," I say. "But out of the three of you, I think Preston's the fucked up one. Everyone loves you."

"They do, don't they?" Colt says, tossing his hair out of his eyes and grinning. "But trust me, Preston is the golden boy in the family. He's just like his dad, and his old man's just like Grampa Darling. You know, the guy's literally gotten away with murder. He can do no wrong."

"The guy at the construction site," I say, my heart picking up speed.

"Nah," Colt says, waving a hand as if that's nothing. "But your family's going to try to make it look that way, aren't they? Because he tried to take the property out from under your dad. That's why they framed him, right? And when they see that he was tried for murder before... I mean, he might have been acquitted, and they'll tell the jurors not to take that into account, but they will."

I'm not touching that topic. But this guy is no fuck-up. He's too smart for his own good.

"I'm not the girl, Colt," I say, closing my locker. Time to close this conversation, too. "Not for you. There's a girl out there who's dying to be with you. Dixie worships the ground you walk on. That's what you deserve. Not someone whose heart is already taken."

"I know," he says. "It's kinda fucked up I even asked you."

"Yeah," I agree. "It kinda is."

I open my bag and pull out one of the necklaces, but Colt holds up a hand. "Keep it," he says. "I meant what I said. You're the only girl who deserves it. You took us all by surprise."

"You know my family won't let me wear it," I say.

"Even if they would, Devlin wouldn't," he says. "I'm surprised he didn't rip it off you."

I swallow again, trying to quell the ache in my throat at the mention of his name. I wonder when I'll stop wanting to cry at the thought of him. I force a chuckle, even though it twists in my gut like a knife. "He's pretty possessive, isn't he?"

Colt laughs at that. "You do bring out his crazy side."

"You going to class?" I ask, nodding in that direction.

"Nah," he says. "I think I'll go sit on the bleachers and lick my wounds. Join me if you change your mind? I've got a medical card and the goods to make you forget your troubles."

"Thanks," I say. The thought of sitting out on the wet bleachers in the chilly December sun sounds a thousand times better than going to class. I know that Colt would make me laugh, even if he's not laughing on the inside. Getting high would lessen the ache for a minute. I know it would be easy and fun to flirt with him, and it would take my mind off Devlin. But I also know I need to stop all of this now, the way I should have a long time ago. I'm not just losing Devlin. I'm losing Colt and even Preston.

But like King said, this is how it has to be. This is what a Dolce does. This is what we get. Family. Money. Status. Power.

It should be enough. That's what everyone wants, what they work their whole lives to achieve. Most people are happy if they have even one of those things. We have it all.

And I'd trade it all in a second.

*

I can't bear the thought of the cafeteria at lunch. Yes, I'm a coward. I don't want to see Devlin, but it's more than that. I don't want to see the other girls staring at me, trying to figure out what I have that they don't. I don't want the attention, the jealousy, the curiosity, or even the admiration. I just want to be some nameless, faceless girl in the crowd like Mabel. How has she achieved this magic?

I shoot the girls a text and head out to the football field, minus the invitation from Colt. It seems as good a place as any. As I walk across the dead grass under the flat grey sky, I can't help but think it's a fitting atmosphere. I don't know if either of the girls are speaking to me anymore, and I can't really blame them if they aren't. Guess I'm about to find out.

I sit on the wet metal bleachers in the damp air and wait. When my friends appear, an odd pair of cousins walking side by side, Dolly in one of her Barbie-pink outfits and Dixie in her goth get-up, I can't help but smile. But the relief is quickly overshadowed by nerves. What if they're coming to tell me we can't be friends? I know exactly how quickly the tables can turn. One day I'm the Darlings' favorite; the next I'm friendless and alone.

"The weather is your friend today," Dolly says, clambering up onto the bleachers in her impossible heels and dropping down beside me.

"How's that?" I'm too cautious to hope for anything, even hearing her normal tone.

"It looks like it's gonna rain real soon," she says, scooting down to make room for Dixie. "At least it's cooperating enough for you to hide during lunch."

"That obvious?" I ask.

"I don't blame you," she says. "This school is cannibalistic."

"Are you mad at me?" I blurt out, looking from her to Dixie, who hasn't said a word.

"I was gonna be," she says. "If you were hiding from us."

"Why would I hide from you?"

"You skipped science this morning," she points out. "But since you texted about lunch, I'll let it slide."

"Thanks," I say, swallowing hard before turning to Dixie. "And you?"

"No," she says, sounding as dejected as the morning after our shame. "He's not my boyfriend. Why should I be mad?"

"For that matter, why would I be?" Dolly asks.

"I know you like them," I say. "You have a right to be mad."

"You didn't do anything," Dolly says. "You didn't ask for the necklaces, did you?"

"No," I concede. "But still."

"They said they were doing away with the Dog, but they forgot to get the collar and ears back," Dixie says.

"You said you wanted to keep them," I remind her.

"He didn't even look at me," she says. "I think they forgot I was even there."

"I'm sorry," I say. "I know how much you like him. But I promise I don't. Not in that way."

"I know," she says. "I just don't get it. How do you get all those guys to like you? Both of you? I mean, besides being hot, is there any other way?"

"Lots of girls are pretty," I say. "It's about more than that. It's about how you carry yourself. And thinking you deserve it."

"You think you deserve all three of them?" she asks, her eyes widening.

"No," I say, laughing. It's hard to say something good about myself, the same way it probably is for any girl to say she deserves the best. In some way, we're all conditioned to take less, to be quiet and demure and perfectly poised like a good Dolce daughter.

But fuck that. Maybe it's time I took something for myself. Time I admitted that I'm worthy. That I'm good enough. That I deserve Devlin.

# twenty-one

*Crystal*

*Tonight I thought I had it. It seemed so simple. That I would take what I deserved. It doesn't matter what I deserve, though. I can't run away from who I am anymore. I'm part of this, whether I like it or not. I was born into my family, and this is how it works. If I take what I want, my family will take it away from me. If I fight back, they'll defeat me. If I stand up for what's right, they'll make me believe I'm wrong. There's no way to win and be a Dolce at the same time.*

I wake to the sound of my window sliding up. I scramble upright in my bed, reaching for the lamp with trembling fingers. My heart is racing as I turn to see Devlin standing inside my room, dripping wet from the rain that seems to take the place of snow as winter precipitation in this state.

"What are you doing?" I hiss. "You can't be here."

He stares at me a second, raindrops running down his cheeks like tears. "Why are you avoiding me?" he asks.

"I told you yesterday," I whisper-shout at him. "It's over, Devlin. We have to stop this before one of us gets really hurt."

I know it's not me who will be hurt, but if he's anything like me, he'd risk himself before he'd risk me.

"It's too late for that," he says. "You can break up with me if it makes you feel better, but it won't change anything. *Boyfriend* is just a word. I'm your man, and I don't need a label to prove it."

"Devlin," I whisper, an ache rising in my throat. "Please."

He stands there dripping onto the hardwood floor, soaked through and shivering with cold, but his words are strong and sure. "You're my girl, Crystal. I've known that for a while, but what I didn't realize until you tried to break me is that I'm yours, too. Whatever forces brought us together, even if it was some asshole who shouldn't be messing in our lives, it doesn't change what we have now. I'm sorry I did thc things I did to you, including what he ordered. If I could take them back, I'd take back every damn one."

"But you can't," I say, tears pressing behind my eyes.

"No," he says. "But I can make it up to you for them."

"You can't do that, either," I say. "We can't be together, Devlin."

"You're wrong," he says, closing the distance between us. He sinks onto the edge of the bed, draws my chin up, and delivers a lingering kiss to my trembling lips. I should push him away, but I can't make myself. I'm as weak as love makes me, and I want him too much. My hand curls into a fist in the wet fabric of his t-shirt, dragging him closer, warming his cold lips with my hot ones.

"Tell me you don't still want me," he whispers, cupping my cheek in his palm. "And I'll tell you that you're lying."

"It doesn't matter," I say, choking back tears.

"You're right," he says. "It doesn't matter if you forgive me or love me or want me. Because I'll spend every moment for the rest of my life making that happen. Proving to you that I need you. That I love you. That this is real."

"What if I can never believe you?" I ask, a tear spilling over my lashes.

Devlin gently wipes it away with his thumb, cradling my face between his hands. "Then I'll still spend every day of my life trying to earn your trust and respect, and if it fails, and you never love me again, at least I'll know my life's work was something worthwhile—making the woman I love feel loved, and worthy, and as treasured as she is."

More tears trickle down my cheeks, and Devlin leans in to kiss them. When they don't stop, he pulls me into his arms. I feel the strength of his body, of his words that are truth, and I can't help but melt into his arms. I believe him already. I love him already. There's no going back, no matter how badly he hurt me, no matter how wrong it is. I can't stop myself even if I try. And I tried so hard.

Now, it feels so good to stop trying to hate him. I wrap my arms around him, burying my face against his strong chest and sobbing. Devlin holds me. He strokes my hair and kisses the top of my head, and he just holds me. When the tears stop, I don't want to look up. I'm terrified that it's all going to slip away again. But he pries me from him and lifts my face, kissing my damp, salty lips.

His blue eyes are soft as the warm waters of the Caribbean as he gazes down at me. "I'm never giving up on you, Crystal," he says. "You can hurt me ten times what you did. You can do it every day, and it won't matter. I'll do whatever it takes to convince you of that. I'll die for you before I let you go."

I shake my head, more tears coming. "You will die, Devlin. My family will kill you. You were right about them. You were right all along, even when I didn't know it, didn't believe it. I didn't want to know it. But they're not good people. I knew I was rotten, but it's not just me. We're all rotten, every one of us."

"Crystal," he says, his voice pained. "You're not rotten. Believe me, I know rotten. I've got plenty of it in my own family. And you, Sugar, are the least rotten person I know."

"I'm not," I say, shaking my head. "I did just as bad as you."

"You had every reason," he says, stroking my wet cheeks with his thumbs.

I shake my head. "I had no right to get mad at you for your grampa setting me up. Especially since... I did something pretty bad to you, too. Something my grandma told me to do."

"What's that, Sugar?" he asks. "What'd you do that could possibly be worse than all I did to you?"

I don't want to tell him, but in a way, I do. If I tell him, he'll go running, and he won't be in danger anymore.

"Remember that day when I brought you coffee?" I ask, swallowing hard.

"Yeah," he says. "It was the first time I thought maybe you cared about more than my dick."

Great. Now I feel even worse. I let out a breath before going on. "I kind of... Put a drop of blood in it."

I want to drop my eyes, to turn away and hide my face. But I force myself to watch his reaction. His eyes darken, smoldering with intensity and lust. "That's kinda crazy," he says, sliding an arm around my back and leaning closer. "But hot."

"It wasn't just any blood," I whisper. "It was... Period blood."

Devlin blinks a few times, just staring at me. "Why?" he asks at last.

I can't bear it anymore. I turn away and throw myself flat on my bed, pulling a pillow over my face. "Because my grandma told me it would make you fall in love," I admit, my voice muffled. "You can go now. I told you I was disgusting."

After a minute, I feel Devlin shift on the bed. He pulls the pillow off my face and leans on one elbow, smirking down at me. "Crystal," he says. "I went down on you in the shower when you were still bleeding. Do you really think that's going to scare me away?"

"But I made you fall in love with me just so I could hurt you," I whisper, my heart beating hard at his nearness. I can feel the heat of him through his soaked shirt, can smell his skin, his hair, the scent making my head spin with desire. I want to reach out and wrap my arms around him, to take it all back and start all over, so neither of us hurt each other.

"Crystal, it wasn't your blood that made me fall in love," he says, pushing his hips against me in the bed. "If anything about that coffee made me fall for you, it was thinking you did something nice for me. I fell for you because you're tough without being a bitch, you never lost your cool even when I was being an absolute monster to you, and maybe a little bit because you dress like my grandmother and then get all freaky when I start fucking you." He leans forward, smiling as his lips meet mine.

"I don't dress like a grandma," I start, but I melt as his lips dip to my throat. He pushes his body against mine, his tongue caressing my skin, tasting me. He sucks and bites, his hot breath against my neck making me squirm. Warm tingles race over my skin, the heat of my need building between my legs as his mouth moves up my neck, his teeth teasing my earlobe.

"Can I do it again?" he whispers. "I want to lick the blood from your cunt and make you moan."

"I'm not bleeding," I whisper, a shiver of forbidden lust going through me at the taboo idea he's suggesting.

"Can I make you bleed?" he asks. "I want to taste you again. I want to be a part of you, to be a part of each other."

"What do you mean?" I ask, my eyes dropping closed and my hands fisting in his hair, pulling him closer.

He lifts up, digging in his pocket and producing a knife. Before I can ask what the fuck he's doing, he opens it and slices the pad of his thumb. Blood beads on the tip, and he lowers it to my mouth, running it back and forth along my lower lips, painting me with his blood. A charge of heat throbs between my legs, and I open my lips. Devlin pushes his thumb inside, a soft growl sounding in his throat.

"Suck it, baby," he whispers. "Taste me."

I close my eyes and draw him into me, shivering with the horrifying yet strangely erotic thrill. Devlin slides his thumb against my tongue, pushing it to the back of my throat before drawing it slowly out. My lids flutter open, and our eyes meet. Devlin's are blazing with that madness I know so well, the one I court and fear in equal measure. The one that says he's past the point of no return, and he's going to fuck me however he pleases, whether or not I want it, and I'm goddamn well going to like it.

I suck harder, feeling a swell of power inside me when the fire in his eyes blazes hotter. He draws his thumb away and throws off my blankets. I lift my hips for him, pulling up my t-shirt while he strips my underwear off. He shoves my thighs open and buries his wet thumb inside me. A gasp escapes my lips as I realize the slickness isn't just my arousal, it's my saliva and his blood. I should be horrified, but instead it makes heat shimmer between my legs, and I let out a moan, lifting my hips to grind into his hand.

Devlin slides down my body, burying his face between my thighs. He spreads me open and tastes me, a growl building in his throat as his tongue sinks into me, pushing roughly into my entrance. He pulls back and looks up at me, his eyes clouded with lust. "Now you. I want to taste yours again."

"Cut me," I breathe.

"Where?" he asks, reaching for the knife lying next to me.

I run my fingers down my bare stomach, spreading myself for him. "Here."

Devlin's breath hitches, and he holds the knife for a second, staring at my cunt with a reverence most would reserve for the second coming. I don't even tremble as he brings the blade to my skin. I know Devlin wants only my pleasure, and he'll give me only the pain I need to increase it.

A pinch darts through me when the pinprick of the knife's point breaks my sensitive skin. Devlin groans, dropping the knife and sinking down as if in prayer to capture the drop of blood he drew. He sucks hard, and I writhe and buck against his mouth as he licks and thrusts and sucks, stroking and biting and pushing me to the edge until I can't breathe, and I have to grab a pillow and hold it over my face to stifle my cries of pleasure as I go over.

For seconds, minutes, I can't breathe or think or even see. There's no thought, no mind, only my body that is so wonderfully, powerfully alive and overflowing with pleasure. And Devlin, who is giving it. At last, I begin to come back to myself, to reality, little quivers still racing through me every few seconds.

"Damn, Sugar," Devlin whispers, his voice rough and hoarse, as if he's the one who's been crying out. He pulls the pillow away from my face before I've caught my breath, resting his elbows on either side of my head as he sinks into me slowly. "We're part of each other now," he murmurs, his lips hovering above mine, his heated gaze holding mine.

"You can't undo what we just did. We'll be part of each other forever. From the moment we met, you were mine."

"I was yours," I whisper, wrapping my arms around his neck, my legs around his hips. "I *am* yours. I never stood a chance. Never had a choice."

"Neither did I. Every inch of me is yours." Devlin skims his lips over mine as he moves slow and deep inside me, to the place where pleasure and pain mix until I can't tell them apart. Then he stills, kissing me gently, letting me feel the perfect, painful way he fills me until I can't take another fraction of an inch without screaming.

"Give me every inch," I pant, rocking against him. "Give me everything." I want it all, from the unbearable bliss to the deep, bruised ache he leaves in my lower belly. I want to wrap myself around him and never let him go, no matter who tries to tear us apart. I want to weather every storm with him, even the storm that is Devlin himself. I want him to break down my walls, to pound into me with the brutal force of a hurricane until he's spent, and he's placid as a calm, blue sea. Until there's nothing left in me to break, no fight left; until my walls are nothing but sand next to his sea.

"We're meant for each other," he whispers, beginning to move inside me. "Nobody else. Just us."

"Just us," I agree, holding his face between my hands. "Always."

Our love is different, deep and intense tonight. Devlin fucks me slow and hard, and our eyes never leave each other's. When we come together, the connection between us pulls so tight it's almost unbearable, infinite and painful in its rawness, as if our souls have woven together and can never be separated from each other, and every ugly, shameful, and hidden part of ourselves has been bared to the other. Even my orgasm is different, echoing in some deep, hidden part of me.

I know then that no matter what our families say, we can't stay apart. We can't even when we try. We're each other's, and there's no way to change that. It was set in motion the first time we met, and it will never stop. I may have joked about Romeo and Juliet with Colt, but now I understand it. I understand love that can't be stopped. I understand two people can't be separated even by death. I understand because we just became those two people.

Nothing will ever come between us again. No matter what it takes, we will be together, even if we have to die to make it happen.

# twenty-two

*Devlin*

"Are we really going through with this charade again this year?" Dolly asks, slipping her hand into my elbow and joining me under my umbrella. I'm annoyed by how familiar it feels—how comfortable. But that's all it is. She doesn't make my head all dizzy and turned around when she's in there, doesn't get my heart all fucked up or send my blood rushing to my cock when she touches me. No, she's just Dolly, the girl I've known since we were young enough to take off our clothes without shame.

An incident that was quickly corrected by a few whacks of Grampa's belt.

"What charade, my darling fiancé?" I ask, squeezing her hand to my side. "Don't tell me marrying a Darling won't make your every dream come true."

She gives that ladylike scoff of hers. "Hardly."

"I don't know how you could want for anything more than our coveted name," I say as we fall into the parade of matched couples under large umbrellas entering Grampa Darling's house for the annual Christmas Eve dinner.

"I don't know, either," Dolly says. "But somehow I manage."

"What else is there?" I ask, smiling for the event photographer. Yes, my family's Christmas Eve dinner counts as an event in this town. No doubt it'll be in the papers tomorrow. Rain or shine, the show must go on.

"Travel," Dolly says. "Fame, fortune, the whole world."

"Don't tell our families that."

"Don't I know," she says. "Is your grampa going to make us give the dreaded have-you-set-a-date talk again this year? I don't know if I can fake my way through another one of those, Devlin."

"I'm sorry," I say quietly as we ascend the wide steps to the front door. We both know I'm apologizing for more than my insufferable grandfather. I'm apologizing for not being able to love her the way she loved me, the way she wanted. The way she deserves. She had to sit through those questions, and as uncomfortable as it was to have to lie my way through, I know it was that much worse for her when she wanted to believe the lies, that we'd get married and have it all.

"Grampa knows you," I say, leaning down to speak to her as we enter into the foyer. "Just be yourself."

"I'm always myself," she says. "That's the problem."

"It's not a problem," I tell her. "It's spectacular."

She smiles, but I catch the shade of sadness there. I feel it, too. This is the end, the last one of these we'll ever go to. I lead her into the next room, where people are dancing and chatting quietly, clinking their glasses together.

"Dance?" I ask, holding out a hand to Dolly.

"We got dressed up, we might as well play pretend," she says with a sigh, sliding her arms around my neck. She feels so different, so much bigger and more solid, her waist thicker than Crystal's in my hands. I wonder what she's doing at home, if she has any ridiculous obligatory traditions in her family.

I'm not the only one thinking of someone else. Dolly's gaze is fixed behind me, and I don't have to turn to know who's there.

"Not him," I murmur, tightening my grip on her waist.

"Who?" She draws back, her eyes widening.

"Whatever you do, Dolly, as someone I care about, I'm pleading with you to find someone else. Go, travel the world, do your thing. Don't step in my family's quicksand."

Our eyes meet, and we sway to the music for a minute, neither of us speaking. She's so close I can smell her bubblegum. But even with her plump lips inches from mine, I couldn't summon even a twitch of my cock for her if I tried. That doesn't mean I want to see her—or my cousin—repeat my parents' mistakes.

"You chose your destiny," she says at last.

"Did I?" I ask, pulling back with a frown. "If I had, I think she'd be here right now."

"You'll find a way," she says.

For a minute, we're silent again. This time, I speak first. "Will you?"

"I don't know," she says. "I'll find some way. I'm just not sure what way it'll be yet."

"Well," I say. "Be careful. His destiny is to follow his father, and his father's father. Our job here isn't to commit the sins of our fathers and forefathers all over again."

"I think the sins of our forefathers is slavery," she says.

I wince. If he really wanted to teach us shame, my grandfather should have started with that instead of whipping us for taking off our clothes when we got wet in a mud puddle. "Yeah, well, let's not repeat any of their sins," I tell Dolly.

"I guess gettin' out of here is a good way to avoid our parents' mistakes."

"You know what's here," I say. "I think you're fucking brave to leave."

"Me, too," she says.

They make an announcement that dinner's about to be served, but we finish out the song. Looking down at Dolly, I see what my life would be if I took the easy road. Like Mom said, I could do a lot worse than Dolly Beckett. She's a bombshell, and in these last few months, I've seen her transform. Not from a caterpillar to a butterfly—Dolly's always been a butterfly—but some other winged thing. Something fierce and brave, who goes after what she wants, flying free of her cage and into the unknown.

If she stayed, if we did what our parents wanted and took the easy road, we could be content. It would be a comfortable life with all a guy could ask for. A nice home, a family, a wife that other men coveted and who could also challenge me. Ironically, that's the one thing she was always missing, and I know who I have to thank for it.

The girl who I'd give up every comfort for, who might not bring me contentment but will challenge me until I lose my fucking mind half the time. The girl who keeps me on my toes, who is so strong she can make even a soft, sweet little southern belle like Dolly reach deep down inside and find her strength. A girl I will fight to be with every day of my life, even if it means giving up everything guaranteed in this life. That girl is *my* destiny.

"What about you, Dolly?" I ask. "What's your destiny?"

"I'm destined for great things," she says. "That's all I know."

"If that's all you need to know, you're braver than me," I say.

"I could have told you that," she says with a grin.

The song ends, and I pull her in and kiss her forehead. I lock eyes with Preston over her cloud of hair, sprayed with enough product to choke a horse if it inhaled near her. "Just don't do anything stupid before you get the chance," I say. "I'd hate to see you get hurt."

"I'm a big girl, Devlin," she says, pulling away. "You don't have to look out for me anymore."

"Well, I know you," I say. "And I don't want to see him get hurt, either."

"Devlin Darling," she says, giving my shoulder a playful push. "I think there was a compliment buried deep, deep, deep in there."

"Maybe," I say with a little smile, offering her an arm. "Don't tell on me."

"If I was going to tell on you, it would be for running around on me with Crystal."

I tense. "I don't think my grandfather cares who his progeny fuck around with, as long as they marry who he thinks they should and don't have illegitimate children." I know I'm being a dick even as the words leave my mouth, no matter how true they are.

Dolly just smiles and pats my arm with her free hand as we move with the other couples toward the dining room. "I'm not going to tell on you, Devlin. And you're right. Most powerful men have affairs. I'm sure he's no stranger to that fact."

"I'm not having an affair," I grit out, annoyed.

"I know," she says quickly. "I didn't mean to imply that. You're not mine, Devlin. You never were. I know that now. You hurt me, but I don't resent you for it anymore. I understand. Some things just aren't meant to be."

"Thanks," I mutter. "I'm sorry I couldn't give you what you wanted. What you deserve."

She doesn't argue. She knows she deserves better. It stings a little, but I'm happy she finally knows it. "Devlin?" she says, looking up at me, her Bambi eyes serious.

"Yeah?"

"Just be what she deserves."

I swallow hard, knowing she's giving me something priceless—her blessing. Not only has she let go of the dream, but she wants me to be happy. We're friends, as we've always been, since long before we knew the implications of the marriage we've known was our fate since we could say the word.

"Hey, Devlin," Chase says, slipping up behind us with Lindsey on his arm.

"Hey," I say, shaking Chase's hand.

He turns to my date while I nod to my waifish little cousin, who looks perfectly polished like all the women here, though I can read the frazzled expression in her eyes. I do not envy Preston his position in the family.

"Why, Dolly Beckett," Chase says. "Last time I saw you, you were krumping at a football game, and now you're looking like a damn fine society lady. Aren't you just a Jack of all trades?"

She laughs, and it's an easy laugh, one that makes me happy. I'm happy that she's happy, that she's excited about her future instead of desperately obsessed with it. I'm happy that she can still laugh that way. That she has enough sense to get out of this town. And I'm happy that I won't have to fake it much longer. For tonight, though, we'll fake it. We'll fake it through the interview with Grampa Darling, when he'll tell us we're graduating in a semester, and it's time I made an honest woman of Dolly. We'll fake it through the one her family will put us through, too. And we'll hold them off a few more months, until Dolly leaves town.

And then somehow, I have to convince my family that I belong with an Italian New Yorker with mafia ties whose family is hellbent on destroying us. Should be a piece of cake.

# twenty-three

*Crystal*

*Christmas is a time of tradition. But what happens when all the traditions are broken, when everything is broken? When families don't trust, don't love, don't even care enough to visit? When no one hangs a stocking, and there is no laughter and merriment in the air. I stopped believing in Santa Claus a long time ago, but this is the year I stopped believing in the magic of Christmas.*

"Are you staying over?" Dixie asks, looking back and forth between me and Dolly. The three of us sit cross-legged on her bedroom floor, eating homemade Christmas cookies Dolly brought and exchanging late Christmas gifts.

"I can't," I say with a sigh. "Royal's outside waiting to escort me home when we're done."

"Let him wait," Dolly says. "You said you'd come for a movie."

"I did," I say, gesturing to my Christmas pajamas. "I just can't stay over. My brother doesn't trust me not to run off with Devlin if I'm out of his sight for a night."

"He's got a point," Dixie says, giggling. "You probably would."

"I would not," I say, swatting her knee. "I'd never leave my BFF's party to hang out with a guy."

"This isn't exactly a party," she says, looking momentarily glum.

"Oh, hush," Dolly says. "It is so a party. I don't make cookies for just anything."

"You made them for Christmas," Dixie points out. "These are leftovers!"

"Are you saying you're too good to eat leftovers?" Dolly asks in a mock scolding tone. "There are children starving in Africa!"

We all crack up, and I snag a Santa cookie from the tin. "So, what'd you girls get for Christmas?"

"I got the usual from my family," Dixie says. "Clothes that don't fit to 'motivate' me to lose weight, a subscription to Weight Watchers, and a cookbook to go with it."

"Oh my god," I say. "Dixie, that's horrible."

"Yeah, Christmas isn't my favorite," she says. "Oh, I did get earrings from my aunt because she couldn't guess my size, and even fat girls can wear jewelry."

"Did she say that?"

"More or less," Dixie says. "I also got a lovely box of dog treats, a collar and a leash in the mailbox. My parents were really confused since we don't have a dog."

"I thought they did away with the Darling Dog," Dolly says.

"Doesn't stop Colt from treating me like one," Dixie says with a sigh. "What about y'all? What'd you get?"

"If it makes you feel any better, my Christmas wasn't all that great, either," I say. "My mom couldn't be bothered to come down for a visit, since she'd miss all the good holiday parties in New York. And my dad decided to install a security camera on the balcony to 'keep me safe.' But it's really to make sure I don't sneak out or Devlin doesn't sneak in my window. They took my phone, too, so I can't even text him."

"That's messed up," Dixie says, her eyes widening. "I thought it was bad when I got grounded."

"The worst part is, I think it was King who did it," I say. "Royal would have murdered Devlin if he caught him sneaking in. My dad, too. But King wouldn't want to hurt me, and he knows hurting Devlin would. So he didn't rat me out, he just had them put up security measures. As fucked up as it is, he's really trying to protect me."

"And he thinks keeping you apart will do that?" Dolly asks.

"Apparently," I say, sweeping crumbs off my lap. "But it's not making me want to give up on Devlin. Nothing is going to make me stop loving him. All it's making me do is want to defy my family."

"What are you going to do?" Dixie asks, her eyes wide.

"I don't know," I say. "But I'm not going to stop seeing him."

"Are you going to the Darlings' New Year's Eve party?" she asks. "I heard it's like, the most exclusive one of the year. It's at Grampa Darling's estate outside town, but he's not there. No adults are."

I turn to Dolly. "I assume you've been to these?"

"Of course," she says, sounding wearied by the whole thing. "But it's not all it's cracked up to be. Last year, one of their Dolls got roofied."

I remember Preston stumbling off into the bushes with some drunk girl at Colt's house, and I'm not too shocked. Some things are the same at any school.

"Did she get... *You know*," Dixie whispers.

"Raped," I say. "That's the word you're looking for."

"Yeah," Dolly says. "By two guys on the football team. Guys the Darlings thought were their friends."

"Did they get arrested?" Dixie asks, her eyes wide.

"No," Dolly says. "They take everyone's phones, so there was no proof, but when Lacey told them, they beat up the guys so bad they ended up in the hospital. One of them had permanent brain damage. Last I heard, he transferred to

Faulkner High where they have more services, and the other guy dropped out of school and is working at a gas station."

"Wow," Dixie breathes. "They really take care of their friends."

"Yeah," Dolly says. "And their enemies."

"The girl was Lacey?" I ask. I remember her telling me about how great it was to be a Darling Doll on my first day of school. Now I understand her loyalty to them, despite her less than desirable experience as a Darling Doll. Still, they took her side over their buddies with no proof, and that has to mean a hell of a lot to any girl in her situation. Because the sad truth is, most guys would just call her a slut and be done with it.

"Yeah," Dolly says. "She's a bitch, but she has her reasons."

"I guess you're not going this year, then," Dixie says.

"Oh, I'm going," Dolly says. "I always go, and it's my senior year, so this is my last one. Skipping it would be like skipping homecoming or prom. I may be leaving Faulkner, but I'm a southern gal at heart. I love tradition. Drape me in mums to the floor and crown me queen all day long."

"Are you going?" Dixie asks, turning to me.

"I don't know," I say. "Devlin asked me to go, but now that I can't leave my room without my family knowing, I'm not sure I'll be able to sneak out."

"I'll take you," Dolly says.

"I don't have an invite," Dixie says, rubbing a velvet teddy bear on the thigh of her pajama pants.

"I'm your invite," says Dolly, who is wearing a pink satin nightdress with a fuzzy white belt. "Both of you."

"Thanks," I say. "But my brothers would do what Royal is doing now. They'd follow me wherever I went, and when they realized it was a Darling party…"

"I'll go," Dixie says, shoving a pecan sandy into her mouth and glancing nervously between us, like she thinks one of us is going to say she can't go.

"Cool," Dolly says to Dixie before turning to me. "Let me know if you change your mind. You have my messenger handle, if they haven't taken your laptop."

"Thanks," I say. "But I'll probably just stay in and have a glass of champagne with my brothers."

"If you're sure," Dolly says, sounding doubtful.

"This is more my kind of party than a big, drunken orgy," I say, gesturing around Dixie's bedroom. "And speaking of, what's up with you and the twins, Dolly? Are they still treating you right?"

She shrugs. "I haven't talked to them since break started. Baron was talking to another girl, anyway. He didn't say who, but it's not like we were ever official. And Duke… I mean, he's fun, and I needed that. But he's a freshman, and I'm a senior. I'm graduating, and even if I didn't leave town, I'd be off at college next year."

"Yeah, that makes sense," I say. I'm glad she's not coming to me asking why he didn't call, which I had to deal with enough at my old school.

"What about you and Devlin?" Dixie asks. "He's graduating, too, and you'll be in school two more years."

I can't help but smile when I remember his promise to me. "He's going to school here," I say.

"Awww," she says, covering her heart and looking at me with puppy dog eyes. "That's sweet."

There are two colleges in Faulkner—a small university and a tiny liberal arts college. I'm sure Devlin could get a football scholarship to the state university, but he said he wanted to be near me. I might feel bad about him staying if his family weren't already insistent that he stay in Faulkner, anyway. I feel worse about the fact that he spent half his final season on the bench because of my brothers. He played in the last game, but I know it hurt his chances of getting a scholarship to a bigger school. Faulkner might look the other way about a scandal, but the whole world won't.

"He's a rich man in his own right now," Dolly says. "He could go anywhere, even if he didn't play football."

"Wasn't he already rich?" I ask, picking up the remote to scroll through the streaming options on Dixie's TV.

"Well, sure," Dolly says. "But he had a really big Christmas gift. You haven't talked to him?"

"No," I say, turning to her. "What happened?"

"He's eighteen, so Grampa Darling made him a full trustee of his trust fund. He basically just inherited four million dollars."

"Holy shit," Dixie squeals. "How do you know that?"

Dolly shifts, glancing guiltily at me. "I was there. Our families do a Christmas Eve dinner together."

"I saw that on the news," Dixie moans. "It looks so glamorous."

"Let me guess," I say. "He's supposed to use the money for your wedding?"

"No," Dolly says. "To buy a home for us. I'm sorry, Crystal. You know I don't want that, and neither does he. He's crazy about you."

"I know." I trust Devlin completely, and I know that he loves me, but it's hard not to be a little jealous of the way his family treats her. She's a part of his world in a way I will never be. Even if we got married, I'd always be the Italian chick from New York who stole his heart, not a real lady, not a tried and true southerner who belongs in the Darling family.

"So, what movie?" Dixie asks, clearing her throat to break the silence.

"I vote Hallmark," Dolly says, and we all agree. It's nice to sink into something so cute and perfect, something utterly predictable but where I know everything will work out in the end without a single trouble remaining. If only life were that simple.

If only I could see a way for any of this to work out so that we're all happy. Hell, at this point I'd settle for half of us being happy. Right now, I'm not sure any of us will end up with what we want. How can I even begin to make a choice between the boy I love and my entire family? Or maybe the choice is simple. Maybe it's a choice between my family or myself.

Maybe the decision is not so hard after all.

# twenty-four

*Crystal*

*King was right. Love makes you weak. But he's never felt it, so there's something he doesn't know. Love also makes you strong. It makes you invincible. No matter what my family does to break my spirit, they cannot break my heart. It belongs to Devlin. It is filled with a love that burns hotter than molten lava, fiercer than the darkest hate. Nothing can stand in the way of a love like ours. It incinerates everything in its path.*

"You're going out?" I ask, looking from one brother to the next. The four of them stand in King's room, staring back at me with expressions varying from resentment to guilt. "I came to ask if you wanted to watch the ball drop in Times Square later, but obviously you have other plans."

"We've got a few things to take care of," King says. "Dad will be here with you."

I sigh, hugging myself and glancing at the window, where once again, sheets of rain are pouring down. "So, on New Year's Eve, I get to stay home with my dad like a loser while you all go out? After you told me I can't go out with *my* friends?"

"It's not like that," King says. "We're not going to party."

"Let her come," Royal says. "She might like it."

"You might be a criminal yet," Duke says, throwing an arm around my neck. They do look like criminals—or a gang. All four of them are wearing black from head to toe.

"What are you guys up to?" I ask, narrowing my eyes at them.

"Nothing you need to worry about," King says. "Go watch TV with Dad."

"You know, you're all a bunch of hypocrites," I snap. "You *say* I'm one of you now, that I'm an adult, you respect me, and I'm your equal, but you don't treat me like it. Even after I proved myself to you, none of you took me seriously.

364

You just shove me aside, leave me to hang out with our parents, and go off to have fun like you did in New York."

"Crystal," King says, his voice stern. "You don't know what you're talking about."

"Yes, I do," I say. "I'm not stupid or naïve anymore, King. I know what you guys do. I know Dad's in the mafia."

"He's just an earner," King says. "And this isn't about that."

"Well, he's connected, and you're going to work for Uncle Al. You told me that, but you won't let me actually do anything. I'm older than the twins and the same age as Royal. The only reason you won't let me go is because I'm a girl."

"Exactly," he says. "We don't want you getting hurt."

"You don't think it hurts to watch you go off like a family and treat me like I'm not part of it?"

"Let her tag along," Royal says. "Once will be enough for her to see she doesn't have the stomach for it."

King looks back and forth between us. "It's no place for a girl," he says at last.

"I'm not a little girl," I say. "I'm a woman. Whatever you're doing, I'd rather do that than sit at home with Dad pretending everything is fine. I know it's not, and I'm old enough to handle the truth. Tell me what happened to you, Royal. Let me go tonight—wherever you're going. Stop cutting me out of our own family."

Royal's eyes are dark and deep as infinity as they lock on mine, and for a second, I think he's going to tell me.

"We're going to take the town tonight," King says. "It's not safe for you."

"And it's safe for you?" I demand.

"I vote to let her join," Baron says. "You never know when you'll need a girl to get shit done. No one expects it. I think she'd be a good asset."

"Yeah," Duke says. "It never hurts to know how to cause a little havoc. Let this be her first lesson in mayhem."

King looks between his three brothers and me. All four of us against him. Still, if he said no, we wouldn't have a choice. What King dictates is law.

"You're part of this family, so if you really want to come along, I suppose you can see how we do things. But you stay in the car where it's safe no matter what. Understand?"

"Okay," I say, nodding. Though I remember Devlin telling me the same thing when we went to get Royal from the Midnight Swans' office. Hell if I'm going to sit back and let things happen. Just because I'm a girl doesn't mean I have to sit on the sidelines of life and watch.

King tosses me a black sweater to put over my white shirt. "Put that on and let's go."

Downstairs, Dad is pouring himself a drink at the wet bar. Unlike Mom, his drinking is controlled, calculated, and never interferes with his work. That one drink might last him 'til midnight.

"You're staying in?" I ask, glancing at the large screen TV mounted on the wall, the reporter showing New Year's festivities in some other country where it's already past midnight.

Dad wraps a strong around me. "Of course we're staying in, Sweetheart," he says. "A quiet night in will be a nice change from the parties in New York. That was always your mother's thing."

I suddenly feel bad for wanting to go with my brothers and leaving him here alone.

"Actually, Dad, Crystal's coming with us," King says. "Don't worry, she'll stay in the car the whole time."

Dad looks from me to my brothers, surprise evident in his expression. No one thinks I can do whatever they're doing. "You really want to go out?" he asks.

*Now* he's concerned about what I want. I nod, looking up at him, that stupid, childish part of me still aching for him to approve of my decision, to tell me it's right.

"We might need a getaway driver," Duke says with a grin.

The irony is lost on Dad. He hesitates, then gives a nod and drops his arm from around me. "I thought you were more of a homebody like me, but I guess I can't keep my little girl from growing up forever."

King checks his phone. "It's time to go, Crys. You coming?"

I look up at Dad. "Do you want me to stay here with you?"

"No, go on and have a good time," he says. "I've got some proposals to look over, anyway."

368

"Okay," I say, turning away from Dad, a hollow feeling inside my chest. It feels incomplete, as if there's something else I'm supposed to say to him. But I know that if I stayed home with him, he'd spend most of the evening working, anyway. Only at midnight, he'd stop for five minutes to watch the ball drop.

"We'll be back after midnight," King says to him.

"Don't come home until you've got the job done," Dad says, clasping his shoulder.

A little shiver of trepidation goes through me when King agrees, but I don't have time to ask. I'm swept up in the clomping feet of my brothers, in the twins' excitement that buzzes through the air around us like an electric current.

We climb into the Range Rover and take off into the stormy night without a word. I try to figure out the reasoning behind the car and our positions. If we were going for stealth, we would have taken Baron's Tesla. King's Evija is too small for us to fit comfortably, not to mention I can make out boxes of different sizes all laid out behind the seat. Duke's Hummer is the biggest, but maybe we needed quicker pickup. And then there's the fact that King is in the passenger seat. King never sits in the passenger seat. If all of us are in a car together, he drives. He's the driver, the leader, the king.

A few minutes later, we pull into a circular gravel drive, one I remember from the day I saw Mabel here in her little Prius and thought she was the help. The day we came looking for Royal. I lean forward, peering at the darkened house through the pouring rain. My heart begins to hammer. "What are we doing?"

"Watch and learn, baby sis," Baron says, wrapping an arm around me and squeezing. Then he hops out with the others. Since there's no one here, I figure it's safe enough to get out and see what's going on. None of my brothers argue when I step to the back of the car, where Duke has lifted the trunk of the car. Inside, I can see a massive stock of brightly colored boxes with cartoon pictures of explosions on them, along with several black tubes.

"We didn't even have to get these illegally," Duke says, peeling plastic off a large, rectangular box. "You can buy fireworks right off the side of the road in this state. Happy New Year, bitches!"

He and Baron run toward the house in the rain. Royal selects a different one, and King takes a fourth. I hear shattering glass, and a whoop, and Duke comes running back toward the car, his eyes full of wild, manic glee. A second later, light flares behind one of the big picture windows. Cracks and bangs echo through the night as the fireworks explode inside the house. More shattering glass, more streams of fiery light, more noise. Baron and Duke grab me and stuff me back in the car, the other two dive into the front seat, and the tires spit gravel as we skid around the drive and shoot back down it.

So, that's what they're doing. Up to some vandalism and mischief, the kind they did in New York. At least, I assume it's the kind of thing they did. But then I remember Devlin saying this was where his parents grew up. I remember Dixie saying the party was at another one of Grampa Darling's houses—but no adults would be there.

"Was anyone in that house?" I ask when the chorus of whoops, panting breaths, and laughter have subsided.

"I fucking hope so," Royal says. "I hope it burns to the ground with him inside it. He deserves worse."

Suddenly, it doesn't feel like such a harmless prank. Suddenly, I wish I hadn't come. Because the night is just getting started, and the trunk is full of fireworks.

I may not like the Darling patriarch, may even wish he was gone, but not like that. I wouldn't cry over the asshole dying of a heart attack, but there's nothing honorable about burning an old man in his sleep.

"What now?" I ask, my hands shaking as I pin them between my knees.

"Now we hit every other Darling house in Faulkner," Royal says, his voice low and laced with hatred.

"You're going to kill someone," I protest.

"Nah, see, that's why we make the loud noises," Baron explains. "So they can get their asses out while the houses go up in flames. See, the funny thing about the fire department in a small town is that they only have a couple trucks. Which means they can't save them all."

"Those assholes laughed in our faces when we told them we were going to take over the school, the town, even their secret society. Guess they won't be laughing tomorrow."

"The Darlings may have run this town for the last 200 years," King says. "But there's a new rule in Faulkner now. Welcome to the Dolce reign."

"While they're all living in rentals and fighting with their insurance companies, our dad will take over," Baron says. "No more obstruction on his building site. No more assholes trying to keep us from owning this place or setting up shop. Preston's and Devlin's dads are already facing trials. Now it's just a matter of time."

"This isn't right," I say, my head spinning. Why was I so stupid as to come on this outing? They might hurt someone. They might get hurt. There's a reason I spent the first sixteen years of my life hiding my head in the sand. I can't face the thought of losing one of them, but more than that, I don't want to know what they're capable of. They were right—I don't have the stomach for this. I don't want to watch my beloved brothers laugh and celebrate burning someone's house, a house full of history and memories from childhood. I don't want to hear the callous, casual way they dismiss the possibility that someone might die, as if it's not even worth worrying about. As if they're monsters who wouldn't worry about taking a life to get what they want.

Maybe I didn't want to know the truth about my family because it's an ugly truth. Somewhere deep inside, I always knew, though. That's why I hid from it. I didn't want to see it because then I'd have to admit that my brothers aren't just boys doing what boys do. Every one of my brothers is capable of things, has probably done things, I can't even imagine—and don't want to.

Baron, with his calculating, brilliant mind, the kind of mind that might see nuclear division and create the atom bomb. Duke is the Joker, a boy with an unhinged kind of hedonism who takes what he wants with no regard for anyone else. Royal, with his brooding anger, who knows it's wrong but does it anyway. Does having a conscience make him better or worse than the others?

And then there's strong King, our leader, trying to save us all from ourselves without noticing he hasn't saved himself, that he's become a man obsessed with his ambition to be the hero, to be the best, to take the world for us no matter what it costs.

Or... Maybe it's not his ambition at all. Because there are two more people in our family. One who had enough and checked out a long time ago, even before she had a chance to wash her hands of us. Who lives in her own little Margaritaville in her mind. And though I can't hold her blameless in that decision—she chose to bring us into this world—I can't hold her completely at fault either.

Then there's Daddy. The man I put on a pedestal all my life, who bought my love easily with lies as sweet as his candy, who put a laptop in my hands and a credit card under my nose, who said, "Go buy yourself a nice pair of shoes, the newest iPhone, the designer dress you'll wear once. Don't worry about how much it costs, sweetheart. Only the best for my baby girl. I'll always take care of you."

And what has he done to take care of me?

He's taken care of his own ambition. He sheltered me, but I no longer know if it was for my own benefit. Did he only want to hide his own actions? Or was there something more sinister? I remember what Devlin said about arranged marriages, that surely the mafia still had them. Is that why he was so obsessed with keeping me pure and innocent? Not for my safety, but so he could auction me off to some stranger, the bidder who could offer him not the most money, but the most status?

After all, aren't we all pawns in a game he orchestrated to feed his ego and his insatiable hunger for revenge against a slight to his pride? My brothers are doing this not to help themselves, but for him. They've already made the football team. They've gotten the parking spot. They've even gotten the Darlings to stop fighting them, thanks to me. They're exactly where they want to be at school. This has gone beyond us. Why would my brothers care about taking down an old family, a bunch of adults? Burning their houses, ruining their name in a town? This isn't for us. This is for Dad, who sits at home sipping a scotch and watching the ball drop while we do his dirty work. He's the gamemaster.

"You don't have to do this," I blurt out as we pull up to a house and the charge of excitement builds again.

"Suck it, Preston," Duke whoops, hopping out of the car without listening to what I have to say.

"You have no reason to ruin anyone's house, let alone their lives," I say, rushing ahead even though they're not paying attention to me anymore. They're caught in the madness of mayhem, the seductive danger of their plan. "What did Preston's dad ever do to you? For that matter, what did Preston? You broke his arm. You took his spot on the team. You ruined his future. Isn't that enough?"

This time, Royal stays in the car, keeps it running. There are lights on upstairs in some of the bedrooms. I remember Preston's sister, all skin and bones, clinging to Chase's arm. Is she in there? Is he? Will they get out?

"You have to stop," I yell, lunging for the door.

Royal taps the lock, trapping me inside. "You wanted the truth," he says, his voice cold. "You said you could handle it. We're only on the second house. We've got a half dozen more. And miles to go before we sleep, miles to go before we sleep." He chuckles, the coldness of it sending a chill down my spine.

"You don't have to do this," I say. "Why are you hurting people for Dad? You don't even like Dad. You've always known the truth about him, haven't you? You're the one who doesn't buy into this, Royal. Why are you going along with it?"

The other three come barreling into the car, Baron pushing me back across the seat and sandwiching me between him and Duke. Trapping me.

Royal takes off, peeling away from the house, but not before I hear screams as the door flies open. I have only a single glimpse of a woman's figure silhouetted in the doorframe before we're gone.

"Did you see that lady jump like a bomb went off when we busted the window?" Duke asks, laughing as he falls back against the seat, his muscles vibrating with adrenaline beside mine.

"Two down," King says. "Five to go."

Five. Maybe I can convince them to stop before they do them all.

"You're going to get arrested," I try. "When every single Darling house gets targeted, they'll know it was us."

"No family gets that powerful without making enemies along the way," King says.

"There's no reason for it," I plead. "You've already won. Let Dad fight his own battles."

"Weren't you the one going on about family earlier?" Duke asks. "We stick together, sis. We're Dolces."

"Yeah we are!" Baron says, reaching across me to slap hands with Duke as we arrive at the next one. There's a gate to the neighborhood, and at first I'm relieved, thinking maybe this house will be spared. But Royal punches in the code with his gloved hand, and we pull through.

"They'll have your car on camera," I say, trying desperately to deter them. "If they know this one is you, they'll figure out they were all you."

"Don't worry so much, little sis," Duke says, squeezing my knee. "Dad's made friends in town."

They're out of the car, shoving me back in when I try to follow. I watch them run across the lawn in the rain, juvenile delinquents dressed in black sneaking through the night. Thunder rumbles overhead drowning my objections. Glass shatters. Volleys of explosions follow. One of them escapes through the broken window, and my brothers duck, racing for the car and piling in, high from the thrill. Fireworks paint the inside of the house with smoke and streams of fire.

"You're fucking crazy," I yell as the car shoots down the street. "What if there are kids in those houses? What if one of those hits a person?"

"Not a person," Royal says quietly, his voice undercutting the adrenaline-fueled chatter of my brothers. "A Darling."

# twenty-five

*Crystal*

By the time we pull up at the next house, my head is spinning, and I think I'll be sick. Royal and King change places, and my brothers hop the fence and run up a long driveway, disappearing into the darkness. "Make them stop," I beg King. "They're going to get hurt. I know you don't want that, King. You're not even going to be here next year. You won't have to deal with it when the Darlings come for revenge. And why do you need to make Dad king in a town you won't even live in? What does it matter? Can't we please just go home? You've made your point."

King drops his forehead to the steering wheel. "I told you to stay home, Crystal. I told you not to get involved, that you wouldn't like what we do."

"Fine," I say. "Take me home. Hell, let me out of the car and I'll walk home. I don't want any part of this."

"But you are a part of it," he says. "This is who we are, Crystal. Not just us. You, too."

Before I can answer, my brothers are leaping over the wrought iron gate. Lightning flashes, blindingly bright, silhouetting them as they come for the car like thieves in the night. I shrink back, stifling a cry when they pile in beside me.

"They're on to us," Royal says, pulling off his black stocking cap and shaking the water from it. "Let's get Devlin's next. His dad's a pussy. He won't fight back."

"No," I say, lurching across Baron and grabbing for the door handle. "He helped you, Royal. If it weren't for him, we never would have found you and gotten you out. Don't hurt him."

"Devlin's not even there," Baron says, dropping me back onto my seat in the middle. "Calm down."

"Mr. Darling is a good man," I plead. I don't know when I started crying, but my face is streaked with tears, and I can barely choke out the words.

"What the fuck is wrong with you?" Royal snaps. "Does Devlin's dick move like a snake, or what's got you so hypnotized you believe their brainwashing?"

"Want us to drop you off with Dad?" King asks, pulling up to the end of Devlin's driveway. He switches off the lights and turns the car around, so we're facing the exit to the neighborhood, as Duke reaches behind us to grab giant boxes of what might as well be dynamite. Lightning licks the sky again, lighting up the beautiful old house behind the rows of bowing trees over the walkway.

"No," Royal says. "She said she wanted to see, so she's seeing. Maybe when it's over she'll understand what being part of this family really means."

He gets out of the car, slamming the door hard. Duke hops out, but Baron grabs me when I try to dive out after him. "I'll stay," Baron says. "This one shouldn't take more than two people."

I kick and scratch at him, screaming for him to let me go, but he pins my arms down and holds me there, forcing me to watch or close my eyes. I don't want to see the door where Mr. Darling kept his evil father out, where he stood up to the most powerful man in Faulkner to defend his choice to let the cops search his house—to give *us* peace of mind. I can't watch the lightning light up my brothers as they skip up to the front windows, full of boyish glee, high on danger and the urge to destroy, to wreak havoc on the world that gave them a mother who can't be bothered to give them the discipline they need, a father who orchestrates evil and hands out approval when they carry it out, and enough free passes to make them feel invincible.

I can't hate any of them. I pity them. I weep for them, and for the unsuspecting town my father has unleashed them upon. I weep for Mr. Darling and his silly little wife, and I pray they get out unharmed. I weep for Devlin, for the grief he will feel when he sees what they've done to his home, the house where he's lived since childhood with the balcony where he's stood gazing at me so many times. And I weep for myself, because I am part of this family, because it's in my blood like chocolate, and I can't escape it.

And I rage for Daddy, who's probably standing at his darkened study window with a drink in his hand, watching the house of his enemy lit up from within like a bomb.

By the time Royal and Duke return, I'm sobbing uncontrollably in Baron's arms. No one speaks as we pull away, the car creeping out of our neighborhood with an unwilling passenger, like the truck that took Royal.

"You did it," I say, sinking back against the seat, spent. "You set up the whole kidnapping, didn't you, Royal?"

"You don't know what you're talking about."

"But I do, don't I?" I press. "Dad would do anything to take down the Darlings. Even use his own children."

"Fuck you, Crystal," he says. "Anything I did, I did for you. I didn't know you'd turn traitor in a week. I thought you were stronger than that. Better than that. I thought you were a Dolce."

"You really did," I whisper to myself, horror growing inside me. "That's why you wouldn't tell me the truth about what happened."

"Fine," Royal snaps. "Here's the truth. Your precious *Daddy* planned the whole thing. Yeah. He was going to get the Darlings framed for kidnapping me. He said that if I didn't go along with it, they'd go after you. And you know what? I shouldn't have bothered. Because when they went after you, what did you do? You bent over and let them fuck you in the ass."

"That's not what happened," I whisper, but I'm too sickened by his words to put any conviction in mine.

"Tell her the rest," King says. "Tell her what happened."

"They put me in that sick old man's house," Royal says. "But he found me before the cops did." He turns to the window and goes quiet, that brooding, sudden silence he falls into lately.

*No*, I think. *Mabel found him. And she told her grandfather.*

I can't speak, though. I feel too sick. I swallow over and over, the only thing I can do to keep the bile down.

"That's when they took him to the Midnight Swans," Duke says, taking over from Royal. He leans forward to squeeze my twin's shoulder. "That's why we're going to take the Swans and everything else from them. Just like they took it from him."

"Who put you in Devlin's attic?" I whisper.

No one speaks, but they don't have to. I already know the answer. I don't want to, but I do. I remember Royal whispering the words through his cracked lips.

*Don't make me move again.*

That's what he said. He called for Dad just before that. Dad, who found him almost dead, and instead of helping him, he kept going with his plan to frame the Darlings. Instead of getting Royal help when he so desperately, obviously needed it, Dad and probably my uncles used the time while Devlin's dad was at a football game to move Royal to his house. He might not be responsible for the battered state we found my brother in, but he's fucking responsible for plenty.

What if those few minutes, those few hours, had cost Royal his life? Would Dad have stopped then? Will he ever stop?

If he would sacrifice his own son in his quest for revenge, would he even blink before taking Devlin's?

Before I can form into words the fury raging inside me, we pull up into a gravel lot beside a house I recognize. It's the one where Devlin left me after that first party. Colt's house. I beg my brothers to stop, but my pleas fall on deaf ears. They're out of the car, slamming the door against me when I try to climb out. I fall silent, watching in stunned horror as they light the fuses, ready to torch the sixth house of the evening.

From the parking area at the end of the house, I can see both the front porch of the house and the back deck, where the wooden bar sits silent in the rain. There's a patio set at the end of the bar closest to us, with a huge umbrella protecting it from the rain. I almost miss the figure sitting in one of the chairs. She's so small, so motionless, she blends into the shadows. But a flash of lightning illuminates her tan coat.

Mabel Darling is sitting outside. She doesn't move. She watches my brothers light the fuse and toss the first block of fireworks through a window. Before they can toss another, the front door flies open, and a far more imposing figure is framed in the light. A figure holding a gun.

I scream, diving toward them, trying to scramble across Baron's lap. King shouts a curse and explodes out his door, sprinting for our brothers. I can't hear the man yelling through the drumming of the rain on the roof, but I can see his face in the light from the windows. I can see the anger, the defensive instinct. And I can see the glimmer of raindrops streaking the barrel of the gun as he raises it. I can see the flash at the muzzle when he fires just as King jumps in front of our brothers.

I scream again, and Baron shoves me roughly back and jumps out of the car. I don't care what they told me. My brother is hurt. That's all I think as I leap from the car and run across the gravel. I don't think about the rain or the danger, that I could be shot. I don't feel the bite of the gravel as I fall on my knees beside King while two of my brothers vault over the railing and tackle Colt's dad. I don't care about him. I only think about King. My brother, my protector, my king.

He's kneeling on the gravel holding his side. "I'm fine," he grits out, his breathing shallow. "I just slipped on the gravel."

"You're shot," I snap, grabbing his arm and draping it over my shoulders. "You're not fucking fine."

"It's just a flesh wound," he says through a ragged breath. Another shot sounds, and I freeze, my blood running cold.

I hear the sounds of fists hitting flesh, of bones hitting the deck as they roll around fighting. My mind is racing, but I try to stay calm. I can only do so much at once.

"Let me help you to the car," I say to King, gripping his arm over my shoulder and lumbering to my feet.

"Come on," Baron says, appearing beside us. "Let's get out of here."

Supporting his weight, I help King into the backseat of the car. By the time he's in, the rest of them are, too, and the car skids in the gravel as Royal floors it. I glance up in time to see that Mabel hasn't moved. She sits watching as we disappear behind the trees.

"Did anyone else get hit?" I ask, peeling King's black sweater off over my head and handing it to him. He balls it up and clenches it to his side, doubling over halfway and holding it in place with his elbow.

"No," Royal says from the driver's seat. "He fired a shot when I was trying to get the gun, but it didn't hit anything. I got his gun away before he could shoot any more of us."

"Fuck," Duke swears, rolling down his window and spitting out into the rain. "I think he busted one of my teeth in half when he hit me with it."

"We need to get King to the hospital," I say.

"No hospital," he says. "It barely grazed me."

"What?" I ask. "King, that's crazy! Someone shot you."

"Which is why it would be crazy to go to a hospital," he says.

"We've got one more to do, and then we'll go home," Royal says.

"What the fuck is wrong with you guys?" I demand, my voice edged with hysteria. "King is fucking shot! Go to the hospital!"

"I'm going to have to get used to this in my new line of work," King says. "Drop the last ones off and let's go home. I wouldn't mind lying down."

"You guys are crazy," I yell. "You're all fucking crazy. What is wrong with this family?"

"I'll tell you what's wrong with me," Duke says, spitting blood out the window. "I'm missing half a tooth. I can't believe that asshole pistol-whipped me!"

"Oh my god," I say, lying my head back on the seat and closing my eyes. I can't deal with this. I don't know what to do. I've been through too many emotions tonight, the shock and horror of what they were doing, learning the truth about Royal's kidnapping, and now this insanity. I just... I'm going to lose it if I have to listen to this insanity much longer. They're like Dad. Nothing will be enough until every Darling house is burned to the ground, until every Darling is nothing but ash.

*One house left*, I tell myself. That's my only consolation. One more.

Then I can go home and figure out what to do. I have to get out of here. Somehow, I have to get out of the mental asylum that is my family. If I don't, I'm going to go as crazy as all of them. I can already feel it bubbling beneath the surface, the urge to break into hysterical laughter and never stop.

Ten minutes later, Royal swears under his breath, and the car slows. I lift my head to see a narrow, one-lane wooden bridge in front of us. A white wooden frame covers the bridge, although it's not enclosed or roofed. Below the bridge, a gushing brown river of water churns past, and around it, darkness and shadowy woods without a house in sight. On the far end of the bridge, two cars sit blocking the road, their front ends angled together, their headlights bathing the bridge in light and glaring into our faces, blinding us to anything but streaks of driving rain.

"Hit 'em," Duke says.

"I don't think I can get enough speed going across the bridge to knock them out of the way," Royal says. The bridge looks sketchy as fuck, with wide boards forming a path for each tire on top of the regular wooden slats that form the floor of the bridge. What kind of bridge is made of wood?

"If they're waiting for us, they're probably armed," I say, reaching forward to grip my twin's shoulder. "Can we just go home? Please. You've more than made your point. I don't want to die tonight, and I'm not planning to bury a brother, either. King can't even fight."

"Bullshit," King growls. "Give me the gun. They can try to come at me."

"The gun?" I ask incredulously. "Since when do you fight with guns?"

Royal's always fought, but he does the underground, bare-knuckle kind of fighting. I was horrified when he said the guys who took him had guns. Yes, my parents have a pistol for protection, but I've never touched a gun in my life. We're rich people from New York. We have security at the front door for a reason.

"I got it off the guy who shot King," Royal says. "Would you rather I'd left it on him?"

"Can we just go home? Please?"

"I bet it's Devlin," Royal grumbles, gripping the wheel tighter. "I bet it's him and his asshole cousins. If they're looking for a fight, we brought it."

"No, no, no," I say as Royal shifts into gear and revs the engine.

Duke grabs me before I can do something stupid like lunge over the console and try to wrestle control from Royal. My breath catches in my throat as Royal's foot hits the gas.

"What if it's a trap?" I gasp out. "What if the bridge collapses under us?"

"There's only one road here," Baron says with complete confidence. "They had to drive across already."

The Range Rover lumbers onto the rickety wood, and all I can do is grip the seat and try not to hyperventilate as nightmare images flash through my mind. It's been raining all month, and though the river below is probably small during most of the year, it's swollen and rushing now. If we go in, we're not getting out.

I'm not going to die this way. I'm done with this mess, with the whole fucked up feud, with the violence and the crazy. I open my mouth, take a deep breath, and make my voice heard. "Let me out," I scream at the top of my lungs. "Let me out of the fucking car right now!"

For a second, a shocked silence fills the car, leaving a vacuum in the space my huge voice just filled. My brothers aren't used to me yelling. Demanding.

And then Royal presses harder on the gas, and Duke holds me tighter. There's no way out.

Is this how it ends? Trapped in a fucking car with my insane brothers because they can't let go of Dad's ambition to win, to be the best, any more than he can. I'm so sick of it I could scream. I didn't want any part of it, from the moment we stepped through the doors of Willow Heights. But I fought for it just as they did, for them, the same way they fight Dad's battles for him. But I'm done. I'm so fucking done. I'm not going to die this way.

I'm done putting my family first. I'm done being an obedient little puppet for my father, done being smothered by my brothers. I'm done putting their needs and wants and petty fights before my own safety, my own life. They're not keeping me safe. They're dragging me down with them. And this time, I choose me.

# twenty-six

*Crystal*

Duke whoops as I feel the drop, and my stomach lurches into my throat in the split second before our tires hit smooth, solid asphalt. But it's enough.

Enough to send my heart blasting into my throat, jackhammering inside my chest.

Royal doesn't barrel into the two cars. He's not here to wreck them the way he did Devlin's old car. He has places to go this time, and nothing's going to stop him. He spins the wheel, the tires biting into the shoulder as he tries to skirt the two cars before they can right themselves to face us head on.

The tires skid, sinking into the soft mud of the shoulder before the car slides to a stop. Royal curses and tries to gas the car, but the tires only spin in the melting earth.

"Let me the fuck out," I yell again, grabbing the door handle and jerking so hard I think it will break off in my fingers.

Royal hits the button, and the locks release. I spill out into the rain, my whole body shaking, my heart racing, my mind numbed with panic. Royal was the one who always calmed me, but now he does the opposite. Now, I have to calm myself, and I haven't mastered the art yet.

My twin gets out of the car, and I turn to him. "What the fuck is wrong with you?" I scream. "You would have sacrificed all of us for a taste of someone else's revenge?"

I watch the conflicting emotions flicker across my brother's face, lit by the headlights of the three cars. Anger. Defensiveness. Guilt.

"Baron said we were safe."

"You didn't know that," I answer. "You don't know what could have happened. You could have killed us all,

Royal. I'm done. I'm so fucking done with all of this. With all of you."

"Crystal…" he starts. But I never find out what he was going to say. A car door slams behind me, and Royal's eyes snap to the road behind me. The cold, hardness returns to his face, and he straightens, glaring over my shoulder at the person approaching.

"You okay?" Devlin asks, moving up behind me and putting a protective arm around me.

Suddenly, everything in me breaks. I'm so relieved that he's here that I can't stop the tears from rising to my eyes. I just want the comfort of him, the safety of this boy who was once a threat and is now my refuge. I want to lie in bed with him on a Friday night and laugh and talk and love. His warm arms around me are everything I need right now, everything I've always needed. He may have hurt me before, but he is not the danger anymore.

I turn and bury my head in his shoulder.

"You're okay," he murmurs, this time not asking.

"Get your hands off our sister," King growls behind me.

I want to hold onto Devlin, but I know I can't right now. I have to be strong now, not fall apart, not let him do the dirty work for me. I force myself to lift my head, drawing strength from the firm certainty of his grip.

I turn back to the Rover, where King sits inside, the back door still open from when I jumped out. "Get back in the car, King," I say. "You're injured. You're going to get yourself killed, and what good will you be then?"

The twins come around the front end, but I only look at King. I can't see his injury, but even in the darkness, lit only by headlights and the occasional flicker of lightning, I can see that his face is stark white. I can see blood covering the hand that holds the sweater to his side. He starts to get out of the car, then grimaces, gripping the door and dropping his head to draw a breath.

Behind me, I hear two more car doors slam. My brothers were right. The Darling cousins came to meet us, to defend their territory from our invasion. This must be the last house, the one with the party. It strikes me then that they're doing what the Darlings did twenty years ago. I heard it from the Dolce side that time. Now, I can see it with my own eyes. I can see that things aren't so simple. I can only hope my brothers aren't consumed by revenge for the rest of their lives. This has gone on long enough. It ends here, tonight.

"She's right," Baron says quietly to King. "Just sit tight for a minute, and we'll get you home to clean that up."

King nods, his lips pinched together so hard they've lost all color. I know it will kill him later, that he'll consider it a weakness that he couldn't fight. But he has the sense to know that he'd only get in the way, that he would put our brothers in danger if he tried to fight like that. He slides back on the seat, and Baron closes the door and turns to us.

And then it's the seven of us.

Colt and Preston fall in on Devlin's either side. I guess Colt's a fighter when he has to be. Royal stands at the driver's side door of the Range Rover. Duke and Baron stand next to him, my three brothers facing the Darlings.

And then there's me, standing in the middle, not wanting a fight at all. It's just as it's been all year, but now it's more than that, too. Now I know more. Now I am more.

"Stop fighting," I say, raising my voice to be heard over the driving rain. "It doesn't have to be this way."

"But it is this way," Preston says from my left.

"You heard my brother," Royal says slowly. "Take your hands off our sister."

"Whoa there," Colt says behind me. "Guess it's time to bring out the big guns."

A second later, I see what he's talking about. Royal lifts his hand slowly, and my heart lurches in my chest. The pistol points straight at my chest.

Devlin tries to move past me, but I grab his hand and step the same way, blocking him from Royal with my body.

"Get behind me," Devlin growls, but I ignore him.

All my focus is on my brother, on the deadly weapon in his hands. "What the fuck are you doing?" I scream at him. "You're pointing a gun at me, Royal. At your own twin sister. Are you really going to kill me for this? For some fight that's not even yours?"

"I'm not pointing a gun at you," he says. "I'm pointing it at your boyfriend. You just happen to be standing in the way, or he'd be dead on the ground right now."

"We're all carrying," Devlin says behind me, his voice calm and even, though I can hear the strain in it. He's pissed as fuck that I'm in his way. "You really don't want to mess with us."

"Don't you dare pull your guns," I snap at him.

He grabs me and tries to pull me back, but I twist away from him, panic tearing through me. I'm the only thing stopping Royal from killing him. I wrench away and dive toward Royal, my heart slamming in my chest and my whole body shaking.

"Royal, put the gun down," I scream, dodging aside when Devlin swipes for me. He doesn't stop until I reach Royal, standing in front of the gun so close that the muzzle presses to my chest. I widen my stance and spread my arms, as if my little body can protect all three of the Darlings, as if it could stop a bullet.

"Crystal," Devlin yells, his voice harsh with panic. "What the fuck are you doing?"

For a second, no one else moves or speaks. I just put a gun to my own heart, and I can feel it racing wildly, careening out of control at the reckless, insane thing I just did, but I don't pull back.

"What I should have done a long time ago," I say, my eyes locked on Royal's. "I'm standing up to my family."

Royal stares at me in shock before yanking the gun down, pointing it at the ground. "So, that's how it is," he says slowly, a slight quiver in his voice. "You're on their side now."

I open my mouth to protest, to tell him that of course I'm not on their side. I'm Crystal Dolce, a flawless Dolce Daughter, a proud Italian, forged with a steel spine and blood thicker than chocolate. This is who I am, who I've always been. Family comes first—always. My twin is my life, and he's in pain, and all I want to do is protect him. How could I take anyone else's side?

Or maybe that's just who I've been told I am. Now I can see my family loyalty for what it is. Something demanded of me, not earned. Now I see the truth. I was too hard on my brothers. They're not monsters. They're just kids, like me. They're kids who have to believe what they do because if they stopped believing, they'd have to admit the truth of who they are. And admitting that truth is too horrible, too painful, for them to bear. So they go on with the charade, keep playing the game, keep letting the gamemaster tell them their next move.

I'm done with the game. They're never going to let me off the gameboard, so I'm taking myself off.

"I'm not on anyone's side," I tell him. "I'm on the side of what's right. On the side where everyone lives. You don't have to fight our parents' battles. This isn't about us. Isn't it time we stop letting them be our puppet masters? Time we stopped playing their game and joined forces to fight back against them?"

Lightning knifes across the sky, illuminating the churning water rising on the banks of the river below. Thunder shakes the earth underfoot, and for a moment, we all stand silent, as if listening to the decree spoken from the sky.

Then the thunder rumbles away into the distance, and Royal speaks. He steps backwards and raises the gun again, steadying the butt on the palm of his other hand as he aims behind me. "If this is a game, then you should know it doesn't end until it's *game over.*"

"No," I scream, leaping toward him, panic clawing up my throat and out my mouth. "Don't shoot! Royal, you'll go to jail. That's murder. Do you really want that on you for the rest of your life?"

"It could be an accident," Baron says. "Anything can look like an accident."

Of course it can, to a boy who will probably be a lawyer like Uncle Vinny. Baron's the quiet one, the thoughtful one, the observer. But he's just as dangerous as the others.

I stand in front of Royal, pleading with him now, needing him to understand. "If you kill him, it'll kill me, too. If you hurt him, it hurts me, too."

He stares at me like he's never seen me before. Maybe he hasn't. "Who are you?" he asks at last.

"I'm your sister," I say, tears streaking down my cheeks with the rain. "And you're my brother, Royal. I want you to be happy again. Don't you want me to be happy, even if it's not with the man you would have chosen for me? What happened to the brother who supported me, who was always there for me, who would give his life to protect me before he'd pull a gun on me?"

Slowly, he shakes his head. "The man you've chosen, the one you want me to be happy with? His family killed your brother. I'm not that guy anymore, Crystal. And you're not my sister. I don't know who you are, but you're not the sister I did that to protect. You're a stranger, an imposter. You're not a Dolce. I had a sister once, but she died in that basement with me."

A sob wrenches from my throat, and I hunch over, trying to keep from sinking into the earth. Cold rain beats down on me, soaking my hair, my clothes. But I'm not shivering. I don't even feel the cold. All I feel is pain.

"Fine," I say. "Then fucking kill me, Royal. But if you're going to kill Devlin, shoot through me to hit him. I don't want to live even one second knowing that my twin brother is the one who killed the boy I love. If you cared about me at all, you would see that I can't help who I love, Royal. I can't help that I love Devlin any more than I can help being a Dolce. Sometimes, you don't get a choice."

"You just made your choice," Royal says, his voice hard. Rain is streaming down his cheeks like tears, but I don't know if he can cry anymore. He's broken, something inside him gone. "You chose not to be a Dolce. You don't deserve to carry our name. Crystal Dolce is already gone. I don't have to kill you. You're already dead to me."

He drops the gun into the mud at my feet. My legs give way, and I fall to my knees, my body wracked with sobs.

"Crystal," Devlin says behind me.

"We're not done with you, asshole," Duke says, stepping forward with his fists up. I don't want to see the fight. I don't want to be here at all.

I am dead to Royal. If I'm dead to him, am I even alive at all? My twin, my other half, just tore me out from the roots, and I want nothing but to end all of it, for the pain to be gone.

Royal steps around me as if I'm not even there, and I hear the first punch connect. I don't exist to him anymore. I'm nothing. And if I'm nothing to him, how can I be something to myself? I pick up the gun, push myself to my feet, and stumble down to the bank to the water.

# twenty-seven

*Devlin*

Crystal staggers off down the bank, and I turn to follow, but Royal steps into my path. "You think you're going to go after my sister?" he taunts, his fists up. The asshole slid on a pair of brass knuckles while I was distracted by the sight of her in distress.

"You just disowned your sister," I say. "She's not your sister anymore. She's my girl. Get out of my fucking way."

Royal's fist comes quick and hard, before I can step past him to go after her. I dodge at the last second, but not quick enough. His knuckles glance off my cheekbone, and I curse under my breath when I feel the metal slice open my skin. I use my own momentum to sink a fist into Royal's middle, going for the solar plexus. He doubles over, cursing and growling.

Beside me, Duke tackles Preston. The guy's only got one good arm, but I don't have more than a second to worry about him rebreaking it and what that will mean for his future. Royal's back up and swinging.

I'm bare-knuckled, but I'm faster than him. I dodge the next blow entirely and sink a left hook into his side. This time, he stays upright, getting in a quick jab before dancing back into a defensive stance.

Colt and Baron are trading insults as their fists fly like a couple of boxers. But Duke's got Preston on his back, whaling on him again and again while Preston tries to block the blows with his broken arm. I duck away from Royal and grab Duke by the back of the neck, flipping him off my cousin and onto the muddy ground. He's on his feet in seconds, diving at me like a left tackle.

I duck him, and he slides across the ground and rolls to his feet. Royal's fist connects with the side of my skull, and I go down like a ton of bricks. Blackness swims in and out of my vision, but I keep myself going, landing on my hands and flipping around, swinging my legs in a wide sweep. They connect with Royal's, and I use one foot to lock into the front of his ankles while I take out his knees with the other foot.

He hits the mud hard, but he rolls free of my legs, untangling himself in the process. My head is still throbbing like a giant is crushing it in his fist from the brass knuckles colliding with my skull, but I'm clearheaded enough to know I need to be on my feet. I'm a better fighter that way, especially against these assholes. They're bigger and stronger than us, and they came to bring pain. My advantage is speed and stamina. If I can dodge enough hits to tire him out, I can get in some good ones and knock him out cold.

I'm back on my feet before Royal, but not by much. He comes in swinging, but I duck and grab his arm, using his momentum to throw him to the ground again. The problem is, the guy's had a concussion recently. If I hit his head, I might kill him. If I wanted to do that, I'd pull the gun from my waistband. Even though Royal made it real fucking clear

selena

he'd have no problem ending my life, I'm not sure I could live with myself if I killed a man. And I know I couldn't if it was Crystal's brother. I vowed to spend the rest of my life protecting her, not hurting her. I know how much it would hurt her to lose her brother, even after he said those things to her.

Royal starts to get up, but at the last second, he kicks out, delivering a sharp roundhouse to my shins. Pain roars up my body, and I stumble. The slippery ground gives way under one foot, and I fall. In the second it takes me to hit the ground, the realization that Crystal didn't return hits me. Maybe it makes me a pussy, but suddenly, fighting is the last thing on my mind. Panic grips me, and dread clenches inside my chest. Rain beats down, and the water's rising higher every minute. If she slipped and fell in…

Before I can get to my feet, Royal swings. His brass knuckles smash into my jaw, pain explodes through me, and blackness snaps closed around me like a trap.

*

I wake to the sound of the rain still beating down and a grinding ache in my jaw, my head, my ribs.

"Devlin, dude, wake up," Colt says, slapping my cheek hard enough to sting.

When I blink the rain out of my eyes, he's crouching over me. "Did you just slap me?" I ask.

"Pass out like a bitch, I'll slap you like one," he says, a relieved grin spreading across his face.

"Who you calling a bitch?" I ask, sitting up and slugging his shoulder hard enough to make him wince. I look around and see the deep tracks left where the Range Rover was stuck in the mud, but there's no sign of the car itself.

"They left," Colt says, hopping to his feet and rubbing his shoulder. "They went toward the party. I'm going to move our cars before they come back and wreck them."

I hand Colt my keys, and he jogs over to the cars.

"Need a fainting couch?" Preston asks, holding out a hand to me. He's peeled off his shirt and is holding it to the left side of his face with his free hand.

I slap his hand away and push myself to my feet. My ribs hurt like a bitch. That asshole must have kicked me while I was down. Not that I didn't have it coming. I did the same to him after he wrecked my car.

"Where's Crystal?" I ask. "Did they take her?"

"No," he says. "They ran like pussies when they saw we were strapped."

"Fuck," I mutter. They might have only brought one gun this time, but if I know anything about the Dolces, it's that they won't be shown up. If my cousins brought out their guns and threatened them this time, they'll bring theirs and shoot to kill next time.

"Come on," I say. "Help me find her. We've got to get her out of here before they come back for her."

The road is a dead end, so they can't get out another way. They'll have to come back through here after whatever shit they're going to pull at the party. The party is the least of my concerns. It's forty degrees and pouring rain out here, and Crystal's been gone for… I don't know how long I was out. Too fucking long.

"What are you going to do?" Preston asks as we scramble down the muddy bank toward the trees, half of them fighting the current as the water inches up their trunks.

"I don't know," I say. "I have to find her, though. To get her out of here. It's not safe. You saw Royal. He's lost it, man. He pointed a fucking gun at her. He's lucky I didn't put a bullet between his eyes for that one."

"Why didn't you?"

"You know why," I say.

"You're stuck in an impossible place," he says. "You're never going to get out of it."

Instead of answering, I call for Crystal. He joins me, and a minute later, Colt does, too. Maybe he's right. If I don't want to hurt Crystal, I can't even defend myself. And if I don't defend myself, I'll wind up dead, which will hurt her anyway.

We scour the banks of the river, walking up and down until our voices grow hoarse and I can't think straight. If she's gone…

Damn it, why didn't I follow her?

At last, I spot a small, crumpled white shape at the edge of the river up near the bridge. I break into a jog, and after a minute, my cousins are beside me. I push myself faster, calling her louder, my heart pounding against the cage of my chest like a prisoner demanding release. I don't dare hope, but I can't help myself. The little form looks so small, it could be a pile of debris or a bag of trash thrown off the bridge.

When I'm almost there, I let myself breathe. Her white shirt sticks to her thin shoulders, soaked through and clinging to her cold skin. She's not even wearing a jacket. I reach her first, dropping to my knees beside her. She's so small, so insignificant looking. It's hard to imagine this girl could be the whole world.

"Crystal, sugar," I say, rolling her over, pulling her up. "What are you doing down here?"

She stares at me with vague confusion, like she can't remember where she is, or why, or who I am. I grab her face and kiss her hard, crushing her cold lips with mine. When I pull back and look at her, still holding her head, she blinks, and a bit of life returns to her eyes. I should have fucking followed her, not stayed to fight her brothers. I shouldn't have let Royal catch me by surprise and knock me out. I shouldn't have fucking spared the ruthless bastard who put that look in her eyes.

"Devlin," she murmurs. "Stop trying to save me."

I just shake my head. "No, baby. I'll never stop."

"It's too late," she whispers. "You can't save me."

"Then I'll fucking die trying," I say, scooping her up and holding her against me. "You already saved me. When I didn't even know I needed saving, you saved me." I want to crush her in my arms, need to know she's here, real, solid. Alive. But I know this isn't the time. This is the time to hold her gently, to cradle her like the delicate thing she is right now. Because that's what she needs. That's what will bring her back to the fierce, loyal, unbreakable, quietly badass little angel that came into my life and made me believe I could be loved no matter how unworthy I felt.

With Crystal in my arms, I push myself to standing. Anger lashes through me when I feel how cold she is. Her whole body is shivering, but she wraps her arms around my neck, quaking against me. "He said I was dead to him," she mutters against my neck, her words almost lost in the drumming of the rain and the chattering of her teeth. "I might as well be."

"No, fuck that," I say. "Just... Shut up. I'm taking you back to the car. You're freezing."

When I reach the car, I open the door and lay her on the back seat. She holds onto my neck, her eyes searching mine. "Don't leave," she whispers. Rain runs down my arms in rivulets, down her body, soaking my leather seats, but I don't care. I only care about her, and how cold and small she looks, that she's soaked through and shivers wrack her body.

"I won't," I promise, pressing my lips to hers. I pull back, and blood drips from the cut on my face to her cheek, running down her face like a tear.

"We'll go back to the party and stop them," Colt says behind me. "We can buy you a little time."

I lean down and kiss Crystal. "One second?"

Her dark eyes search mine, and then she nods, releasing my neck. I stand and face my cousins. For a second, none of us speak. I can see the knowledge in their eyes, that there's not going to be a happy ending to this. Not at the party, not in this town. Maybe not for any of us.

"Be careful," I say, pulling Colt in and hugging him hard. None of that bullshit guy hugging. I hug him like I did when we were kids, before anyone told me guys didn't hug that way. An ache forms behind my eyes, in my nose, in my throat. He hugs me back just as hard.

"Go on," he says. "Get her out of here."

I release him and turn to Preston, pulling him in. One of his arms is barely functioning, with a short cast still on his wrist and his shirt still held to his eye, but he makes do with the other. Preston's a tougher nut than Colt, and I expect a smartass remark, but he gives my back a slap instead. He starts to pull away, but that's not the kind of goodbye I want if something happens. I grab his head with both my hands, pressing my forehead to his.

"You gonna be okay?" I ask.

"I might have lost an eye," he says. "He got me with the brass knuckles."

"Shit," I say, letting out a breath. "Thank you."

"She better be worth it."

"She is."

We don't say more. How can I say what I want to my boys, who might be walking into a death trap? Grampa Darling has lots of guns, and I'm not stupid enough to think they're all in the safe. The guy has a lot of enemies. He probably sleeps with two under his pillow. Hell, my cousins might not make it there at all. The Dolces have a bigger vehicle, and they're not above using it as a weapon. They almost killed Colt with it already. We should have been harder, meaner, from the start. We should have seen how serious they were.

But it's too late to go back now. Now, I have one chance to get Crystal to safety.

The only question is, what's safe now? The Dolces bombed all our houses. They live right next door to me. They could storm our house and drag her back. When my cousins walk away, I turn back to Crystal. Her eyes are glassy and faraway as she stares at the ceiling. Her lips are colorless.

"What do you need?" I ask, sinking onto the edge of the seat beside her. She doesn't answer.

I think of the flash of life that came into her eyes when I kissed her. She needs to get warm, that's what she needs. Dry clothes. Heat.

Maybe I should take her home, turn her over to her dad. Maybe I should leave her alone, never speak to her again, and hope that would be enough to keep her safe.

But I'm not going to. I know that's not what she needs. She needs me.

And I need her.

"I'm going to move the car," I tell her. "It'll just take a minute."

I get in the driver's seat, and I turn on the Ferrari. After powering the heat to high, I turn down the opposite side of the road, down a steep embankment toward the river. The trees grow up this side all the way to the road, but they were cleared to make way for the bridge, and I aim the car down the narrow strip of cleared red dirt and gravel. I know I may never get my car out, but I don't care. It doesn't matter now. What matters is getting her away from the road, where her brothers might see her.

Taking her home won't keep her safe. Delivering her to her brothers won't keep her safe. That's not where she belongs anymore. She's not a Dolce. She's mine. Her family doesn't deserve her. I'm done playing their game. I'm done sharing her. If I brought her home, I wouldn't just lose her. She'd lose herself again. Tonight, she broke free, and I won't be the one who delivers her back to her cage.

# twenty-eight

*Crystal*

"What do you need, baby?" Devlin asks, sliding into the back seat and covering me with a fleece blanket he got from the trunk. He kneels on the floor, wedging himself into the tiny space while I lie on the seat.

I can't answer. I can't begin to explain to him how it feels to lose a twin, like half of me died on that bank out there. Royal isn't just my brother. He's half of me—the good half. He's the boy who kept me upright when I wanted to collapse, the boy who picked me up no matter how many times I fell until I learned to stand again. He's the one person in all the world who understands me to my very soul without me having to say a word. The boy who offered help and strength and silent companionship in moments when I didn't even know I needed them.

He said I wasn't his family anymore.

That I wasn't his sister.

That I was dead to him.

Fresh tears spring to my eyes, and Devlin leans down and kisses them away from my cheeks. The gash across his cheekbone is still bleeding, and a deep bruise is swelling on his jaw, but pain only enters his gaze when he sees mine. He kisses down my cheeks, then my lips. I don't respond. My lips are cold, frozen, as immobile as the heart that has died inside my chest.

Devlin kisses me harder, his mouth warm and commanding. I submit, opening my lips when he pushes his tongue against the seam between them. His tongue is hot and forceful, and he arches up, angling himself over me. A minute later, I feel his hand on my body, pulling at my clothes. I don't know how he can want sex now. I'm dirty and wet and bedraggled, my eyes swollen, my makeup long gone, and my skin cold as the dead when he peels away my clothes, stripping me bare.

But he kisses me hungrily, roughly even, his teeth clashing with mine and his tongue pumping against mine. He pulls back only to pull off his wet shirt. His nipples pebble in the cold, water clinging to his skin. I swallow hard, watching the muscles in his chest and his arms while he unbuttons his wet jeans and shoves them down.

"I'm gonna fuck you now, Sugar," he says, his fingers wrapping around his thick shaft, which is hard and ready to destroy me. I swallow hard, raising my eyes to his. The burning hunger in them makes me shiver and cower from him, not sure I can take his roughness tonight. I open my mouth, and his lips crash down onto mine, devouring, demanding, dominant. He lifts the blanket and slides on top of me on the seat without breaking the kiss. His chest and arms are cold, but when his pelvis meets mine, the heat of his skin makes me gasp into his mouth. He growls in response, grinding his stiff cock against my cold, bare skin.

It's so hot I can't breathe for a second. I feel like I'm being burned, branded. I don't want to think about that much life being inside me again. I don't want to feel alive again, but he makes me. His tongue sweeps over mine in an irresistible rhythm, his body moving against mine until I can feel myself blooming under him, wetness springing to life for him. Shame burns through me. I shouldn't want this so soon, shouldn't be able to feel so alive after what Royal said to me.

But I am still alive. Devlin's bringing me to life, warming me with his heat, waking parts of me that I didn't know could be woken at a time like this. "What do you want, Sugar?" he whispers, his breath hot against my neck. "Tell me you want it."

"I want you," I say, my voice hotter than I expected, breathless with desire. "Fuck me back to life."

He does. He draws back, reaching down to position himself at my entrance before pushing into me hard and deep, filling me with one thrust. I cry out, tensing at the suddenness, the painful fullness of him inside me. He doesn't slow. He pounds into me hard and fast, until I can't help but respond or be crushed to dust under him. I dig my heels into the seat, lifting for him to go deeper, to hurt me more. I move with him until we're both panting for breath as our bodies crash into each other, until I can't hold back. I crest hard and fast, the orgasm like a shock of heat blooming inside me.

I cry out, gasping and clawing at Devlin, but he's not done. He grabs my hands, pinning them and pushing himself up on the seat to watch me as he hammers into me, his breath coming as fast as mine, his eyes glinting with fiery intensity. He moves even faster, until I have to beg him to stop, that it's too much.

"Can you come again?" he asks, grinding his bare, raw cock into me until his pelvic bone crushes my sensitive bud.

My body answers for me. I can't hold back my cries at the intensity of this one. I buck under him, trying to wrench my hands free as my toes curl and climax grips me, squeezing his length as it pulses thicker inside me. He gives one more quick thrust, and then his heat spurts into me, warming me from the inside, filling me with life—his life. My whole body jerks under him, and helpless cries escape my lips again and again. Devlin holds himself up on his hands, grinding into me until I'm whimpering for it to be over. When it finally ebbs, and I begin to come down, Devlin lowers himself onto me.

I hold onto him, shaking though I'm no longer cold. He knew what I needed before I did. He knew, and he gave it to me. If I lost him, I'd die. He's all I have left. All I want.

For a long time, neither of us moves. My heart is thawed, now racing in my chest. The heavy, hard rhythm of Devlin's heartbeat bolsters me, makes me remember that I'm his, that we're one. That we're alive. Together.

Outside the car, the rain has stopped at last. The world is quiet, the night swallowing everything but us, the little world we've made together. I don't want it to ever end, but I know that too soon, I'll have to face reality again.

"What am I going to do?" I whisper at last.

"We'll think of something," Devlin assures me, squeezing me tighter against him.

"It's too late for that," I say. "We're out of time, Devlin. My brother spared you tonight, but my dad won't. He's going to kill you. And don't say you're not scared. I mean it, Devlin. Your life is in danger."

"Do you have anything on him?" Devlin asks.

"Maybe," I whisper, my heart thudding hard in my chest. I know what I have to do, something a thousand times worse than protecting Devlin when my brother held a guy. I have to do the right thing.

"What is it?" Devlin asks.

"They'll kill me," I say. "You know what happens to people who squeal."

"Then I'll die with you," Devlin says, holding me harder. "It's worth it to have had the time I had with you. I told you I'd die for you, and I meant it."

"Let's do it," I say impulsively.

Devlin lifts his head, his eyes searching mine. "Do what?"

"We live and die for each other now," I say, taking his hand and linking my fingers with his. "You said we were part of each other now. Nothing can tear us apart, Devlin. Not even death. So, let's die for each other."

# twenty-nine

*Crystal*

Devlin looks at me for a long moment. "What do you mean, Crystal?"

"They're going to kill you," I say. "I'm not living without you, Devlin. I'm in this to the end. I'm yours, forever. My life ends the day yours ends."

"You want to… Die?"

"No," I say, my heart lurching at the thought. I couldn't do that even if I wanted to. I have other people to think about now.

"Then what?"

"Devlin," I say slowly. My heart is hammering so hard I can barely breathe, or swallow, or even think. "Can we sit up?"

"Sure," he says, lifting himself from me. He helps me sit, maneuvering in the tiny back seat until we're both sitting. Then he wraps the blanket around us both, pulling me against his side and keeping an arm around my waist. I take comfort in the solid sensation of his strong body beside mine. He will protect us.

"I didn't mean we'd really die," I say. "But we could die to the rest of the world."

For a minute, he doesn't speak. Finally he asks, "How do we do that?"

"We can run away," I say, my words coming faster as the idea grows, strengthening more each moment. I can't believe I didn't think of it earlier. That's the Dolce solution to everything. It's not always the right solution, but this time, it's the only option. This is the last Dolce tradition I'll ever honor. "But we have to do more than that. They have to think I'm dead. If I just ran away with you, my family would hunt us down. They'd find me."

Devlin lets out a quiet scoff. "I bet they would. The mafia's probably better at finding people than the FBI. That's why they have witsec, right?"

"But if they thought we were dead…" I search his eyes, my heart drumming in my chest. "Like Baron said, anything can look like an accident."

"Crystal…" Devlin starts, then shakes his head. "Where would we go?"

"Anywhere," I say. "California. Canada. Mexico. Somewhere far from here and far from New York."

"You wouldn't be able to say goodbye," he says. "Not to your friends, not to your family. We'd have to make a clean break. No note, no blog post, nothing."

My heart begins to hammer as I realize he's agreeing to my crazy, desperate idea. It seemed crazy even to me, but what choice do we have? I won't let anything happen to Devlin, and I sure as hell won't be the reason he's hurt. I won't let my family keep us apart.

"I know," I say, raising my chin. "I don't belong to the Dolce family anymore. If it was as easy as Royal disowning me, and they'd all go along with it, maybe we could stay. But they won't let me go, Devlin. This is our chance to start over as ourselves. No pressure from my family or yours. We'll leave the burden of our names and just be us, where no one knows us as anything else."

Devlin works his jaw back and forth for a second. Then he nods. "Okay."

"Okay?" I ask, my heart doing a little flip. "Really?"

"If that's what it takes for us to be together, that's what we'll do. I took some money out of the trust already. I just need to go get it. And we'll need to buy a car with cash. It won't be anything like this one. Nothing flashy. We'll have to change who we are."

"Oh… Devlin…" My heart sinks when I think of what he's giving up. His beautiful new car. Football. Graduation. College. His family. "I can't ask you to do that," I whisper, my throat thick with tears. "Your family isn't like mine."

"I think my dad will understand," he says. "Even if they don't know I'm alive, they'd be happy if they did. They'd be happy I was safe with you. You're all I need, Crystal."

"There's something I have to do first," I say, knowing I should fight harder but also knowing I won't change his mind. And selfishly, I don't want to. I don't want to lose him. If his family has to lose him for him to be safe, then that's what has to happen.

"Anything you need to do," Devlin says. "Let me help you."

I nod, my throat aching with the hard truth stuck in it. "I have to send a letter," I say. "I have to tell the truth about Royal. You were right, Devlin. It wasn't your dad. It was mine."

Devlin nods, his eyes so kind it makes my heart ache. He knew. He's not surprised. His grandfather did something horrible to Royal, but so did my father. I sit up, and I compose an email on my phone. It takes a while, but I give every detail I can think of while Devlin looks up contact information for his dad's lawyer, the judge, and the newspaper.

When I'm done, my thumb hovers over the send button. Maybe it won't do any good. But maybe it will. I only know it's the last email Crystal Dolce will ever send.

After hitting send, I sit there with my heart racing, feeling like the worst traitor in the world. I sold out my family. I turned on the Dolces. I'm a snitch. I know what happens to snitches in the "candy" business.

"Okay," I whisper, my hands shaking as I set down my phone and reach for Devlin's comforting grip. "It's done. There's no going back now."

Devlin takes my face between his hands and kisses me gently. "Then let's do this. Let me prove I can be there for you, Crystal. I'll take care of you."

I nod, gripping his strong arms with shaking fingers. "You and me," I say. "'Til death."

Devlin strokes my hair back and kisses my forehead. "You're all I need. Just this. Just us. You and me."

Suddenly, I know I can't do this. Not yet. Not like this.

I pull away from Devlin and lean back against the seat, close my eyes, and take a deep, shaky breath. "Devlin," I whisper. "It's not just you and me."

"I know." His voice is low but firm, but my heart lurches at his words. His hand finds mine under the blanket and squeezes.

I turn to look at his face, searching his gaze for signs that he's talking about what I am, signs that he's as desperate and terrified as I am. But he looks calm, as steady as his body feels next to mine.

"You do?" I whisper.

He slips his fingers from mine and slides his hand over my hip, letting it come to rest gently on my flat stomach. "Is this what you're trying to tell me?"

"How did you know?" I ask, dizzy with nerves. I want to hold onto him, to make him carry the weight of this terrifying, wonderful secret with me. But I don't want him to feel what I've been feeling the last month. I don't want him to feel trapped. I don't want to feel him pull away, to see the terror in his eyes. Somehow, I've convinced myself it will hurt less to watch him go if I let him do it, if I don't hold on or beg him to stay no matter how much I want to.

"Well," he says, smiling a little, his hand still resting on my belly. "I'm no expert, but it's been almost two months since that day I tasted you in the shower, and I think most girls have a period every month."

My cheeks warm at the memory, but I force myself not to drop his gaze. "How long have you known?"

"Not that long," he says. "When you told me about the coffee, I started counting backwards. We've been together enough since then that I probably would have noticed if you were bleeding."

"Why didn't you say anything?"

"I was waiting for you to tell me when you were ready," he says. "Or to tell me you were on some kind of birth control where you don't have them."

"You're not freaking out." I let out a shaky laugh that's a mixture of relief and terror that I'm still missing something. "Why aren't you freaking out?"

Devlin lifts the arm that's around my back, burying his hand in my hair and turning my face to his without taking his other hand from my middle. He gazes into my eyes with such tenderness that a lump forms in my throat. "I love you, Crystal. You're my forever girl. The only thing that scares me is someone taking you away from me. And this little baby isn't going to do that, so why would I freak out?"

"You're my forever, too," I say, laughing even as tears blur my eyes.

"Good," Devlin says, pulling me in and gently pressing his lips to mine. "Then nothing has changed except that now there's one more person in our forever."

"You're still in?" I ask, pressing my forehead to his and slipping a hand behind his neck.

"Until I fucking die."

"Okay," I say, relief melting me against him. For the first time since I realized I was late, and then more than late, I feel like I can breathe. Like there is hope. Like maybe, by some miracle, we'll be okay. After what we've been through, I think we deserve a fucking miracle.

"You don't think this could've changed your family's mind?" Devlin asks.

"No," I admit. "I already asked King. He said Dad would put a hit on you."

"Well, that's not going to happen," Devlin says. "No one is going to take care of my girls but me."

"Oh, so you already know it's a girl?" I tease.

"I know it's mine," he says, his voice close to a growl. "And so are you."

"Then let's go somewhere where that's possible," I say. "Somewhere no one will ever find us."

We pull on our wet clothes in silence. I'm not cold anymore. Every inch of me is vibrating with adrenaline. I can feel us careening toward the edge, toward the point of no return, but I'm not afraid. I know this is our miracle. That we won't fall. We'll fly.

When we're dressed, we climb out of the car, leaving our phones and all our possessions inside. Devlin leaves his gun in the glove box and sits in the front seat, the door open. The water has risen so high that it's only a few feet in front of the car now. I look at Devlin. He looks at me.

Thunder rumbles overhead, mingling with the roar of the water. We may freeze our asses off walking into town to buy a crappy car, but I know it's a blessing that the storm isn't over. More rain means our footprints will be washed away. But the storm is over for us.

Devlin tosses his soaked jacket into the back seat, turns on the car, and looks at me.

This is it. This is the end. The point of no return. The moment when we cut ties with Faulkner, with our families.

The moment our identities disappear, and we become our own people.

He sits for a second, then climbs out, pulls the brake, and steps back. Gravity does the rest. The car rolls forward on the slope of the bank. The water catches the front end, and we watch it sink in and disappear beneath the churning water. And then it's gone. I no longer carry a Dolce ID. I no longer carry a name that was a noose around my neck for too long. I once said I sold my heart to keep my name. Tonight, I washed away my name to keep my heart. I belong to no one but myself and this boy, this boy with no family, no past, no name. He's no longer Devlin Darling. He's only mine.

He takes my hand in his, pulling me closer as the rain begins to fall again. Laughter bubbles up inside me, and I turn and run. My darling boy keeps his fingers laced through mine, and we don't let go. My clothes are wet and cold and heavy, but I've never felt lighter. I'm free. I'm finally fucking free. I'm ready to fly.

"Come on," I yell above the rush of rain and river. "Let's disappear."

# epilogue

*Crystal*

The sound of the key in the lock startles me. I didn't hear the Honda pull up outside our little two-bedroom house. I struggle to sit up, pulling down my shirt over my big belly. I shove my phone under the couch pillow just as Devlin walks in. He studies me as he pushes the door closed with his foot.

"How's my favorite girls?" he asks, leaning down to give me a kiss and setting down the shopping bag on the coffee table. He sinks onto the couch beside me and puts a possessive hand on my belly. "Has she done anything new today?"

"I think she discovered her future career," I say, smiling as I rest a hand on the top of my belly.

Devlin arches a brow. "I'm intrigued."

"Yep," I say, reaching for the food. "She's going to be a boxer. She's decided my bladder will be her first punching bag. She's been practicing all day."

He laughs and pulls me in, kissing me softly. I wrap my arms around him, kissing him like I do every time he comes home from work, every time I have to go a whole day without feeling his touch. He pulls me into his lap, and I move to straddle him. Devlin runs his hands up my thighs and around my hips, grabbing my ass and pulling me forward as he pushes his hips against mine, letting me feel his hardness through his work pants.

I rock against him, already wet for him. Hormones are a blessing and a curse.

Devlin pulls back, wariness in his eyes. "Are you going to be thinking about ice cream while I fuck you?"

I can't help but laugh, though my cheeks warm with embarrassment. "Probably," I admit, sliding off his lap. "First, ice cream."

He loops an arm around me, pulling me against his side and nuzzling my ear. "As long as I get to eat you next."

I pull the bag into my lap, hoping to hide my blush, but Devlin plucks it away.

"Hey," I protest, swiping for it as he holds it out of reach.

"This is my favorite part," he says with a grin.

I cross my arms over my chest and give him a playful pout. I can drive now, and after ditching half a dozen cars we bought with cash as we crossed the country, I even have my own car, bought used and registered under my new name. I could have gone out for ice cream myself, but I know how much Devlin loves to bring me home whatever I'm craving.

His eyes dip to my swollen breasts, which my position put on display, and he swallows.

"Well played," he says with a grin, dragging his eyes from my cleavage. He takes a pint of ice cream from the bag. "Cookies and cream." He sets it on the edge of the coffee table, then continues pulling more from the bag, naming each one as he lines them up. "Strawberry. Mint chip. Rocky

Road." He ends with a pint jar of pickles. I try to laugh, since this is our little joke, even though I've never craved pickles. He keeps saying it's going to happen, so he gets a jar every time I ask for ice cream. But this time, tears blur my eyes as I stare at the rocky road, the memory of King bringing that flavor to my room suddenly fresh in my mind.

"What's wrong?" Devlin asks, alarmed at seeing my tears.

"It's just the hormones," I say. "And... And this." I pull my phone from under the pillow and hand it to Devlin, burying my face in his chest. I can't risk touching any of my old social media or even my private blog, but I read the news from Faulkner even when I know I shouldn't.

Devlin holds me, letting me cry so I don't have to look at him while he reads about Preston's dad finally going down for a crime I know my grandfather committed. It's been six months since we've seen our families. Six months since we dumped the car in the river and disappeared. Since we took Devlin's money, bought a junky old car for cash, and drove away from Faulkner. Six months since I left my world with no goodbyes.

I still miss them every day, and I know Devlin misses his people, too. He never reads the news from back home. Not anymore. Not since the first month, when we watched with beating hearts and breath held, with fingers crossed that they wouldn't come looking. That they'd believe the car was washed away by the floods with us in it, even though they didn't find our bodies. Because of the jacket and certain other "evidence" in the back seat, the police eventually reached the conclusion that after sending the damning email, Devlin and I crawled in the back and were so caught up in each other that we didn't notice the water rising until it was too late. We joke that at least they think we died doing what we love. I did once tell him it would be the perfect way to die.

Devlin swipes the story from the screen and lays my phone facedown on the coffee table. "Why do you look at that?" he asks, his voice almost pleading as he lifts my chin. "We can't go back, Crystal. You know that."

"I know," I say, nodding and wiping my nose.

"I just hate to see you sad," he says, kissing my teary face.

"It's not fair, though," I say. "Maybe we can send an anonymous letter or something."

"Crystal," he says. "You know that's too risky. You were brave to do what you did for my dad, but I shouldn't have even let you do that. We can't save everyone."

"I know."

He runs his thumb across the fat pink diamond of my ring, the lone extravagant purchase we've made. It cost more than it did for us to buy new identities. I would have been happy with a twenty-dollar ring from a department store, but Devlin wasn't having it. After watching him agonize about the fact that it would take him ten years working as a grunt for Nyso Records to afford something nice, I suggested he dip into our savings, which we've left mostly untouched. I don't need more than the simple life his income provides. But he wanted to give me more.

His voice softens, and he holds my hand gently in his. "Remember what you told me when I didn't want to use the trust fund money on your ring because it was Grampa Darling's?"

I nod, remembering how hard it was to see him feel unworthy when he couldn't give me the things he wanted to. "I said you earned it."

"Well, Preston's dad may not have killed that construction worker, but believe me, he earned whatever he gets."

I nod, feeling slightly better. I reach for the rocky road, my heart filled with bittersweet memories. "I just miss them, you know?"

"I know, Sugar," he says, handing me a spoon.

I know, too. I know this is worth it. The past six months have been the happiest, most freeing, contented months of my life. Devlin is rich on his own, but we decided it was safer not to live that way. We don't have a big fancy house, a designer wardrobe, or an expensive car. But we don't need it. We have each other.

Despite the things we did to each other in the past, or maybe because of them, I know nothing will ever come between us. Maybe it's fucked up, but I'm glad we did those things to each other. If I can love and forgive him after what he did to me, he knows it's real. And if he can love me and trust me after what I did, I know it's real. We're two fucked up people, and we know we have something that was worth every minute we fought for it. If it came easy, we wouldn't know it was worth fighting for.

I may look back more than Devlin does, but I'd never risk what we fought so hard to win. I know that once the baby comes, I'll only look forward to her beautiful future. We're making our own family now. Our own rules. In our family, no one will have to be anything they don't want to be. Their futures will be theirs to decide. Our kids will be loved for who they are, just as Devlin and I love each other.

Fiercely. Unconditionally. Until death.

# author's note

I hope you enjoyed reading Crystal and Devlin's story! This is their happy ending. There are no more books planned in this series. However, a few familiar faces will star in upcoming series of their own.

Royal's will be the start of another series of bully romances featuring him and his girl.

King's will be the start of a mafia series where each book features a new couple. Read the blurbs below for more details, and a note on pre-order dates below that.

selena

# *It's my duty to the family...*

*King*

When I go to work for the Valenti's, I don't expect my first assignment to be my biggest challenge—marry the daughter of a rival boss.

Wild and smart-mouthed as she is beautiful, Eliza Pomponio's nothing but a bratty princess who's always gotten her way. Taming her won't be easy.

But everyone is counting on us to keep peace between the New York families, so that's exactly what I'll do.

I may answer to mob bosses during the day, but at night, I'll give the orders.

*Eliza*

In one moment, my freedom is snatched away when my father tells me I have to marry a man I've never met.

I expect an eighty-year-old retired boss who craves my virgin flesh in payment for his service. Bright side—in a few years, he'll be gone, and I'll be free again.

I'm not prepared for the dangerously gorgeous soldier my father presents. Like anything that looks too good to be true, so is my new husband. He's cold, cruel, and worst of all, young. Suddenly, marriage is a life sentence.

That is, if I don't show him from day one that no one controls Eliza Pomponio.

# Bury Me

## *Bad Apple*

My name is Harper Apple, and people say I'm rotten to the core.

*"Girls like you get one shot."*

When my shot comes in the form of a scholarship to Willow Heights Prep, you can bet your ass I take it. If getting out of this hellhole town means spending my last two years of high school at an elite academy full of rich, entitled pricks, then bring it on.

*"Girls like you don't belong."*

The arrogant and infuriatingly gorgeous Dolce brothers reign supreme in the hallowed halls of Willow Heights, and they don't welcome my kind. Especially when I get in their way, don't play by the rules in their twisted games, and refuse to bow to the cruel tyrants who run the place.

*"Girls like you are bad news."*

Royal, Baron, and Duke Dolce set their sights on me. They think a poor girl will be an easy target, that they can break me and bring me to my knees like the girls who came before me. But the Dolce boys underestimate me. In this town, even girls from the trailer park hide deadly secrets. Secrets that could destroy them.

After all, it's those from the wicked world of wealth and privilege with the most to lose.

451

Printed in Great Britain
by Amazon